Meet Love Through My Eyes

A Novel
Inspired by True Events

DeAnna L. Alexander

Archway Publishing books may be ordered through booksellers or by contacting:

Archway Publishing
1663 Liberty Drive
Bloomington, IN 47403
www.archwaypublishing.com
844-669-3957

Because of the dynamic nature of the Internet, any web addresses or
links contained in this book may have changed since publication and
may no longer be valid. The views expressed in this work are solely those
of the author and do not necessarily reflect the views of the publisher,
and the publisher hereby disclaims any responsibility for them.

Any people depicted in stock imagery provided by Getty Images are
models, and such images are being used for illustrative purposes only.
Certain stock imagery © Getty Images.

ISBN: 978-1-4808-9325-2 (sc)
ISBN: 978-1-4808-9326-9 (e)

Library of Congress Control Number: 2020913064

Print information available on the last page.

Archway Publishing rev. date: 09/17/2020

Prologue

The day is lovely, and the walk to the office is enjoyable as the breeze prevents the glaring sun from scorching me. I take the fifteen-minute stroll often. Mostly, when I need to clear my mind from all my cluttered thoughts. Lately, they've been on love and the meaning of *genuine love*. Victor is a great husband to me, but I often question his love for me, or if the great sex is what he loves. Is the sex what holds us together? We do little communicating outside of making love or him telling me about a new artist, and we only go out to business functions together. Since I've known Victor, business is always his number one priority. I occasionally wish I could talk to him about my thoughts, but since he always turns the conversation to himself, my wish immediately goes faint.

I love my husband, but am I truly in love with him? Does he make me happy mentally, physically, emotionally, and sexually? There are so many questions I should've asked prior to marrying him. Have I settled because I was lonely? Was I desperate? I know it's not love that made me say yes to marrying him because I don't know what love was. Is it too late to take it all back? If only I could turn the hands of time. Do I know what love is now? Is sex love? These thoughts stay consumed in my brain since I've been too busy to express them in my journal.

"Good morning, Serenity. You have a message from your husband," Savannah informs me.

I'm at the office before I realize it. Lately, I become so confined in my thoughts that I either lose track of time or I'm at my destination sooner than expected. At my desk, I listen to Victor's message, "What's up Baby! I've changed our dinner reservations to lunch reservations. I got an important dinner meeting I must attend after work. I'm not sure how long the meeting will be, but I don't want to cancel any plans. I'm sure you understand. See you soon."

I hang the receiver up and stick my head out my office door. "Savannah, can you make sure you clear my lunch schedule and arrange for a car to pick me up at 11:30, please?" Mr. Chow's is too far to walk, so I'll have my driver, Mark, take me.

"I've already cleared your schedule, and I will have a car ready."

I run through my appointments and send my clients on their way, and as usual, time does not wait for me. It's already 11:10, which means there's only twenty minutes left to fix my make-up, change my shoes, and get downstairs. I wore the dress I picked out this morning as a shirt because I dare walk down the street in it. In my walk-in work closet, I remove my pants and the dress transforms from a nice shirt to a sexy dress. I'm wrinkled. I skim through the garments and choose a similar Valentino dress; same color, length, and style, but reveals more cleavage. Dressed and ready to go, Savannah speaks through the intercom, "Mark is downstairs waiting."

"Let him know I'm on my way down." I pick my purse up and leave my office.

"Well, don't you look stunning," Savannah says as I pass her desk on the way to the elevator. I wink at her and laugh on the inside as I take in the gasps from the other assistants.

"Nice dress Serenity," Felicia says as she joins me on the elevator. "What's the occasion?"

"Victor and I are having lunch at Mr. Chow's. I'm meeting his new artist, and, well, you never know what may happen afterwards."

Felicia laughs. "Oh, I understand that, trust me. Have a

wonderful lunch, which I'm sure you will," she tells me as we exit the elevator into the lobby and go separate ways.

Riding in the back seat, my mind wonders to my husband's new artist and a ball of anxiety suddenly hits me in the abdomen. My interest grows, but I try to disregard the fact that I'm so intrigued. I've never met her, but stress takes over not just my stomach, but my entire body.

We reach Mr. Chow's and Mark comes around, opens my door, and extends his hand to help me out. "Have a great lunch, ma'am," he says, then asks, "Shall I wait, or will you text me when you're ready?"

"No, Mark, you don't have to wait. I'll text you if I don't catch a ride with Victor." His eyes remind me of someone, but I can't put my finger on it. I've never paid attention to that until today.

I glide through the restaurant with the supermodel walk that would slay anybody's runway. My curls bounce on my breast as I sway from side to side in the perfectly fitted, size six dress. All eyes are on me. At the table, Victor sits with the most beautiful woman I've ever laid eyes on. The same emotion of anxiety occurs again. She looks familiar, and it feels like we've met before, but I can't recall when or where.

"Hazel, this is my wife, Serenity White. Serenity, this is Hazel Brown," my husband introduces us. As Hazel shakes my hand, chills run through my body, causing every hair on the back of my neck to stand on end. I know her. Did we go to school together? She reminds me of Carmen. Could this be her? Could she have found me? Is she the woman of my dreams? Am I dreaming?

I sit nervously as we order lunch. Victor does his usual babbling of how great an artist she is and how he's excited to work with her, but my mind is not on the conversation. Instead, it's on the weird feeling that I know her. I try to figure out where from, but I'm at a loss.

As my husband speaks, I catch her glaring at me several times.

There's something behind those eyes that makes me tingle. This woman is doing something to me. She's doing something to my body, something to my mind. It's a feeling I've never felt, or have just not with my husband. I'm confused. I glance at my watch. I've only been here for ten minutes. Time is drifting for the first time since I can recall. My armpits sweat. I take a gulp from the glass of the water in front of me, but that doesn't help, so I excuse myself.

"Is everything okay, Baby?" Victor gets up to pull my chair back.

"Yes. I just need to go powder my nose," I say in a quiet voice and not showing my anxiety.

Staring in the mirror and trying to calm myself down, I close my eyes and take slow, deep breaths as an attempt to ease the pain in my stomach. It doesn't go away. Instead, it speeds up as I feel someone's breath on the back of my neck. Only Victor knows this is my weak spot, so my eyes remain closed as I assume it's him taking this as an opportunity for another one of our perfect getaway sexcapades. His hands run along my sides, caressing me softly. He's being gentle with me, considering we're pressed for time. I enjoy the feeling. It's a fresh feeling that's calming me down, so I embrace it.

"I've been waiting many years for this day," she says in the sweetest, most sensual voice I've ever heard. I open my eyes to see Carmen standing behind me. *My* Carmen. It's the same Carmen it took me months to get over, years. How did she find me? My intuition was right. I'm puzzled. Unable to speak, I refrain from asking questions.

"You left without a word. I looked for you. No one would tell me where you'd disappeared to." She whispers in my ear. Still unable to move, I continue to listen. "I refused to give up and then finally, I saw a picture of you and your husband on a magazine cover while in the grocery store. You changed your name. That's why I couldn't find you. But that face, those beautiful eyes, and that smile… I'll never forget. I've missed you so much. We were young back then, but there's not a day that goes by when I don't think of you." I'm trying to process everything she's saying.

"Se-re-ni-ty," she slowly whispers in my ear, allowing each syllable to roll off her tongue in the sexiest way. I don't move. Holding back the tears, I blink as they fill up in the wells of my eyes. "Mel-o-dy," she whispers just as slowly. She says my name. A name I haven't heard in so long. A name I thought no longer existed. Melody. That's me. My knees weaken beneath me. She holds me up. A tear falls. Our bodies face each other. My arms wrap around her as I cry quietly into her neck. We speak no words. Time is still. The room is still. Our hazel and light brown eyes finally meet.

The woman I fell in love with stands before me. The woman I ran from because of my confusion stands before me. My evil mother made me feel like a confused sinner. My feelings made me question myself and my sexuality. I did everything in my power to forget about her and erase her from my mind. Victor was my scapegoat. He helped me forget about her. Thunderstruck, my hands touch her soft hair. It has grown to be long and beautiful. Oh, how she has changed in the physical aspect, but the amazing feeling she gives me remains the same. It's like I'm in my senior year of college again, back when we first met. It's a feeling that's becomes more powerful with this interaction; a feeling too powerful to describe.

My thoughts speed up. Time moves swiftly. My husband pops in my head. Muddle sets in and it shows. She sees the panic, grabs my face, and says, "Don't worry. I have it all figured out." Her demeanor is calm and refreshing. "We have little time. Your driver, Mark, is a great friend of mines. He's waiting out back for us. I've been watching you for the past two years, waiting for the right moment. I don't want to sign with your husband's company. It was all a front. Everything that I'm doing, I'm doing to have you back in my life. Will you come with me?"

Flabbergasted, I think about the love I had for her and how I was ashamed to admit it. My thoughts take over my being again. I think about the malicious things my mother told me about the women she referred to as 'dykes'. I think about how my success is because of my mother. The talks Carmen and I used to have, and the way she made me feel all circle in my brain. I think about my husband and how he would feel. While I'm doing all this thinking, I think about my happiness, its importance, the opportunity to be free, and the opportunity to embrace love; true love. I think about my dreams and desires.

Looking in her eyes, I nod my head up and down, not caring about my husband, my career, or what I'll do. Nothing matters at this point. My body and mind both eases. My heart eases. A safe feeling overcomes me. For the first time in my life, I feel wanted. Not sexually or physically, but more mentally and emotionally.

She takes my hand as we sneak our way through the restaurant, and to the back door where Mark is waiting. We get in the back seat, and as the car pulls forward, I don't look behind me. I fixate my eyes on hers. I realize I'm doing it again. I'm running, just as I have before, but this time, I don't look at it as running. I look at it as trading a life where sex is my only means of staying for a life of freedom.

1st Phase

Chapter 1

It's the first semester of my senior year at St. Xavier University, and I'm exhausted from the move back to campus. I had a decent summer at home in Miami, and I finally broke up with Jarmaine, my no-good ex-boyfriend. We dated for two years before I realized I wasn't the only girl he was entertaining. Once it became clear, I refuse to be his or anybody else's number two or three when I can be my own number one. So, kicking him to the curb was easier for me to do than it was for him to accept. It feels like the more time passes, the more my feelings for him dissolve, and the easier it is to not miss him. I don't have time for him anyway since school is my focus right now. Getting a degree in business management requires a lot of attention and long hours of studying. Jarmaine wanted too much responsiveness that I couldn't give. It was him or school, and I chose school.

I'm twenty-one and fine, so people automatically assume I'm the partying type, when honestly, I'd rather go to a local bar and throw back two Heinekens with a lemon. My fellow classmates think I'm a nerd, so that should tell you the number of friends I have here... zero. I don't feel like I really need a circle to survive, so I let others think whatever they want, as long as they don't fuck with me. My mom sheltered me my whole life, which made it hard for me to trust others. I trust my housekeeper Lucia though. That's my girl! I can tell her any and everything and she gets it... she gets me. She may not always understand my English because she's a Cuban native and her English is bad, but I understand her perfectly fine.

I pick up Lucia's picture from the bottom of the almost empty box. A chill comes over me and I feel myself missing her more now than five minutes ago. When I sit on the edge of the bed, I'm flooded with a memory of laying on her lap as she brushed my long hair until I fell asleep. And now, because of her, I brush my hair every night before bed, one-hundred strokes. My long, jet-black, natural mane has grown down my back, and it complements my extended frame and legs. I stand five-feet-nine inches, and I'm naturally fit in all the right places, with the physique of a model. My caramel skin tone and perfect teeth contribute to my beautiful smile. Let my mother tell it, I look just like my father, except for my light brown eyes—which she swears I get from her—but I'd rather not have any resemblance to either of them.

The door creeps open and distracts me. A girl who looks my age peeks her head in first, "Um, is this dorm room 256? It looks like somebody scratched the numbers off." Her deep voice confuses me because her face doesn't match her voice.

I laugh at my own thoughts and respond, "Yes. You must be the new roomie. You can put your things over there since I've already started unpacking on this side." I point to the other bed, stand, and turn my back to her and begin placing random things back in the empty box to prevent from socializing any more than I'd already done.

I hear her enter the room and close the door. I walk to the desk next to my bed and I get a better look at her. Not only is her voice deep for a girl, but she's dressed like a boy. She's about five-feet-seven inches with an athletic build and shoulder-length hair. Her Michael Jordan shoes, basketball shorts, and T-shirt give me the impression that she's a basketball player or one of those lesbian girls. If I base it solely on her looks and voice, she must be one or the other, or hell, she may be both.

I'm not sure if I'm comfortable having a lesbian roommate. Who knows, she might try to hit on me. And as soon as she does, I will fuck her up. I probably should let her know that, but if I do, then the fuck up might not be as good. I won't say anything just yet. I'll feel her out for two days and see how she is. Only because I hate when people judge me before knowing anything about me. She could be a tomboy and here I am labeling her a lesbian the same way others label me a nerd. A proper introduction could break the ice… I'm good.

"Hey, you don't mind if I hang a few things around the room to give it some jazz, do you?" She asks.

I shrug, "Nope! I don't! As long as it's on your side. I'm Melody. What's your name?"

"What's up, Mel? I'm Skylar." She extends her hand.

Her handshake damn near breaks my wrist! I knew she was one of those lesbian girls! Talking about some… what's up, Mel? Who in the fuck is Mel? I know I told her that my name is Melody! I may have to put her in her place. To make matters worse, she's started hanging half-naked pictures of different video vixens on the wall. I'm so ready to snap on her and get her out of here, but I finish unpacking instead.

School doesn't start until Monday, so a drive to the city might do me some good. By the way this day is going, I can already tell I will need a few beers to calm my nerves. I'll try not to have too many, but if I do, I'll just crash at my parents' condo, so I won't have to make the forty-five-minute drive under the influence.

I'm planning out my evening when I'm distracted by Skylar's loud phone conversation that she has on speaker phone. Her ghetto habits are irritating my soul, so I gather my things and make my way to the shower. As I close the bathroom door, I hear Skyler say, "Ooooh, girl, the new roomie is too fine. Thick in all the right places with legs I'll crawl up any day. And she got some pretty ass hair with some beautiful, almond-shaped, light brown eyes. Now I can fuck with her. Shit, I bet you I can fuck her. She'll be another one of my victims," she snickers to the person on the other end of the phone.

That's it! She has officially fucked up! I snatch the door open, walk to her and get in her face, staring her square in the eyes. "So, check this out. First, thank you for the compliments, but there will be no fucking me in any shape, form, or fashion. Second, I would appreciate it if you took some of these naked ass posters down. Third, I don't care if you like men, women, or animals, please don't disrespect me or this dorm room. Meaning, if you want to have company, fine, but *no* fucking while I'm here! Last, I'm not gay and if I were, I wouldn't be the damn victim, you would! Got it? Get it! Great! And oh, in case you didn't hear me, my damn name is *Melody*, not *Mel*! I would appreciate it if you called me that and nothing else!"

I quickly turn and rush back into the bathroom and slam the door. I wanted to say more, but I didn't. I wanted to call her a "dyke bitch" or something like that to piss her off as much as she'd just pissed me off, but I didn't. I should've said more. Or maybe what I said was enough to help her understand I mean business… "Lord, please hold my mule." I pray out loud, turn the shower on, get undressed and step in.

My old-school Whitney Houston radio station is jamming on Pandora. I'm grooving and not caring how loud or out of tune I am as I sing the lyrics to Toni Braxton's "Seven Whole Days". I thought I heard the dorm room door open and then close. *Good! I hope she left!* I hurry and finish my shower so I can leave before she comes back.

The room is empty when I come out of the bathroom. "Thank goodness!" I say. Some posters have been taken down and I don't care if I offended her. I don't think she realizes we're in college and not high school. I didn't know people even still decorated their walls.

I rush to get dressed and throw on a yellow Express V-neck T-shirt, white Express shorts, and all-white Converse. My keys and clutch are on the desk, so I grab them and head for the door. On my way out of the building, I spot Jarmaine hugged up in the corner with some tramp. All I can do is roll my eyes and shake my head. If she only knew how many other tramps he had, she would run for the border. When he looks up and sees me, he backs away from her. That's funny to me because he's old news and I couldn't care less about what he does and who he does it with.

I speed up my pace, so he doesn't catch up with me. Once at my car, I turn and see him trotting towards me. His trot turns into a jog as I turn the ignition. By the time he gets to my door, I'm pulling away. I open the sunroof and throw up the deuces and then drop the one. "Fuck you, Jarmaine!" I yell and skid off, leaving him standing in the dust.

I'm cruising down the Dan Ryan in my jet black '07' Audi A4 (I call her Pepper) and jamming to the tunes playing on V103 when I think back to the episode with my new roommate. I can't believe she said she would fuck me. Little does she know that if she ever tried anything with me, she would get cut from her asshole to her appetite in a New York second. I may be single, but I'm not desperate. TLC's "Scrubs" come on and I turn the radio volume and my voice volume to the max.

Chapter 2

By the time I get back to campus, I'm tipsy and ready to relax. Sounds of moaning fill the hall and get louder as I get closer to my door. I unlock the door and freeze at the sight of Skylar making out with some light-skinned chick in my bed.

"Now *this* is some bold shit!" I say and run to the bed and snatch both of them to the floor, one-by-one. I can't believe my eyes. It's like Skylar wanted me to walk in and catch them; like she's intentionally trying to piss me off.

"Damn! Be easy, baby," Skylar says while standing and helping the other girl off the floor. "You are more than welcome to join us."

Spit from her mouth lands on the other girl when I slap the shit out of her. "Now, you join that!" I step back. "Yeah, you should leave before shit gets worse than it has." It must be the three beers in me that gave me the courage to put my hands on her without second guessing.

"Whoa, hold up, Lil Mama. Now this room is mine just as yours," she says while snickering. "You might *need* to get your rocks off, and maybe that'll get your panties out a bunch. You don't know what you missing until you try it, so until then, my advice to you… is don't knock something you ain't never tried."

I'm livid that she insists on insulting me. But instead of acting a complete fool with her, which is what I assume she wants me to do, in a calm voice, I politely ask her and her company to leave for the night. She doesn't pick up her pace, so I yell, "LEAVE! NOW!" at the top of my lungs. They both hurry to find the rest of their clothes and exit. My head pounds, and I just want to go to bed, but I refuse to sleep on the same sheets they were just fuck-ing on top of. I'm glad my mom taught me to keep extra linen. I find a clean set in my drawer and remove the dirty linen. I spray the mattress with Febreze and put on clean sheets. I'm too tired to brush my hair or write in my journal, so I change into my nightshirt, take a BC powder for the headache and get into bed.

After being in bed for Lord knows how long and unable to fall asleep, I turn and lay staring at the wall. The moaning and an image of Skylar having sex forms in my mind. I feel myself moistening between the legs, and it captures my entire body. To make sure I'm not fantasizing a sensation, I wiggle my hand in my panties and sure enough, my cookie is wetter than Hurricane Harbor at Six Flags Great America. I snatch my hand from in my panties. Is it weird that I'm turned on by the image of two women having sex? I ask myself. I touch between my legs again and my finger rubs against my button and sends a charge of energy through my entire body. It's an unfamiliar feeling that I've never had. One I never knew existed. Jarmaine never touched me between my legs like that. He just stuck it in, and we got down to business. Or he would penetrate me with his fingers, assuming he was doing something. There was never a time when he and I had sex and my cookie got wet like it is now. That might explain why it was always so uncomfortable. Sometimes, it hurt me… well, most times it did.

I run my finger across my button again. My heartbeat speeds up and something in the pit of my stomach rages out of control, turning me on more. I try to take deep slow breaths to calm myself, but it doesn't help. I turn on my back, take my Victoria Secret panties off, and eagle-spread my legs. I use one hand to enter my cookie jar and the other to caress my nipples. I am turned on but have no clue of what I'm doing. The rhythm of my hips matches my finger as I enter and exit my opening in a slow motion. The wetness of my opening is turning me on more and more. I remove my wet finger and message my button in soft, circular motions. I mirror the same motion on my nipples, one at a time. I can hear my cell phone ringing, but I can't stop myself. Something is happening to me on the inside. My motions speed up. I spread my lips further apart as I open by legs as wide as they can go. I work my button with the opposite hand. I can't stop. The build-up is getting stronger and more intense by the second. I move faster, and faster… and faster, until… until my entire body explodes. I exhale deeply and close my eyes.

~

I wake up the next morning full of energy and ready to start the day. It's still early. The sun hasn't even come up and Skylar is sound asleep in her bed. She must have crept in in the middle of the night. I ease out of bed and notice I don't have any panties on and there's a wet spot in the middle of my bed. I must have had a wet dream that ended very well. I remember smacking Skylar, but I don't remember nothing else after that. Next time, I won't drink so many beers. I snatch the fitted sheet off the bed and stuff it in the dirty clothes hamper on my way to the bathroom.

In the bathroom, I turn on my tunes and jump in the shower, allowing Tyrese to take me away. This man sure knows how to serenade a woman. "Sweet Lady." He went from being the voice on the Coco-Cola commercial to having a number one hit. This song will never get too old, and I'll be his "sweet lady" any day.

After my shower, I get dressed and Skylar is awake when I come out the bathroom. I ignore her when she tries to speak. I collect my belongings and make my way to the door. Skylar blocks the door with her arm.

I look her directly in the eyes and say with emphasis, "*Move.*"

"Is there a way I can make this up to you?" She pleads.

She doesn't move when I give her a final warning, so I reach back to smack her again. She catches my hand and squeezes it.

"Just say you'll forgive me, and I'll let you go."

"You have every bit of three seconds to let me go, and to move your ass or—"

"Or what? What can you do?"

I knee her between the legs without breaking my firm glare. She may not be a man, but apparently it worked because she lets go of my hand and clenched over in pain. "Now, when I say move, I mean *move!*" I step over Skylar and leave when she falls to the floor.

She laughs and says, "I wonder what you was thinkin' about when you was masturbatin' last night." I reach over Skylar and she ducks. I grab the closest thing I could find, which was an umbrella, and whack her across her back as she tries to get up from the floor.

"Masturbate that, bitch!" I quietly say and slam the door. As I rush down the stairs to proceed with my Saturday morning, I wander to myself exactly what she is talking about.

Chapter 3

I'm startled out of my sleep by a sudden loud ring. I jump up and see Skylar snooze her alarm. I throw the pillow over my head after I flop back on the bed. What seems like only ten minutes later, the same loud ring wakes me again. This time, it doesn't stop. After a minute of constant ringing, I throw the cover off me and get up and turn the alarm off. The sun is barely up, so I crawl back in bed and cover my head again. I can hear the shower going as I try to dose back off.

The loud buzzing of my alarm awakes me at 6:30 AM. I snooze for an hour before I finally peal myself out of bed. I feel exhausted. Skylar isn't in her bed and her shoes are missing from the door. Good, she's gone. I should've known better though. As soon as I open the bathroom door, Skylar stands naked in the mirror and freezes while combing her hair.

Disgusted, I say, "Ugh! Yuck! Hurry," and slam the door. I get back in bed until she's done.

After dozing back off for thirty minutes, I'm finally dressed and trying to maneuver my way through the early morning campus grounds. What normally takes five minutes feels like forever once I finally get through the hustle and bustle and drag myself to the Management Building. I'm not in the mood for any bullshit today! But that's short-lived when I get to class and see Skylar sitting in the lecture hall's front row with her typical basketball shorts, T-shirt, and Jordan's.

I slide in the back row by the door, so she doesn't see me. After the Professor introduces herself as Dr. White, she summarizes the first assignment, assign groups and dismisses class. I was in the clear until Dr. White assigned me, Skylar, and some chic named Vanessa as a group. As soon as she said my name, Skylar turned around and instantly spotted me. *Thanks for nothing, Dr. White!*

Once I gather my belongings and turn to exit, Skylar is approaching. By the time I get to the door, she's on my heels, "Sup, Mel? Oh, wait, my fault, I mean Mel-o-dy," she corrects herself. I ignore her and speed up my pace. "Wait! Hold up," she yells! The faster I walk, the faster she walks to keep up and the more she ran her mouth. "Man, how long you gone give me the cold shoulder? I've apologized a million times. You know we got to live together, and now we have to do this assignment together. At some point or another, you gone have to say somethin' to me, you know?"

She runs into the back of me when I come to a sudden stop. I quickly turn and push her off me. "Would you stop fucking following me?"

"But we h—," she begins.

"An assignment that we have to work on together. Yeah. And? So what!" Skylar looks confused. "We can start on it when you find out who the third person is." I turn to walk off and she follows. I look back, "Don't you have class or something?"

"I'm done with class—"

"That was not a question," I say and start jogging. Thank God she doesn't follow.

From a distance, I see someone putting something under my windshield. It's Jarmaine. Got damn, it seems like I can't catch a break to save my life.

"What in the fuck are you doing, Jarmaine?"

He jumps and turns when he hears my voice. "Melody, can we please talk for a second? I messed up and I'm sorry. Please, just give me another chance. What do I have to do to win you back?" He pleads.

"Well, let's see, Jarmaine. You can start by moving away from my car." He's standing in front of the car door, so I push him out of the way to get in.

"Damn! Why are you so pushy? You weren't like this when we were dating," he says.

I hop in my car, start it up, and put it in reverse. I speed off and leave him standing in the dust. Jarmaine had his chance with me and he blew it. I'm tickled at how badly he's trying to get my attention now that I'm over him. When he had me, he didn't know what to do with me, and now that we're no longer together, he thinks begging will win me back.

I flip through the CD book in the front seat and pull out one of my favorites; it's my girl Lauryn Hill. She knows she did the damn thing with The Miseducation of Lauryn Hill album. I press on the gas as her voice feels my soul going ten miles over the speed limit. Traffic is clear, but the further I get into the city, the worse I know it can get.

I make it downtown in no time because traffic tricked me today. I find a quick parking spot in North Avenue Beach, but finding a posting spot on the beach didn't happen as fast. After ten minutes of looking, I finally find the perfect spot, not too close to the water and not too far. I spread out my purple beach towel and let out my beach chair. Just as I'm getting situated, a ball comes flying my way and collapses my chair. Without looking to see who threw it, I annoyingly toss it back in the direction it came from. I take a deep breath in and then out and whoosah to calm myself down.

The heat shortened my relaxing evening at the beach. Before leaving, the same dick face that made my beach chair collapse, called himself hitting on me as I was leaving. He was an interesting guy, but fine as hell at the same time. So fine, I named him Sexual Chocolate.

The sun is breath-taking today, but the tall buildings along Michigan Avenue serves days like this justice. A nice quick stroll is the perfect thing to keep me away just a little longer from the clowns on campus. Walking past Tiffany & Co, I see the Silver Man on the corner doing his usual thing; pose in a stance, move, and awe the crowd, pose again, move again. This man has been doing this for years; ever since I've been coming downtown. The tourists get a kick out of him, especially the children. I've always wondered if it's the same man. Or do they have different men that take turns wearing a platinum silver suit and painting the rest of their visible body platinum silver? I put money in his tin can every time I see him, no matter where he's posted.

Besides the Silver Man, on just about every other corner in downtown Chicago you have a bum or two, or maybe even three. I give them money too because you never know a person's situation. Some of them buy liquor with the money they collect, but how are givers to determine the difference between the ones that buy food and the ones that get drunk? Being homeless probably takes a toll on them. If it were me, hell, I'd need a drink too. I wouldn't lie about it though. I would tell people straight up, "You got some change to spare so I can get me some beers?" I would drink something harder than beer; something like… Everclear.

～

It's almost three, and I make it back south just in time to beat the traffic. Before going back to campus, I stop at Harold's Chicken on 95th and order a four piece with ketchup, mild sauce, hot sauce, and fries.

It's always a ghetto mess in Harold's Chicken, no matter which one I go to. Every time I step in this one, though, I try my damnedest not to snatch somebody's weaves or wigs off their heads. That's why I call my order in advance.

"Can I take yo order?" The girl at the register asks, smacking her gum and blowing bubbles.

"Yes, I have a call-in order for Melody."

"What cha got?" She asks, still popping that damn gum.

I tell her my order, and she tells me it'll be ready shortly. My morning episodes had me a little uptight. She better be glad I've calmed down since I've done a little retail therapy, although I spent more than I expected. That's what shopping while frustrated does to me every time. It never fails. I should probably work on getting that under control before it gets out of hand.

"Sit cho mufuckin ass down, boy, befo I beat da shit outta you in dis place," a youthful girl says to her son who is running around like a wild duck.

I wonder what this world is coming to. These little girls get out here and have these babies and then don't know what to do with them. Shit, he wouldn't be so damn bad if she chastised him at home and gave him that ass whooping at home. That way, when she brings his bad ass out in public, he wouldn't embarrass her ass. That's how I see it, anyway.

"Foe piece wit fries." The ghetto cashier calls out my order as I watch the little boy act a complete nut. I tried to not wear my feelings on my face, but that was an epic fail because I could feel my shit face as I get up and walk to the cashier. I take my order, check it, and leave. I hop on Western Avenue to avoid the traffic.

After I take my shopping bags and food back to my dorm, I make my way to the cafeteria to get dessert for later. Students fill the dorm halls, couples are on the grass smooching and making out, and doors are open as students decorate their rooms. Distracted by a hunger pain, my pace picks up. Trotting across the lawn, I notice Skylar from the back, standing around a group of other students. I assume they're all girls because they're all dressed like her, except they have hair hanging from under their caps or no cap at all but overlong flowing hair. Those must be her dyke friends. I cut through a crowd to prevent from having to walk past her and enter the cafeteria.

"Yo, Melody, what's up?" Damn! It's Skylar! I can't shake this chick if I wanted to. "I saw you running across the lawn, so I thought I'd come speak since you blew me off earlier."

"What do you want?" I ask. I don't care what she wants, but I know if I ignore her like I've been doing, she will only keep talking and might follow me back to the dorm room. I don't want that just yet.

"I just wanted to tell you I got our other teammate for the assignment." She has a stupid grin on her face, like she's expecting me to be proud of her.

"Good for you." I pay for my ice cream and leave the cafeteria. Skylar follows.

"Here she comes right now." I see a girl walking towards us, and the closer she gets the more familiar she looks. I never forget a face. Realization sets in when I notice it's the same girl she was having sex with, in my bed the other day. I barely stop when Skylar introduces us, "Vanessa, this is Melody. Melody, Vanessa," Skylar introduces us.

"You have got to be fucking kidding me!" I ignore her extended hand and continue walking away.

Chapter 4

I'm not sure how I'm supposed to work with one annoying ass girl, let alone two, but I can't deal with this today. I'll cross that bridge once I get to it. Since I don't have the class again until Thursday, I have plenty of time to figure it out. Today, I need some time to just me, myself, and I. I get an idea that sends me in the opposite direction and back to the cafeteria to find Skylar. When I locate her, the group of girls from earlier have now joined her and Vanessa by the cafeteria door. She's turns around and looks surprised when she hears me call her name. I quickly pull her to the side and speak before she opens her mouth, "Hey, you think you can find somewhere else to crash tonight and let me have the room to myself?"

"And what am I supposed to do? I just—"

"Thanks, roomie," I interrupt. "You can come back in the morning before you go to class," I say walking backwards.

Once I turn around, she yells from behind me, "Can I at least get clothes?"

"Come now!" I turn and yell back.

"All right. Hold up." I speed up. "Why the rush? Everything good?" she asks once she catches up with me.

"Yup!" I smirk. "I'm just trying to get back to my food before it gets cold."

"Oh, you got food. Word? What you got?"

"Nothing for you."

Sasha, the evening resident's assistant, is sitting at the door when we enter. She nods at me and winks at Skylar. "What up Sash?" I take the stairs two steps at a time and Skylar takes three to keep up. "Hey, this ain't no trick, is it? I mean, you've been giving me nothing but tude, and now all of a sudden you having small talk wit me."

"Please don't be delusional," I say and unlock the dorm room door. Skylar packs her backpack with clothes from off the floor. I remove my food from the microwave and plop down on the sofa.

"Man, what's up wit you?" Skylar asks while zipping her backpack.

"Nothing." I open my container of food and start eating.

"Yea, I'm sure it's nothing. You bipolar or something? Or weird as fuck?" Skylar pauses for an answer. I continue eating and without looking up. "Man, whatever! I'll see you tomorrow."

"Hey, can you lock the door for me?" I catch her before the door closes. She doesn't respond, but I can hear the lock turn a few seconds after she slams the door.

I can feel the "itis" kicking in, so I get up from the sofa and clean my mess. After I'm done, I dig through my beach bag for a something to read. As I'm fumbling through the bag, a piece of paper with a name and phone number falls out when I pull out my favorite book. I pick it up and slowly read it out loud, "Malik (773)-606-2575." The name doesn't ring a bell, so I put the piece of paper in the back of the book and get comfortable on the sofa.

Snuggled in the sofa's corner and sitting Indian-style, I allow Zane's "The Sex Chronicles: Shattering the Myth" take me away... until a light knock at the door interrupts me. I ignore it until they knock louder. I throw the book on the sofa and stump barefoot to the door. Jarmaine stands pitifully on the other side of the peephole. I slowly back away from the door, trying not to make a sound. "Come on, Mel. I know you're in there. I saw your car parked in the parking lot." I creep into the bathroom and gently close the door.

I had to shower anyway, so what better chance than now. I turn the shower on, undress, and step in. The scorching water sends a calming effect over my entire body. I close my eyes and an image of Skylar pops into my visual. Maybe I've been a little too bitchy with her. Not just to her, but just about everyone. I don't like it when I'm mistreated or misjudged, so what makes it right for me to treat her that way. Maybe I should cut her some slack the next time I see her.

Standing naked in the full body length mirror, my flaws are unnoticeable. This body of mine, perfectly formed, has flaws that no other eye can see. An hour of me embracing myself mentally, physically, and emotionally has gone by. The loud knock at the door distracts me. Peeping through the peephole, a short, brown–skinned girl stands on the other side. It's the Vanessa girl from earlier. "I said I would try to be better, but I for damn sure didn't mean tonight," I mumble under my breath. I tell her through the door that Skylar isn't here, and she turns to walk away.

Not even two minutes later, someone knocks again. This time, I ignore it and continue putting on my nightgown. I let the knocking continue for several minutes before becoming annoyed. I open the door wide enough for my face only to fit. "Skylar left for the evening, and I'm trying to rest."

"I was hoping I could talk to you."

"It's late, and I'm in bed. Can't this wait until tomorrow?"

"Sure, but can you promise me you'll talk to me then?" She looks like a lost puppy.

"Okay, we can talk tomorrow," I agree. She nods and leaves. Vanessa is a cute girl with a short Toni Braxton hairstyle that matches her brown and round face perfectly. She's much thicker than me, but it fits her well. The best way to describe her shape is short with thick hips.

I close the door, and as I'm walking back to my bed, another knock at the door stops me in mid-stride. Frustrated, I swing the door open, and to my surprise, it's Jarmaine. "What the fuck do you want?" He invites himself in. "Really, Jarmaine!"

"I just wanted to come by and talk to you since you wouldn't talk to me earlier. I came knocking at the door not too long ago, but you didn't answer. When I saw some girl coming out, I tried again."

I slam the door closed and cross my arms in front of me, "What makes you think you deserve any of my time, after all you've put me through?"

"I just wanted to apologize and tell you how much I miss you," he says walking closer to me.

I back all the way to the door, "You've done that already. Several times to be exact."

"I know, but you haven't said if you forgive me or not." I watch him walk to the window and turn to me. Walking back towards me he continues, "Is there any way we can go hang out sometime? I know I fucked up, and I can't apologize enough. I was stupid. Ain't none of these girls got nothing on you. They all look for the same thing; somebody to take care of them. You are different. You take care of yourself and don't ask for shit. You're not just beautiful on the outside, but you're also beautiful on the inside. I didn't notice that at first, but once you left me alone for good is when reality sat in."

I respond with a blank stare. Jarmaine has tried to play me frequently while we were together. The two times I caught him red-handed, I forgave him and took him back both times. I can't do that this time. That would make me a fool. Fool me once, shame on you. Fool me twice, shame on me. If I let it happen a third time, I'm the fool for allowing him to disrespect me when I know better. As attractive as I am, a clown ass can't keep playing me for some ratchet tramp. And he is the biggest clown of them all.

"Well, Jarmaine, right now my focus is completing my last year with a 4.0 GPA and living single is the only option I have to fulfill that goal. You know… find who I am in every aspect. There are other goals and aspirations I want to accomplish after graduation, and I need no distractions. Your honesty is very much appreciated though," I tell him without sarcastically saying, "I told you so."

"So, you're saying I would be a distraction?" He weirdly gets excited.

"Out of everything I just said is that the only thing you heard?" Maintaining my annoyance becomes difficult.

"I was—"

"You know what, don't even bother answering that. I have an early class tomorrow, so I need to finish getting ready for bed. You've said what you've had to say and so have I. I accept your apology, so there's no need to keep apologizing because I forgave you as soon as you did the same shit a third time. One thing for sure and two things for certain; just because I forgave you, does not mean I'll ever forget. I won't hold any grudge against you because that only hinders me from living my life. The best thing right now is to just not fuck with you at all. With that said, hanging out together is not an option." I turn and open the door, "Now, since that's out of the way, can you please leave so I can get some rest?"

Before the door is open, Jarmaine slams it closed from behind me. He places an aggressive hold on me from behind and begins kissing my neck. His grip is too tight for me to turn around. "Jarmaine! What are you doing?" I try to ask.

"Come on, Mel. Just one last time. You know you want this." He pulls me closer and holds me tighter. I can feel his dick getting hard on my back because he's that much taller than me. "Just one more time." His breathing picks up.

"No! What the fuck has gotten into you?" I try to elbow him in his stomach, but he catches the blow. He locks the door with his free hand and then hugs me with both hands and squeezes me so tight that moving becomes impossible. "What are you doing, Jarmaine?" I yell, trying to fight him off. He covers my mouth with one hand, locks both my arms using one limb, and force me to my bed.

The harder he presses my face in the pillow, the harder it becomes for me to breathe. Suddenly, I feel him jam his fingers inside me. I can't breathe and I'm getting dizzy. My body becomes weak. Restrained, I give up and lay still, trying to catch a breath. *Focus on your breath.*

Chapter 5

The pressure on my head releases and I feel Jarmaine's entire body fall limp on my back. Suddenly, his weight is off me and I hear him hit the floor. I turn my head and Skylar is standing over Jarmaine with one fist balled up and a mini bat in the other hand. I sit up slowly and cover myself with the sheet. Skylar bends over and drags Jarmaine to the door by one arm. The door is open and the same group of girls from earlier fill the hall at the doorway. Two of the girls from the group help Skylar drag Jarmaine into the hallway.

I don't know if he's dead or just passed out, but either way, he's not responding. Skylar steps over him and back into the room and closes the door. Before she could ask, I tell her I'm okay, and lie on my side with my head facing the wall. I'm not okay, I'm just not in the mood to discuss this right now. I just want to sleep this pain away. I'm hurt right now. Not because he tried to take my cookie, but because he was someone claiming to love me. I never knew that loving someone meant hurting them. Since when does love become pain? I'm familiar with neglect being love, but not pain too.

"Do you want me to call Sasha?" Skylar's voice is calm and sincere.

"No." I say snobbishly while trying to hold back the tears.

"You sure?" I feel her sit at the foot of the bed.

"No." I turn my body to face her with a cry for sympathy in my eyes. "What made you come back to the room?"

"I forgot some stuff, so I came back before it got too late. When I opened the door, I saw him ramming his fingers in you. I could tell you wasn't enjoyin' it cause of how he was holdin' you down. I'm a fast reactor," she straightens her back with pride and continues, "I'm glad I came back when I did."

"Yeah. Me to. Thanks." I bury my face in my pillow and cry from my soul. Skylar scoots closer and places her hand on my shoulder.

"You ain't got to thank me."

Now looking into her eyes, I respond, "But you saved my life. I don't know how I'll ever repay you," I say in between snuffles.

"Well, you can repay me by not being so damn mean." She flashes a big and beautiful smile.

"That's a start, huh?" I chuckle and all the tears that's been sitting in the well of my left eye fall. I sit up and get a Kleenex from on my desk and blow hard. "Excuse me." When I wipe my tears, a sudden feeling of violation rages through my entire body. I throw my head in my hands and sob excessively.

"It's okay to cry, you know. Believe it or not, I cry sometimes too. I remember when my family found out I was into the ladies, and my uncle tried to molest me sayin' it was for *my* good and was to help me like men. It's a good thing I used to be heavy into that workout shit in my younger days, cause I gave him an ass whoopin' he was not expectin' from a chick," Skylar takes a moment to reflect, and then under her breath, laughs at something only she can comprehend. She snaps out of her thought and redirects her attention back to me, "I understand how you feel right now. You feel violated cause you thought he loved you. Which sucks cause most men don't even know what love is. They think they can love a woman with their limp dicks and their money, and that's all they got to do. They don't understand that love requires more than that," she explains.

I'm shocked because one, she knows my emotions, and two, she's been in a similar situation. "But what makes you think I feel the same way as you and your situation."

"I don't for real. I'm just assuming and hopin' I don't make an ass out myself. I see you holdin' back your tears though. That's why I say it's okay to cry. As far as you feelin' violated, well, let's just say that any woman who don't volunteer to give their pussy away *should* feel violated. I don't know," she shrugs. "How do you feel?"

"I don't know." I shrug. Skylar stands up and goes to the door. She opens it. The doorway is clear; no friends, no Jarmaine. She then turns to me, "Ol' boy is takin' care of and I know for sure he ain't comin' back."

"It's cool. You don't have to leave." I softly respond. I figured that's the least I could do since she saved me from what could have been a tragedy. "I just need a minute or two to get my head right. I will take a shower and see if that helps." I wrap my bottom half with the sheet, even though my gown is long enough, and take short, quick steps to the bathroom. As I pass Skylar, she snatches me up and gives me an enor-mous hug. I do not reciprocate her gesture but freeze in place. Eventually, she lets go and I walk into the bath-room showing no emotions. I turn the shower on, let the sheet fall, undress, and step in. My knees weaken when once both feet hit the bottom of the tub. Sitting in the back of the shower, I hug my legs and bury my face in my knees. I let the tears fall freely until there are no more tears left to cry, and then I pray.

"Please forgive me for all the awful stuff that I've done. I don't know what I did to deserve this, but I'm so sorry. I need strength from you, God. Strength to make it through this situation. I know that nothing happens by mistake, and everything happens for a rea-son, but why me and why now? I pray that you give me the strength to forgive Jarmaine for what he's done to me. I pray that you fill me with peace. I pray for peace in my mind, body, and soul. I want my heart to heal because right now it's broken, and it hurts. Forgive me for judging Skylar. Thank you, God. Amen."

As I sit in the fetal position in the back of the shower, my thoughts are all over the place and going a thousand miles per second. The past few days have been so challenging, I feel like I'm being tested. I can get through this. I will and I can. I need someone to talk to. I should call Lucia, but I don't want to worry her with my mess since she has so much of my mother's mess to tend to. I wish I had a better understanding of why me? I know I've been a little bitchy lately, but not deserving of this. It almost makes me wonder if my bitchiness is really bitterness. How can I be bitter when I was the one who left Jarmaine, not the other way around? I allow the tears to flow.

The crying suddenly stops. *God sure works fast;* I think to myself. I stand and scrub my body several times, but I still feel dirty. I scrub until the water is cold. The floor feels cold when my feet hit the tile. Standing in front of the mirror shivering, I stare at the reflection that stares back. I am filled with flaws, but now there are more flaws than before. The knock at the door stuns me.

"You okay, Melody?" Her tone is so low, I could barely hear her.

"Yeah, I'm okay. I'll be out shortly." I step away from the mirror.

"Okay. I'm going to lie down. If I'm asleep when you get out, you can wake me up if you need to."

I get dressed in my nightgown and tiptoe to the closet and quietly find my panties and shorts. It's pitch black in the room, so I must feel my way around. I trip over Skylar's foot and almost fall forward.

"What the hell are you doing, Skylar?" I hit the nightlight on the side of the desk.

"Come." She pats the bed.

"Why are you on my bed?"

"Just come. I ain't gone try nothin' with you. I just want to be here as a friend. That's it. You can take my word." Her voice is persuading, but I don't know who I can and can't trust at this point.

Nervous and not knowing what to expect, I meander and sit beside her. "I just want to go to sleep and wake up to a better day."

"Bet! I got you! Lay down, and I'll be here for comfort." She stands and swing my feet onto the bed and covers me up to my chin.

She lies down beside me on top of the covers and tells me, "If you want to talk, I'll be right here."

Why is this chick so nice to me when I've been so mean to her, are my thoughts as I close my eyes and try to sleep. She takes my hand and squeezes it. I don't move. My eyes drift. It feels good to have a friend, but is she my friend? I guess so since she just saved my life. Only a friend would go the distance she's gone to save me and keep me safe. Or does she want more from me? More is what I can't give because I like men. I *love* men!

Chapter 6

Night sweats wake me in the middle of the night. I realize Skylar is still in the bed when I try to remove the covers but can't. Our hands remain locked. I slither my fingers loose, trying not to wake her. I remove my shorts and underwear with one hand and use my feet to kick them to the foot of the bed without disturbing her. Skylar smells good lying next to me. I sure could use a shoulder to lie on right now. I look at Skylar and figure, why not? I turn towards her and rest my head on her shoulder. She doesn't budge. I wonder if she's faking. I softly place my hand on her chest. She moans, causing my reflex to pull my hand away. I bury my face in her neck when she turns her head towards me. She's still sound asleep. Stillness comes over my body because if she isn't faking, I don't want to wake her, but damn, her smell is intoxicating and is pulling me in. I try to figure out a way to get my head from caught up in her rapture before I become drunk from her scent. I lay there thinking of a master plan and it finally hits me. I place my hand back on her chest. As soon as I do so, she turns her head back the other way. I smile and quickly move my hand.

"Everything aright?" Her voice is sleepy, but sexy. Much sexier than that dominant voice she usually has.

"Yes. Everything is fine." My head remains on her shoulder.

"I wasn't talkin' in my sleep, was I? I've been told I do that from time-to-time."

"I didn't hear you." I glance over her to the clock and notice that I'd only been asleep for an hour. "I didn't wake you with all of my moving around, did I?"

"You did, but it's cool." Skylar turns to look at the clock. "You ain't been sleeping long, go back to sleep, you need your rest."

"I don't have class until the afternoon, so I'll be okay. Plus, I can't sleep right now."

"Melody, can I ask you somethin'?"

"Yeah, you can, as long as it doesn't pertain to earlier tonight."

"Why are you layin' on my shoulder?" Her question sends me on a loop.

"I don't know. I need a shoulder to lie on, and yours is the only one available now." I'm giving myself nothing but attitude on the inside for such a dumb ass response.

Quietly, she turns her head back towards me but doesn't suffocate me and says, "Then what do you know, since you say you don't know?"

"I know I need a shoulder."

"Can I ask you somethin' else?" Oh shit! Here we go with the thousand damn questions. I like her better when she's sleeping.

"One last question and that's it." I respond.

"Why you put your hand on my chest? And don't say you don't know."

I knew her ass was faking. "To see if you were still breathing," I respond with a smirk.

"Yea, sure. Let that be the reason, while you smirk and shit."

"Can I ask you something, Skylar?" My nerves kick in.

"Yeah, you can." Her voice is soft.

"Remember when you made a statement about me masturbating?"

"Yeeeep…"

"What were you talking about?" It feels like we're having pillow talk.

"Seriously! You mean to tell me you really don't know?"

"No. I've been wondering about it since you said it."

"I came in the room and you was masturbating. I mean, you was so into it, I was kinda turned on. Thinking about it now is turnin' me on." She waits for me to respond, but I don't. I just listen. I must admit that I'm getting turned on too, but I don't understand why. Damn, she smells good. Like a cool breeze of water on a beach in paradise. She turns to look at me and for the first time, I notice her beautiful eyes in the dark. "Why was you masturbating? Was you turned on by what you saw? You can tell me. I won't judge you like you judged me. Every woman has a curious side when it pertains to another woman. At least that's what I believe." Skylar shrugs. "Even if you don't like women, you have that curiosity and the only way to entertain that curiosity is to try it." She's speaking softly; different from her usual tone.

Skylar's gaze locks me in and I embrace her face with the palm of my hand and kiss her lips. They're soft. She doesn't reciprocate the kiss. Did I do something wrong? Did I not kiss her right? What the fuck did I just do! That kiss came out of nowhere. "Are you sure this is what you want? Even if you don't like it, promise me we'll be able to room together and establish a friendship? I don't want you to do nothing you don't want to do." Her breathing picks up. I can tell she's turned on. At least her nipples are if she's not. She has me feeling something new. Not just down there, but all over. I want to kiss her so bad, but I tried that. Her breathing picks up. Her breath smells fresh and makes me want to taste it. When her lips touch mine, a warm electricity runs through my body.

My breathing picks up and I bite my bottom lip. "Uhmmmm," I moan. "I don't know why I was masturbating. I don't remember doing it. And yeah, I'm sure. I'll tell you to stop if you do something I don't like." I lean in closer to inhale her sweet breath. "I don't know what I'm feeling but it feels good, and it feels like it's something I need. I want you right now. If I am confused, so what. I can deal with that later. I just want to kiss you." I speak into her mouth.

Skylar flings the covers back and grips me by my waist. She doesn't have to use much strength to get me on top of her, because I'm just as ready. I straddle her and she grips my hair seductively, pulls me down to her, and kisses me in a way I'm not familiar with. Her hands are soft on my skin as she caresses my butt cheeks and grinds me up and down in a slow motion. The friction from her basketball shorts and her bare stomach against mine is driving me wild. My cookie vagina gets wetter, and I kiss her harder. I completely relax at the abrupt loss of control. Skylar wraps both her arms around me and holds me tight as our kisses grow more passionate. She does something I cannot take. With one of her hands, she reaches for my clit from behind. At her gentle touch, I wail and my body collapses. She grabs my face with her other hand and plants soft kisses on my lips as she continues exploring. Another wail exits my mouth. This time, she doesn't stop. She caresses gently and slowly, while kissing me with every rotation.

"Melody... Melody..." she whispers.

"Yes," I whine.

"Melody! Wake up!" My eyes barely open. "You aright?" she asks. I rub my eyes and look at the clock. It's 2 am. Skylar gets up, turns the lamp on, and sits on her bed. "You good?" She asks again.

"Yeah. I must have been having a terrible dream." I sit up and rub my eyes again to make sure I'm not still dreaming.

"A *terrible* dream? You mean a *wet* dream?" she asks.

I shoot her a nasty look. "Don't flatter yourself."

"Don't front. I know you want me. At least that's what you said in your sleep." She chuckles and continues, "And *you* say the dream was terrible. Ha! No dream with me is ever terrible, Baby. I'm the one that can make all those dreams come true." She laughs with confidence.

"Ha! Ha! I don't get the damn joke! And what makes you so—. You know what, fuck it!" I'm not in the mood to entertain her, so I flop back on my pillow.

"Right! Just like I thought!" She snickers, then ask, "Aye man, what you think about me? You think I'm some little dyke broad, don't you?"

Still lying on my back, I turn my head towards her, "Why would you say that?"

"I don't know. I guess cause I get that a lot. Allow me to introduce myself to you though." Skylar sits on her bed and cross one leg across the other. "I always knew girls attracted me. At an early age, too. I was a young girl trying to play with the vagina. Like ten-years-old little. That shit that happened to me with my uncle, didn't leave me scorned cause I was gay before that. It just gave me more of a reason to not even want to *try* men after that. I eventually found that I don't have a desire for men. Shit, they can't do nothin' for me I can't do for myself. Not only that, but they couldn't even handle a thoroughbred like myself." Skylar stands, flexes her muscles, and turns side to side. I guess she's trying to sell me tickets to her "gun show". She must have read my thoughts through my expression because she says, "Oh stop! You know you think I'm the shit!" She sits back down. "Anyway. I know you feelin' some way from that shit that happened earlier. Don't let that shit fuck you up like that. I know it's easier said than done, but I know so many chicks that start fuckin wit other chicks just cause they heads are fucked up by the penis. That's today's generation of gays, anyway. They only doin' it cause they think that's the in thing and the thing to do. Like this shit a trend or something. Just don't get yourself caught up in this trend cause of what that asshole tried to do to you, is all I'm tryna say."

I chime in when she pauses, "Trust me, I won't."

"Yea, that's what they all say in the beginning. I got a lot of fine friends that'll be coming over to kick it wit me. Don't be trying to hit on them either." She pauses for a few more seconds as if she had to think about her next statement before saying it, then continues, "You know what, your ass grown, if you want to play around in the va-jay-jay, you go right ahead. That way, if you get turned out, it's on you and not me. I'll be damned if I be the one to turn you out though. You'll probably think I'm a dick anyway cause I give no fucks about these broads. But just a head's up, I'm single, and I only like to play. I keep a victim or two cause I can, and these broads thirsty for a chick like myself. Call me the thirst quencher, baby." She finally stops and stares at me, waiting for a response.

"To be honest with you, that was my original thought when I first saw you. I thought you were exactly what you're describing."

"I can be all that, but I'm a lady lover too. I love the ladies. It's just that none of them love themselves enough for me to love them the way I could... or should. Enough to have straight people like you dreamin' about me." Her laughter annoys me.

"Fuck you, Skylar!"

"You wish." She replies with more confidence than before.

I turn to face the wall, pull the cover over my head, and inhale and exhale slow and deep. I can't believe I had a dream about this girl. It's almost four in the morning.

I turn my head towards Skylar. "Skylar."

"Yes, Melody."

"You sleep yet?"

"Almost. Why, what's up?"

"Thanks for coming back to the room when you did?"

"You thanked me already. Make sure you thank Vanessa too. She's the one who reminded me I got conditionin' for basketball tomorrow. If she didn't, I would have forgotten my shoes and bought a new toothbrush instead of comin' back here. I think she low key knew somethin' cause she said as she was leaving the building, he was comin' in, and he asked if you was around. I don't think she knows who he is though, but thank her just cause." She pauses for a moment before continuing, "You see there, victims *are* good for somethin'." She stops and turns to face the wall.

Just like I thought, Vanessa is one of her *many* victims.

Chapter 7

On the way to class the next day, I see some of Skylar's home girls. "Yo! What up, Mel?" They all say in unison.

It's Mel-o... oh, never mind. "Morning, ladies." Vanessa is walking with them, but I'll catch up with her later. I must find a subtle way to thank her because I don't need any of Skylar's other "victims" knowing any of my business. As I skim the area, I wonder where Skylar is, anyway. She wasn't in the room when I got up this morning, and I'll be damn if I ask any of her friends. I'll see her later, at one point or another.

Jarmaine is sitting in class when I enter. Damn, they fucked him up! He has two black eyes and one of them is swollen shut. I don't feel bad for him. He tries not to look my way when I pass his row. The whispers among the other students seem to grow as I scan the room for an empty seat, "Damn, he looks bad," one person said.

"I wonder what happened to him," I hear someone behind me say.

"Somebody said he got jumped by some dudes."

"I heard he was in a car accident."

There's an empty seat in the first row, next to a white girl that I've seen in a lot of my classes throughout the years. She must be a business management major too.

"Hi Melody. How was your summer?"

"It was good, thanks for asking." I sit.

"I'm Casey. I'm not sure if you remember me from any of the other classes we've had together." She extends her hand.

"I remember you. Just never knew your name." We shake hands.

"Maybe we can hang out sometimes. I've been here all these years and still have no one to hang out with."

"We'll see." I'm not sure if she's someone I would enjoy hanging out with. This is my fourth and final year, and I've stayed to myself. I'd like to keep it like that.

"Okay cool. Here's my number if you decide you're up to it," she says, writing her number down and then giving it to me with confidence that I will call her. I slide it in the pocket of my notebook. I direct my focus to the instructor and straighten myself in my seat as the professor begins her introduction. No soon as she shares her background, there's a loud interruption from another student.

"Someone! Please! Call 9-1-1!" they yell.

The entire class turns their attention to Jarmaine, who has passed out cold on the floor. "Check to see if he's still breathing," someone says. Oh God, I hope he's still breathing. I know I was glad they whooped his ass, but what the fuck did they do to him.

"He's not breathing!" another student shouts.

A crowd gathers around him. So I don't look suspicious, I join them. The teacher begins CPR. I go into complete panic mode. I swear I didn't want them to kill him. Please let him come back to life.

He chokes after the third round of mouth to mouth. He spits up blood, and the professor demands something to wipe it with. A student gets a t-shirt out of his gym bag and hands it to her. Professor Whitehall wipes the blood from his mouth and sits his head up on her leg to help him catch his breath. "Stay with me," she says. She rubs his head, trying to comfort him.

I need to get in touch with Skylar, but leaving class right now might make me look suspicious. I wait to see what happens so the information I share with Skylar and her crew is exact. When I just so happen to I look up, one girl that was talking to Skylar the other day is peering at me as if she knows something. I quickly divert my eyes in another direction. Just as I do so, the professor dismisses class, "We will resume on Thursday." I rush to my seat and collect my things but wait a minute before leaving.

"Okay, people, clear the way." The paramedics arrive and push their way through the now thickened crowd. They reach Jarmaine and immediately start asking questions as they work on him. "Sir, are you able to tell us what happened?" Jarmaine doesn't respond. "Sir, can you hear me?" He nods his head yes. "Can you tell me what happened?" He nods his head no. The paramedic looks at Professor Whitehall and says, "Ma'am, can you tell me what happened here?"

"He passed out and stopped breathing. I performed CPR on him, and when he came to, he choked up blood." Professor Whitehall remains calm.

"Okay, I need for everyone to back up and give us some room." The even now thicker crowd backs up as they put the oxygen mask on Jarmaine and place him on a stretcher. Some students are leaving, so I follow the small crowd. "Are you hurting anywhere?" I hear the same paramedic ask as I'm exiting.

In the hallway and out of the crowd, I see Skylar. She looks at me as if she's telling me not to say anything. Duh! Does this girl think I'm slow or something? I casually approach her, "Hello, Skylar. Shouldn't you be in class?" I disguise my knowledge with a question.

"My class across the hall. When we heard all the commotion, we started being nosey, even the damn teacher."

"Yes, there are a bunch of nosey asses everywhere I see."

"Heard dude even stopped breathin'." Her face turns serious.

"He did. The professor did CPR on him and brought him back to life. He was gagging up blood too," I update her.

"You got another class?" she asks.

"Not for another couple of hours. Why, what's up?"

"Head to the room." She turns and walks away. I follow behind her as does the rest of the crowd because the paramedics are pushing Jarmaine out to the ambulance. We got a head start on the crowd, so by the time we get outside, Skylar's pace speeds up. We pass some of her friends, and one of them asks what's going on. Skylar nods her head, then turns to look at the other girls. After we pass them, I look back to see them trailing in the same direction as us. It's cool that they know how to read each other without saying a word.

When we all get to the room, Skylar immediately questions me about Jarmaine, "Ya'll two didn't say nothin' to each other in class, did you?"

"No. He didn't even look my way." I explain the events as they took place from beginning to end.

"Okay, good." The door bangs open. It's the three home girls that handled Jarmaine the other night along with the girl that stared me down in class. They come in and close the door as Skylar paces the floor. What did they do to him and why is she so nervous? She's starting to make me nervous, but I do everything in my willpower to contain it.

One by one the girls find a seat and speak to me as if they've known me for years. "Hello again, ladies. I think it's only fair that I know your names since all of you know mines." I look with a raised brow.

Skylar stops pacing the floor, "Oh, my bad. This is Carmen, Meek, Brit, and Jay," she introduces pointing them out individually.

Carmen is the girl from my class. She's beautiful. She reminds me of myself, except her style of dress is… different. She looks feminine, but there's some dominance in her. Her clothes don't comprise the typical basketball shorts and a t-shirt like the other girl's, and the chrome design on her nails match her toes. Carmen has a swag about her that's intriguing and interesting. Her dark brown, chin length hair compliments her hazel eyes, and gives them a genuine shine. Both her skin-tone and eyes are the color and shape an almond. Of all the girls, she's the tallest, with an athletic build that's highlighted by a tight, plain purple V-neck and slim fitting jeans.

Meek is appealing with a laid-back demeanor. Her long and beautiful dreadlocks match her long, athletic frame. She's wearing the typical Skylar crew gear—basketball shorts, t-shirt, and jersey— but her shorts aren't hanging half-way off her ass, and her jersey and T-shirt fits tighter than the other girls. She's wearing Nike flip-flops and carrying a basketball. When Skylar introduces her, she corrects her by telling me I can call her Meeka. She and Carmen both sit on Skylar's bed.

Brit and Jay are the complete opposites. They enter the room acting like heathens, and I mean ugly, or shall I say unattractive. Either way, they both have braids and are dark-skinned. They look rough and dirty, like they're from the West Side of Chicago. Dressed in their basketball gear and gym shoes, and they have a smell to them that's breathtaking. Literally. They're stink is hitting from every direction, so I politely ask them to have a seat on the floor.

I'm glad everyone finally sat down because the funk was becoming overwhelming. I didn't want to be rude and start spraying air freshener in here, especially not my quality stuff. Bath and Body Works Room Fresheners always gets the job done, but they cost too much for such a small can. All it takes is one spray, and I don't think that would've been enough for the stench that filled the room. They smell like they just came from playing basketball, having sex, and swimming in onion soup nonstop for the past week without considering a bath. They smell like they haven't even drank water… let alone used it.

After everyone is calm and seated, Skylar speaks. "Aye, none of ya'll have opened your enormous ass mouths, have you?" Once they all confirm they haven't, she continues, "Cool! This shit stays between us six and us six only. I don't want to have to fuck nobody up behind this shit. Don't even say shit to the hoes ya'll be fuckin' wit. You know how chicks like to talk now days. And Melody, never mind. I ain't worried about you sayin' shit to nobody. Carmen, did you take care of him to make sure he forgets everything?"

"I did. That's what you paid me to do, right?" Her voice is sweet and low, and it matches her looks. That explains why she was eye-balling me in class, because she knows who I am and is a part of this entire thing. I'm curious now so I speak up, "What does that mean?"

"Carmen is a med student who takes her general courses here and her main courses at U of I in the evening. She conjured up some shit to stick Jarmaine with that made him forget everything after they whooped his ass. I told you we knew about him being here after I saw Vanessa," she stops. "OH SHIT! VANESSA!" She directs her attention to Carmen. "We may have to give her some of that shit too before she goes blabbing off at the mouth." Now to Meeka. "Hey Meek, hit her line. She wants to fuck you, anyway." She throws Meeka her cell phone and looks back at me and continues, "I wasn't sure why he came over here after I'd already seen and heard him on the lawn talking shit, so I came prepared with my girls and I'm glad I did."

"Thanks guys," I say to everyone.

"Anything fa yo sexy ass. I was tryna get at chu, anyway." Jay moves closer to me, giving me a whiff of her fiery ass breath. I laugh at her. I mean, I literally laugh out loud at her. Carmen and Skylar laugh too.

"Aye bitch! What da fuck is so funny?" She's offended and embarrassed.

Out of reflex, I smack her in the mouth, "Watch who you're talking to. Bitch, I am not! Not yours or anybody else's, unless you do or say some dumb shit like you just did to make me act like one." She gets up like she wants to do something to me, so I stand with her. Skylar and Brit both rush between us.

"Man, sit yo ass down. How you gone try to get at her when you just disrespected her. I wooda smacked the shit out yo ass too," Brit says in her ghetto Westside voice and mispronouncing some words.

"Shit, I would have punched your ass," I hear Skylar say. Jay snatches away from them both and goes back to sit on the floor, only this time, further away from me. She's rubbing her face and rolling her eyes.

Skylar looks at Meeka and asks, "Did you get hold of her?"

"Yea, I did. She said she'll be over here after she's done eating."

"Naw man, hit her back and tell her I said come NOW," Skylar demands.

Meeka gets back on the phone with Vanessa. Skylar continues her ranting, and I can feel Carmen's glare beaming on me. I glance quickly out of my peripheral, and sure enough she is. It seems a little creepy. Why is she mugging so hard?

"MELODY!" Skylar yells interrupting my thoughts

"Yeah, what's up?"

"Damn! You ain't hear me calling your damn name? Where the fuck is your head at?"

"Who do you think you're talking to, Skylar?" My response is soft and calm.

"Man," she smacks her lips and wave me off. "Anyway, ain't nobody got time for this extra bullshit. When you get to your next class, try to find out as much info as you can." Skylar walks to the window and swiftly turns back to me, "Oh! And you might have to bite the bullet and go visit that Jarmaine in the hospital to get some accurate 4-1-1. Aright? Aright," she answers herself. She's lucky she saved my life, or I would curse her ass out. I don't know who she thinks she's talking to, but she must've forgotten that I'm not one of the chicken-head ass girls that she's screwing, or "victims" as she calls them. "MELODY!" Skylar yells again.

"What!" I yell back.

"Imma need for you to get yo head out the clouds and pay attention."

"Hell, I thought you had finished." I try not to laugh in her face because she's doing too much.

"Naw, I ain't done yet. When do you have this class again?"

"Friday."

"Okay, cool. I think you should check out the buzz around campus and go to the hospital tomorrow." When she finishes her sentence, there's a knock at the door. Skylar looks out the peephole, and then turns to Carmen, "You got some of that shit with you now?" That must be Vanessa.

"No. Why would I be carrying around some shit that's not legal, nor required for any of my classes?" Carmen has a point.

"Shit!" Vanessa knocks again. "Go with the flow, guys." Skylar swings the door open, and sure enough, it's Vanessa's chipper ass.

"Oh, hey, guys. I didn't know it was a party. Y'all hear what happened on campus. Some dude passed out, then died and came back to life. That shit is crazy. I wonder who he is. They say it was some basketball pla—" She's jabbers away before Skylar cuts her off.

"Aye, Carmen has that present I told you I got for you. It's over at her apartment. Don't you want to take a walk with her and go get it?" Skylar grabs Vanessa around the waist and pulls her close.

That shit was right up Vanessa's alley because she melts as soon as Skylar touches her. "Okay, baby." She's such a fool. I want to laugh so badly, but I don't feel like having to smack the hell out of two people in one day.

"Cool!" Skylar looks at Carmen and says, "I'll meet up with you after my four-thirty class."

"That works for me. Just make sure you have my package when we do. You want to meet here or at my apartment?" She gets up to leave, but not without brushing up against me and sending a shock wave of electricity through my body. It almost knocks me off my feet. She looks at me and smiles and continues on her way. She was so smooth with it, nobody noticed.

"Your apartment, since it's bigger." Skylar force Vanessa out the door behind Carmen. Vanessa was too giddy to notice she was being ridden.

After they both leave, Skylar locks the door, and then turns back to the rest of us, "That was a close call."

I look at the time and realize I have an hour before my next class. It's my Professional Writing class, and I need to go by the bookstore to get some materials and the book. "I have to get to class, guys." I stand, grab my things, and walk to the door.

"Aright," Brit says.

"Later," Meeka says.

When I get to the door, Skylar grabs my hand, "Hit me up on my cell after class."

"I don't have your number." I move my hand.

"It's on the board." She points to the whiteboard above my desk.

"Okay."

There are police and detectives scattered throughout campus talking to students. A familiar face walks towards me with a female officer. I never forget a face. The closer he gets to me, the more I try to figure out where I know him from, but nervousness and sweat takes over. Oh shit! I hope they're not coming to question me. What if they find out I was the last person to see Jarmaine? Oh shit! Should I turn around? I must go to class. I just act like I don't see them and walk with my head down.

So caught in my thoughts I don't realize how close they are, but I can feel the male officer eyeballing me. Thank goodness they walk past me without stopping me. I think I would've peed my pants if they had said something to me.

"Ma'am do you mind if we ask you a few questions?" Damn! I think I just wet my pants.

Chapter 8

"Excuse me. Are you talking to me?" I ask as if I don't know the answer already.

"Weren't you at the beach the other day?" he says so surely of himself. "It's me, the douche who made your chair collapse with the ball."

I softly laugh. "You said it."

"Did you find the number I slipped in your bag?"

"Oh! That was you? I didn't know where that number came from. Maybe I'll give you a buzz later. I'm in a rush right now. I have to make it to the library before class."

"Cool! That'll work!"

"It was good seeing you," I say turning to rush off.

"I have some questions, Ms. *Beach Baby*? It won't take us long," the female detective says sarcastically, stopping me in my tracks.

"Oh, let her go, Reed. I'm sure she knows nothing about this incident," Sexual Chocolate says while keeping his eyes on me. I look at his name tag, and it reads Det. M. Jackson.

"Thanks, Detective Jackson! And he's right, Reed, I don't know anything about any-thing. I have to get going now. If I hear some-thing, I will let you know," I promise Detective Jackson.

While rushing to the library, I make a mental note to talk to Vanessa and Skylar about our assignment. Maybe that's what Vanessa wanted. But damn, she will not remember she went to the room wanting to talk to me once they give her that shot. I must talk to Skylar to figure this out.

At the library I purchase my supplies and book, and just as I'm leaving, I hear my name. "Melody! Melody! Over here!" I see Casey waving and trotting towards me.

I really don't have time for her right now. "What's up? I'm running late for class, so make it snappy," I say, hoping she tells me never mind and that she'll catch me later.

But she doesn't. "I was just wondering if the police questioned you. They are interviewing everyone in our dorm since some girl named Vanessa said she saw him going there last night. Weren't you and he a couple last year?"

"Yes, we dated, but it's been over. I have had little to say to him since our breakup."

'Oh wow, I didn't know that. I thought you guys were still together," she pauses, "What class are you headed to?"

"Professional Writing." I glance at my watch.

"Oh, okay. I have that class too."

That's just my luck, but I don't entertain it. Instead, I continue to class. Casey follows me across campus, and we make it right on time. I sit in the back, while she goes to the first row. In case I need to let my head down and take a nap, no one will see me. I can tell this will be a long, drawn out course because the teacher is talking slowly. Not even ten minutes in, sleepiness kicks in so I pull my journal out and write instead.

Tuesday, August 26, 2006

3:10pm

I haven't been in this class for ten minutes, and I'm already over it. This damn professor needs a slapping for being so boring. It's been an interesting past couple of days. "Sexual Chocolate" slipped his number in my bag, Jarmaine tried to take my cookie, Skylar and her girls whooped his ass and almost killed him, and one detective investigating the case turns out to be the same "Sexual Chocolate" from the beach. I've been super horny lately. Maybe I'll give Detective Jackson a.k.a. Sexual Chocolate a buzz to see what he's talking about. Or I could use him for sex only.

Someone nudges me just as I'm getting into it. I look up, and its Detective Jackson and Reed. "Can we speak to you in the hall, please?" I pick up my things and follow behind them. All eyes are on us. I keep my head down.

"So, Ms. Moore, how do you know Jarmaine," Detective Jackson asks as soon as we get in the hallway, wasting no time.

"He and I dated for a little over a year, but we ended it at the start of the summer," I answer.

"Two people say they saw you and him talking at your car." Reed steps closer to me.

"Let's just say he was the one doing all the talking. I may have said four words. Why does this matter, Reed?"

"That's *Detective* Reed to you. We're asking because they say they also saw you guys talking outside of your building yesterday. Is this true?" She checks her notepad.

"Again, he was doing all the talking, or shall I say begging," I inform them.

"Do you know a Vanessa Phillips?" Detective Reed asks.

"Yes, I know her. She's in one of my classes."

"Do you have any idea why she would say she saw him going in your building yesterday evening, and that he asked about you?" Detective Jackson chimes in.

"Look, Jarmaine is a whore which is why we're no longer together. There's no telling who he isn't fucking, or who he would not see. He has groupies everywhere and in every dorm. Why he asked *her* of all people about *me*, I don't know." I try to contain my frustration.

"Do I sense a little bitterness, Ms. Moore?" Detective Reed asks.

"Bitter?! Why would I be bitter when I'm the one who broke it off with him, and I'm the one who ignores him when he tries to talk to me? We must have two different definitions of bitter." Now I'm ready to slap her.

"Calm down, Ms. Moore," Detective Jackson says calmly. "We're only following protocol by questioning everyone from that building. You're free to go back to class now."

"Thank you," I say snobbishly towards Detective Reed. I look at Detective Jackson, "I'll call later on this evening."

"Please do." His smile is cute and shows off his perfect teeth.

"Good day, Ms. Moore. We will be in contact if we have further questions. Don't stray too far." Detective Reed rolls her eyes and smacks her lips.

As she walks away, I take Detective Jackson's arm and say, "Check your partner before I do it for myself."

"Don't let that offend you, she's just doing her job." Detective Jackson rests his hand on my shoulder.

"Whatever! Her doing her job can be the same reason she loses it." I turn and go back into the classroom. I go to my seat, ignoring the stares and whispers. I continue writing in my journal.

3:30pm

That was a close call. That damn Detective Reed acts like she has a problem with me, and she doesn't even know me. She must be jealous or something. What she cannot realize is he wants me. All I'll do with him is hang out and have sex here and there. I know one thing, she better calm down and stay off my back before I go to jail for assaulting a police officer. Detective Jackson is good eye-candy, and fine from head to toe. He's not worth all the fuss if that is what her issue is. Maybe I'll call him tonight and see if he wants to get a bite to eat, just to ruffle his partner's feathers. I can use him to get information on Jarmaine since he's one officer working the case. The damages are so bad, whoever did this to

him will have an assault and battery charge, plus attempted murder. I
couldn't fathom going to jail for assault and battery, let alone attempted
murder. I'm not trying to be nobody's bitch behind bars.

"Class dismissed," I hear the professor say. I immediately close
my journal, place it in my bag, and run the entire way to my dorm
room.

Skylar is sitting on the floor. "Did those officers talk to you?" I
ask, bent over and out of breath.

"Yea, they did. I ain't have shit to tell em'. You talk to em'?" She
looks up to me from the game.

"Yes, I did. They told me Vanessa said she saw Jarmaine coming
into our building yesterday and he asked about me. Now they will
question everyone in the building." I throw my backpack on my bed.

"Well, I talked to Carmen and Vanessa's taken care of. If she told
anybody anything before this, her ass won't remember."

Relieved about that, I then remember our assignment. "Will she
remember we have an assignment together?"

"Shit, honestly, I don't know what all she will or won't remember. We'll just have to see what happens."

"Okay. Or how about I just outline who can do what by assign-
ing each of us equal portions. If she doesn't remember, I'll explain
everything to her." I suggest.

"That'll be cool. I have an evening class in a little, so I'm gone
change and head out." She takes her basketball shorts off and puts
on jeans. She's wearing boxer briefs. Damn, she's sexy. I shake my
head, trying to change my thoughts. It doesn't work. I'm just admiring the beauty she hides. There's nothing wrong with that. At
least *I* don't think it is. "I should be back no later than five or six.
What are your plans for food later? I'll be out, want me to grab you
somethin'?" she asks.

"I'm cool. I'll find something around here. If I can't find anything, or I change my mind, I'll hit you up and let you know. You

look better in jeans." I wink my eye. She looks nice, and they fit her well. Not too big and not too small, but exactly right. Now that she's not wearing baggy basketball shorts, I notice how nice her body is.

"Okay, now you gettin' weird." She picks up her backpack and tosses it around her shoulder.

"So, me giving you a compliment is weird?"

"I'll holla at you after class." Skylar opens the door just as Carmen is about to knock. "Hey, what's up, Carmen?"

"My pay please." Carmen invites herself in.

"I got you damn. You don't waste no time, do you?" Skylar comes back in, goes in her backpack, and gives Carmen four one hundred-dollar bills.

"One, two, three, four," Carmen counts out loud.

"It's all there," Skylar says.

"I'm just making sure." Carmen grins, and turns to me and says, "Hello again, Melody."

A warm, tingling something covers me from head to toe. Unsure why, I reply nervously, "Hey, Carmen, again."

She grins as if she knows the effect she just has on me and then goes to sit on Skylar's bed. "How do you think you will like this Financial Accounting class we have together?"

"Math is one of my favorite subjects so it may be a piece of cake," I lie knowing I don't like math.

"While you two are playing fuzzy toes, I got to get to class." Skylar walks towards the door. I forgot she was here.

"Later, Skylar. Don't forget to contact Vanessa after class so we can discuss our assignment."

"I got you! Don't forget to hit me up if you change your mind about food." She closes the door behind her.

"I can take you to get food," Carmen says.

"No, I'm good. Thanks though."

"You sure?"

"Very." I pick up my backpack to retrieve my books.

The door bursts open and it's Brit. "That dude died! Have you guys heard? As soon as he got to the hospital, he died. Said it was internal bleeding that caused it. What the fuck is we gone do? Man, I can't go to jail for beating the shit outta that dude. My entire basketball career will be ova. What the fuck I'm gone do?" She paces the floor in fear.

Chapter 9

Brit is going crazy and so am I. I pray this is just a rumor and people don't know what they're talking about. I need to get to the hospital. I can't drive right now! I need to relax, then I'll drive. Should I even go to the hospital?

"First you need to calm the fuck down, Brit." Carmen gets up to lock the door. "You trying to get everybody caught up acting like that. Where did you hear this information?"

"Vanessa!"

Carmen looks confused. "Not since she left my apartment about thirty, forty-five minutes ago. When did she tell you all of this?" Carmen asks Britt.

"Just now when I was on my way here. She seemed… different. She pulled me to the side and told me he died. She said she heard it from another student, and that she just left from over here with you Melody. Did you give her that shot?" Brit eyes Carmen for reassurance.

"Yes, I gave it to her," Carmen responds, still confused.

"Okay, so all of this is some crazy shit." I say to the both. "Are you sure you gave her the right shot?" Carmen nods. "Okay… I need a second to think." For a moment, I ponder a plan as Carmen and Brit stand staring at me. "How about I go to the hospital and Brit, you find Vanessa and bring her back here?"

"No, I will not let you go to the hospital alone, Melody. You look shaken up. I can drive you. First, try calling the hospital to see how much information they can give you over the phone. Brit, you go see if you can locate Vanessa like Melody recommended," Carmen orders as Brit gets up and leaves the room immediately. I do as I'm asked and get the number to every hospital close by and start making calls. After calling three of the local immediate care hospitals, I finally get some information on Jarmaine.

"They would only give me so much information, but the nurse at the hospital down the street said that he was there briefly, but then had to get rushed downtown to Northwestern Hospital for immediate surgery. I will go in the bathroom and call his mother to see what she knows, and if I'm not out whenever Brit brings Vanessa, smack that bitch for me," I say to Carmen with rage and frustration. I want to ask Carmen what she gave Vanessa, but I let it go, walk to the bathroom dialing Jarmaine's mother, and close the door.

"Hi Mrs. Wheaton, I was calling to see if everything is okay with Jarmaine. We were in class today, and he suddenly passed out and the ambulance came and rushed him to the hospital. Do you have an update on him?"

"Thank you for calling. Jarmaine will be fine. God favors him, so you need not worry. You know those doctors only tell you what they want you to believe, when God has the final say so. If God were ready for him, He would have kept him dead when they had to resuscitate him. He didn't bring him back for nothing, you know. There's a lesson that's being taught through this experience, whether it's for him or the individuals that did this to him. I'm not worried and neither should you. Just keep the faith and believe in your heart that he'll have a speedy and full recovery. I know you two are no longer dating, but your call shows how good a friend you truly are. Of all those little floozies he dates, none of them have attempted to call. They all have my number. I sure wish he'd done right by you, but you can't tell a grown man anything, not even me as his mother. He must learn by and by. All I can do is continue to pray for him.

Oh dear, I'm just going on and on. How are you doing? You know you can call me whenever, not just during an emergency," she says when she realizes she's talking my ear off.

"I'm doing fine, ma'am. Had a few trying times but nothing God won't see me through. So, I can't and won't complain." I tell her, hoping she's ready to end the call.

"Well, that's the right attitude to have, Dear. Just keep that mindset and you'll continue to prosper. Hold on a minute, Dear, my husband is calling on the other line." She immediately clicks over and leaves me no option but to hold.

As I hold, I hear Brit and Vanessa enter. I wonder if she's hallucinating from that damn shot Carmen gave her. I must remember to never get on her unpleasant side. She's liable to poke my ass with some shit.

"Are you there, darling? Hellooooo! You still there?" Mrs. Wheaton says on the other end.

"Yes, Ma'am, I'm still here."

"Okay, that was Mr. Wheaton at the hospital with Jarmaine. He says he's still in surgery, and the doctors told him he's doing well and going to make it. They finally got the internal bleeding to stop. The boy didn't know he has broken ribs, and a collapsed lung. He thought he could get one of his old crutches and everything would be okay. You see how good God is? That's why you make sure you say your prayers and put God first. Nothing should ever come before Him. You always give thanks unto the Lord. Mel, when you pray for things all the time without giving thanks, God sees that. I pray for my son every day, and I also thank the Lord for guiding him and directing his path. Without him covered in the blood of Jesus, I'm not sure he would've made it. So I thank God right now for saving his life. I will have to pull him out of that school. He may not like it, but I think it's best for him. Not sure what he's done to deserve this, but I pray all is forgiven, and I forgive whoever hurt him. Melody, are you still there?"

"Yes, ma'am."

"Well, okay, I won't hold you much longer. You remember to say your prayers and give the Lord thanks for everything. I will get off here now and let you tend to your classes. Thank you so much for calling. As soon as Jarmaine gets better, I will let him know you called to check on him. They say he doesn't have too much remembrance of anything, but I'm sure he remembers you. I just hope he forgets about all those other no-good heifers. I'll call you next week sometime to give you an update on him."

"Okay, Mrs. Wheaton. Thank you so much for the update and the encouraging words. It's a pleasure speaking with you. I will send flowers to Jarmaine. Does he have a room number yet?" I ask.

"He's in room 610. It's a joy hearing your voice. You keep in touch now you hear?"

"I will, ma'am. I hope you enjoy the rest of your day." We end the call. Although Mrs. Wheaton is long-winded and known for talking my ear off, it was a well-needed conversation… at least some of it. This entire situation has me feeling awful. Like all of this is my fault. Do I whole-heartedly forgive Jarmaine for what he did to me? I need someone to talk to. Maybe I'll call Detective Jackson for a conversation, since I promised him I'd call.

It's only the first week of school and all this drama is giving me a headache. A nice get-away from campus would do me a lot of good. I'll call my mom later to see how things are and ask if the downtown condo is available for the weekend. Walking into the room, I find everyone staring at me inquisitively, Skylar, Brit, Jay, Meek, and Carmen. Vanessa is knocked out cold, lying on Skylar's bed.

"So, what up? What she say?" I assume Carmen filled everyone in since this is the first question Skylar asks.

"Everything is cool now. He had internal bleeding that the doctors could stop, a few broken ribs, and a collapsed lung." I give the rest of the details about his condition and take a seat next to Carmen on my bed. An electric shock radiates through my body. "His mom is a prayer warrior, so he'll be fine," I continue.

"That's what he gets if you ask me," Skylar says, pushing Vanessa's limp body over and lay on her back with her feet crossed and hands behind her head.

"I second that." Meeka is sitting on the floor.

"Have a little sympathy for da clown, ya'll. We fucked him up bad. I wasn't tryna kill his ass though," Brit includes.

"I agree that we *could* have some sympathy for him." My eyes fixate on my twirling thumbs.

"Are you okay, Melody?" Carmen puts her hand on my shoulder. I jump at the electrical wave. She didn't touch my button, but I get the same feeling every time she touches me as if she touched me down *there*.

"Yes, I'm fine, just feeling bad for him right now." The lump in my throat pains me.

"You should be da one happy he fucked up! He should have neva put his hands on you! Not the way he did, any damn way!" Jay exclaims.

"I agree with that shit." Skylar rolls her eyes.

"Look, I see how all this is my fault, but I must forgive him for what he did to me. I can't allow that to dwell in me and cause me anger. He may have gotten what he deserved, but it still doesn't make any of it right. I think you guys should forgive him too. I'm the one he hurt, and if I can forgive him, I'm sure you guys can. Let's not be so juvenile about the situation. Do you realize the importance of forgiveness? Forgive him so that each of you can be free. Get over it. What's done... is done and we can't take it back, but we can move forward and continue to hope for his recovery. He's still living, but what if he were to die? Then we all would not only be facing assault and battery charges, but murder charges. If you don't want to forgive him, just know that he forgives us, and be grateful that he's still alive; if not for the sake of him, do it for the sake of your own serenity.

Good he remembers nothing. I mean absolutely nothing," I conclude in hopes they all take heed.

"Man, here you go being all religious and shit." Brit sounds agitated.

"No, I'm not *being* religious because I'm not a *religious being*. I'm a spiritual being. If you try letting it go, then maybe, just maybe, you'll have better luck and won't be so damn negative all the time, just sometimes," I advise her with attitude.

"You're right, Melody. We all played a major role in his condition, except you, you were being protected, that's all," Carmen speaks up in my defense.

"I'm over this. I forgive the dude for what he did to you, but only cause you do." Skylar gets up to leave.

The rest of the girls all get up and follow suit, except for Carmen. "In case I need to give her another shot, I'll stay until she awakes. I need to make sure she remembers nothing from the past twenty-four hours."

"Oh! I sure would hate to get on your grim side." I say to Carmen once we're alone.

"You don't have to worry; I would do nothing to hurt you. Ever. You're too precious," she assures me with a tone that warms my insides again, but also makes me nervous. An anxious nervous. The unthinkable happens when she sits next to me much closer than before and puts her hand on my leg. I flinch at the sensation that tickles my clit. I scoot away, not knowing what else to do. She scoots closer. I scoot again. She scoots again. What the hell!

"You have no reason to run. I won't bite you. I'm an affectionate woman and I just want to hold you. No sex just hold you. From the moment I laid eyes on you, I have felt an undeniable admiration for you. I think about you day and night and even find it hard to focus. That's probably why I fucked up the concoction for Vanessa the first time, because my mind was on you. I know that you're not into girls. So, I will never force you to do anything you don't want. I just want you to know what you do to me. No one, I mean, *no one* has ever made me feel this way." Her voice is low and soft.

I ignore her confession. I can feel the moisture between my legs, so I get up and go to the bathroom. As a straight woman who loves and prefer men, I don't understand how she, another woman, is making me feel this way. Carmen knocks on the door some minutes later, but I ignore it. She knocks again and asks if I'm okay. I don't answer. She knocks again and I swing the door open. Just as I do, she picks me up, sits me on the bathroom sink and kisses me passionately. So passionate I unconsciously return the kiss. I wrap my legs around her waist. When she pulls me closer, I become weak and everything goes black.

Chapter 10

"Melody! Melody, are you okay?" I can feel Carmen shaking me and can hear her voice in my dream. "Wake up. Are you okay?" She taps me lightly on my cheek. Everything is a blur when I finally open my eyes. What the fuck happened! Who passes out from a kiss? I'm dumbfounded! She continues to call my name and ask if I'm okay. My eyes are open, but I don't know if I'm too embarrassed to speak or if I'm in a state of shock. She picks me up, takes me to my bed, and lays me down. She lies beside me and rubs my face. "You'll be all right. I'm sorry for doing too much."

"That caught me off guard," I finally respond while lying in the dark. I question my calmness and I look over to see that Vanessa is no longer in Skylar's bed. "How long was I out? Where did Vanessa go?"

"Not long. As soon as you went into the bathroom, she woke up and seemed cool, so I sent her on her way. Are you sure you're okay?" She rubs my brow.

"Do you always make women pass out when you kiss them?" I question.

"I've never felt the desire to just kiss anyone the way felt to kiss you."

"Why me? Is it because I'm straight, vulnerable, or both?"

"It's neither of the two. The connection I feel for you is undeniable. No matter how I try to disregard it, it only grows stronger." I feel myself tensing up more throughout my entire body. Should I fight myself for questioning my sexuality? I don't know what it is, but I suddenly feel myself fuming as she proceeds. Her lips are moving but all I hear is a loud ringing sound in my ear. A connection. Is that what I'm feeling and don't want to admit it? A connection. I wonder what type of connection. Why am I thinking about her this way? What is it? Maybe I have gay tendencies. Maybe I'm a lesbian myself. A connection. I need to leave. I'll leave and call Detective Jackson, as promised. "What's on your mind? Did you hear anything I just said?"

Oh! She makes me feel so good. I should leave before I do something I can't take back. No! She should leave! "I remembered I'm supposed to hook up with an old friend for drinks tonight," I say with a straight face. It feels like she's ready right through my bullshit. Is it just me or is all lesbians like that? Skylar makes me feel the same way; like she can see straight through me, to my soul. "You don't have to stay, you know? I plan to be out for a while," I conclude.

"I don't mind. Eventually, I'll get my clothes for tomorrow and then come back here and study. Are you sure you're okay with going out? Are you driving or getting picked up?" She asks one too many questions. Is it strange that I like it? I hate it when Skylar asks me a trillion questions because her questions are always stupid as hell, but Carmen's make me feel like she cares.

I glance at the clock on the microwave. It's after seven. I wonder if Detective Jackson is off work. Instead of answering Carmen, I go to my beach bag and pull out his number. I read the name written on the piece of paper and remember the name on his badge. Malik Jackson. Pleasant name for a detective. I get my phone to call him and notice I have a missed call from my mother. To have some privacy, I go in the bathroom to return her call.

The relationship between my mother and I is different. Her way of showing she loves me is through material things or providing financially. She's not affectionate, and she never tells me she loves me. As beautiful as she portrays to be on the outside, her inner spirit is one big, evil, ugly sin.

My father showed us more attention than my mother did, but not the way they should show it from a parent. His form of affection got him in the trouble he's in now... locked up. They sentenced him to fifteen years in prison for molesting my younger sister Sabrina, may she rest in heaven, and has served only four so far. Apparently, the judge was not lenient on him and demanded that he serve every single day since my little sister wasn't the only child he was molesting. He caught a major case here in Chicago while here on business. Once the authorities caught him, they locked him up and found out about several other cases within the city, and my sister's case and other cases in Miami. I think he knew I would've cut his manhood off if he ever came at me like that. I have always been the feistier child. My mother and him remain married, but she has a boyfriend she's been dating for four years. It's clear she wasted no time moving on.

"Hello, Mother. What's going on?" I close the bathroom door.

"Hello Mel. How is everything going in school? I thought you would have been and called before now, but I haven't heard from you since you left Thursday. Is everything okay?" She sounds concerned. This isn't normal because my mother lives in a little bubble with only herself and her man.

"Yes, Mother, everything is fine. I've been busy settling in. I made plans to call you before the weekend. I want to go to the condo on Friday and stay until Sunday. You guys don't have any plans for it, do you?" My mother sometimes has parties there for the elite business class, or they sometimes rent it out.

"No, there are no plans. Enjoy. Are you taking anyone with you? Have you met someone new yet? I heard what happened to Jarmaine, such a tragedy. His mom called me earlier today and gave me the news. It's good to know he's hanging in there. Aren't you glad he's doing well? How are your classes? Do you have that International

Business class? I hope so. It would be a significant benefit for you when you graduate." My mother's boyfriend must not be around because she's asking more questions than normal.

"Slow down, Mother. You sure have an awful lot of questions." She, of all people, knows how I feel about a lot of questions, but I reply with short and sweet answers. "No one is going with me. I have met no one worth discussing. Yes, I'm glad Jarmaine is doing well. My classes are okay so far, and yes, I'm enrolled in International Business." My tone becomes dry as I realize she wasn't being concerned; she was being nosy. If Mrs. Wheaton hadn't called her, I'm sure she wouldn't have called me.

"That's wonderful. I have to go now. Oh, and Melo go see your father, please. He wrote a letter asking about you. He says he misses you and begs for your forgiveness. I'll be buried in my grave and still won't forgive him." That's the evil, self-absorbed type of person my mother is. I get a lesson of forgiveness from one person, and then this from her all in the same day. No wonder I'm always confused about everything in life.

"I've forgiven him, Mother. I just haven't had time to go see him."

"I will have to let you go. Sam is calling me." He's such a controlling boyfriend.

"Okay, Mother, I'll talk to you soon. Tell Lucia I'll talk with her soon." We say our goodbyes and I hang up. My body relaxes on the toilet as I think about my mother's success. I just wish she were a better mother. My memory is vague as I try to recollect a time when she's shown me any love or affection. School and work consumed most of her time, which she did more than my father. The housekeeper, Lucia, is the one who made sure there was always a hot meal on the table. Could this be the reason I don't know what love is? I've been learning to love myself unconditionally, but that even becomes questionable. With loving someone else, I'm a complete failure in the department. Is wonderful sex love? Is great sex love? Is money love? Will I ever have it? My mother does everything to keep and love a man but does nothing to show me unconditional love. She never sat me or my sister down and explained what a menstrual cycle was and how it worked, talked to us about boys and sex, and she never gave advice on the meaning of love. I'm learning everything on my own through experience, and it's teaching me well. Lucia tells me all the time about how I'm the opposite of my mother with men. She says we're like night and day. Jarmaine was lucky to get a second chance, but I was adamant on not giving him a third one.

My sister resented my mother because she felt my mother allowed horrible things to happen to her. My father would creep in her room every night for over four years—from the ages of nine to fourteen—and take her innocence. When my sister told my mother, she didn't believe her. After my father got caught and punished for his wrongdoings, my mother still refused to acknowledge the situation with my sister. This caused her to commit suicide on her fifteenth birthday. All she ever talked about was how she wished my mother loved us and showed us the same attention she showed my father, work, and school. She didn't want the attention my father gave her, and she didn't deserve it. I was two years and five months older than her and distracted myself with reading and writing. I would write in my journal about all my deepest darkest secrets, desires, and passions. My journals know more about me than my mother does.

"Do you mind leaving me your key?" Carmen says through the door.

"Yes, I'll leave it for you," I say, remembering I would call Malik to see if he wants to hang out.

"Okay, cool. I'm going to my apartment to get clothes now. Will you be here when I get back?"

"Wouldn't I have to be to let you in?"

"Oh yes, that's right! I'll be sure not to take too long. Can you come lock the door behind me, please?" Carmen is waiting at the door when I open it. "You good?"

"Yes, I'm good." I hold the door open as she exits.

"I'll be twenty minutes at the max."

"That's cool. I'll be here." She finally leaves and I lock the door. I go sit at the desk and call Malik. He answers on the third ring, sounding just as sexy as he looks. Tall with muscles in all the right places and dipped in chocolate. His eyes are a dark maroon looking color, and his waves are those of the Pacific Ocean. My ass instantly gets nervous. "Um, hi Malik? It's Melody."

"Hello, Melody. I'm surprised you called." I can feel the grin on his face through the phone.

"I'm a woman of my promise. Are you busy?" I probe, hoping he isn't because I could use a beer, and it wouldn't hurt to get the scoop on Jarmaine's case.

"No, I'm wrapping things up here at the station. What's up?"

"I was wondering if you wanted to grab a bite to eat," I ask, trying not to sound as nervous as I really am.

"That would be excellent. What did you have in mind?" His excitement tickles me.

"There's a Hooters not too far from here on South Cicero. Their wings and shrimp sound delicious right about now. We can meet there in an hour." My stomach growls at the mention of food.

"That sounds great. See you then." He sounds like a kid in a candy store.

I hang up and go to my closet to find something to wear. I remove a pair of denim American Eagle jeans, a white tank top and purple thong sandals and place them in the bathroom, along with matching bra and panties because who knows what might happen afterwards. My grandmother told me to always go outside prepared by wearing clean and matching underwear. In case you have to go to the hospital or in case you luck up and get some.

I wonder where Carmen is. Just as I pick up the phone to call her, there's a knock at the door. Through the peephole, Carmen stares back at me. After I let her in and turn to walk to the bathroom, she grabs me from behind.

"I don't want you to go," she whispers in my ear.

"What do you mean? I've already made plans to meet someone." Her embrace paralyzes me. And not because it's too tight. I feel my body relaxing. "Please stay. These feelings I have for you are hard to shake now that I've officially met you. Just tell me if you feel it too and if you don't, I won't mention it again and I won't come on to you again." Her words travel through my body like the melody of a sweet love song.

"I have to go get dressed." I turn and stare into her hazel eyes. I don't want to deny or admit my feelings because I'm confused about them.

She lets go. "I'll be here when you get back." I'm glad she understands.

Once in the bathroom, I turn on the shower and some tunes, undress, pull my hair into a ponytail, put my shower cap on, and step in. The water feels great. A good shower always gets my mind right. All the filth from the chain of events over the past couple of days is scrubbed off by the Dove body wash. There's a breeze that causes me to turn and notice Carmen stepping in to join me. My body instantly freezes. She closes the shower curtain and approach me slowly while the scorching water runs down my back. The closer she gets, the more the electricity emerges. Still frozen, she removes the towel from my hand and washes me. She starts at my shoulder and moves down, gently washing in circular motions. As my body slowly relaxes, I clench her shoulders for balance and support as she kneels to wash my feet. Not understanding why I haven't flipped out *again*, I allow her to wash my entire body, not once, but twice. She stands, grabs me by the waist with one hand and washes my cookie with the other. She knew this would make me weak as my legs wobble below me. She uses all her strength to hold me up. The rubbing from the towel and the motion of her hand is driving me wild, and every time she touches my button, I hold my breath, trying not to moan. She does this repeatedly until my body explodes and then becomes stifling.

"Here's something to think about while you're out," I hear her whisper in my ear. She stands me straight up and reminds me I must get dressed. Unable to speak, I gather myself, or at least try to, and point to my dry towel. She reaches behind me, turns the water off, and then turns to recover my dry towel that's hanging on the other side of the shower curtain. She dries me off from head to toe and wraps me with the towel. Carmen is still standing wet and naked, looking like a tall glass of water. She steps out the shower and holds my hand as I follow. Standing motionless, her soft hands rub lotion on my body from top to bottom. Once she's done, she looks at me and asks, "Do I need to dress you also?" I don't speak, but my head moves up and down. She takes my panties and puts them on, followed by my bra and the rest of my clothes. Then she takes my Burberry Brit perfume and sprays it in all the right places. Turning me around to face the mirror puzzles me. To my surprise, she does the unthinkable, and takes my ponytail holder off—allowing my hair to drape past my shoulders—and brushes it softly. "There," she nudges me closer to the mirror. "All done." While observing myself in the mirror, I notice an unfamiliar but radiant glow.

Finally able to muster up a few words, I view her naked body through the mirror and say with big and bright smile, "Thank you."

"No, thank *you*." Carmen reaches in the shower, turns the water back on and steps back in. On my way out of the bathroom, she peeks out the shower and says, "I won't tell if you don't tell," and disappears behind the curtain.

Chapter 11

Malik sits at an empty table when I arrive at Hooters. I'm running late because the episode with Carmen left my mind in the clouds and I had to get myself together mentally before leaving campus. *Damn he looks good and smells good,* are my thoughts as he stands to great me with a powerful hug.

"I thought you forgot about me." He's such the gentlemen when he pulls my chair out for me.

"Now how could I forget about you?" I sit and wink.

Malik walks to the other side of the table to take his seat. "Well, considering that you're running about an hour behind and didn't answer my phone call when I called you, I thought you'd either forgotten about me, or something happened. Is everything all right?"

"Everything is fine. I didn't realize you'd called. My apologies, I lose myself from time-to-time when I'm in the shower."

"I know how that can be sometimes, especially for a woman. I'm getting on my mom's case often for hogging my shower when she has her own."

"Did you say your mom?" I ask, hoping he doesn't live with his mother or vice versa.

"Yes, my mom," he chuckles. "I let her stay with me until she's able to get back on her feet. Times are hard for her now."

"Oh! Is that so?" I'm so turned off. He's just another pair of pants.

"Yes, she left her husband and needed somewhere to stay until her divorce is final and her alimony kicks in."

"I see, I see," I reply as I decide on whether I want to give him the benefit of the doubt. There goes the sexy panties and bra. I couldn't give him any tonight if I wanted to because Carmen is staying in my room. Oh, my goodness! Carmen... I can't believe she made me cum by washing my cookie. What kind of shit was that? It was truly something amazing. She is damn good at what she does. I wonder what she's doing. I pick up the napkin from the table and fan myself.

"Melody," I hear Malik whisper aggressively.

"I'm sorry. So, you stay with your mother? I mean, your mother lives with you. How long has she been there?" I eagerly ask so he doesn't question my thoughts.

"She's only been there two months. I told her she has until the end of the year to move out, even if that means I help her get her own place. I don't need her invading my privacy. It makes me feel awkward. Somewhat less than a man," he utters. It *should* make him feel less than a man.

"So what do you do about having company?" I expect his answer; not sure if I want to know for my sake or if I'm being nosy.

"Well, luckily my four-year relationship with my ex ended about three months ago. I haven't focused on anyone else because I was taking time out for me. You know, finding what makes me happy, finding myself. It hasn't been a straightforward process, but I think I have it figured out, mostly. I want to concentrate on my career as a detective. I was doing good focusing until I saw you at the beach that day. Ever since then, all I can think about is you. And then I coincidentally get assigned to a case at your school. That's definitely fate. Fate that brought us here." He smiles big. He couldn't possibly believe I'm impressed by this bullshit.

"What's so special about little ole me?" I ask.

A perky waitress appears. "Hi! Can I start you two off with something to drink?"

"Yes, I'll have a Heineken draft, please, with a lemon twist." I say.

"I'll have the same." I hope he really drinks Heineken and not just ordering it to impress me.

"Oh, can you also bring me some water with no ice and lemons?" I ask politely.

"Sure, I'll be right back with your drinks." She looks at Malik and it's obvious she's flirting with him as she flaunts off with those little bitty ass shorts they're required to wear.

"Do you know her?" I lean towards him and question.

"No, I come here often, and she's flirts with me all the time."

"That explains it." I laugh at her youthful behavior.

"Enough about me, tell me about you. How much longer do you have at St. Xavier? Are you originally from here? What's your major?"

Malik is very charming, but I find this conversation boring all ready. "Whoa, easy with the questions."

While we wait on our drinks, I tell him as little as possible about me without being too subtle. The waitress returns and we place our order. It turns out that he drinks Heineken. He says that it's the only beer he likes. We both know what we want without looking at the menu. Our non-interesting small talk continues over another round of beers, which are running straight through me.

"Can you excuse me while I go to the restroom?" I get up from the table, and he rushes to my side to pull the chair out. I stride away and then glance back to see if he's checking me out, and he is. The "new message" alert goes off as I push the bathroom stall door open. It's from Carmen: *I hope you're enjoying yourself,* is all it says. My mind goes back to our escapade in the shower and my body becomes weak. God, what is this woman doing to me? Skylar doesn't even have this effect on me. Shit, NO ONE has ever had this effect on me. I use the restroom and wash my hands. As I'm doing so, the Hooters waitress comes out of another stall and begins washing her hands in the sink next to me. While drying mines, her statement catches me off guard.

"You know he's gay, right? Or bisexual; it's one or the other." She has the stupidest smirk on her face.

"Who are you talking to?" I'm now feeling the beers, so my sassiness is through the roof.

She looks around sarcastically and then turns her body towards me. "You." She points at me and then continues, "The guy you're with. He's gay. I see him all the time at the gay clubs. I'll admit that the first couple of times I saw him in here, I found him to be attractive and I flirted with him, but then I saw him in different gay clubs dancing with and hugging on unfamiliar men."

"Are you saying all of this to piss me off, or because you're jealous? If you're not into him anymore because he's gay, why do you flirt and flaunt your little ass around when you bring things to our table?" I'm asked confused.

She laughs hysterically. "*Flaunting* is a part of my job. He's not aware that I've seen him, but I know he's a down-low brother trying to cover some shit up. I laugh because as fine as he is, he's a waste of a man and a waste of space on this earth. You better be careful. You know how these down-low brothers are. They use women to cover up their sexualities, and before you know it, they give women diseases that is preventable if they just keep it real. His partner is a prime example, the female officer, that's a total bitch, he uses her to cover his shit up. I see them all the time coming in here giving each other the magic eyes and drinking beer and shit. He has her ass completely fooled. Don't let him fool you too." She walks past me and out the door.

I stand immobile in disbelief, trying to figure out how I'm about to ditch this dude. I don't have the energy to confront him tonight. To each their own. Just don't lie to me or use me, and we're good. What a person does and how they do it is their business, just keep it real. Him fucking another man is one thing while him fucking his partner to cover it up is another. No wonder she was so hard on me. I knew she wasn't bugging out for no reason. A woman only trips when she's fucking a man that someone else has, or she wishes she were fucking him. I see why Skylar and most of her friends are lesbians. I know how we women and our emotions can be, so I'm sure they deal with the same issues. What I really want to do is leave right now without saying a word, but I also want to get some information on Jarmaine's case. I remember Carmen, so I reply to her text and tell her to call my phone in fifteen minutes. When she does, I can say there's an emergency and I must leave. It's one of the oldest tricks in the book, but it has to work. I conjure up the nerve to go back out and face this clown without spitting on him.

As I approach the table, Malik gets up and pulls my chair out again. I order my third beer just as I take my seat. Good thing campus is only a few blocks away.

"You better slow down before I might have to give you a ticket," he says jokingly.

"And I'll gladly pay it off," I respond sarcastically.

"Is everything okay?" He picked up on my sarcasm, but I don't care.

Instead of beating around the bush, I come right out and ask, "So, how's the case coming along? Is Jarmaine okay? I talked to his mom, and she said he's doing much better."

"Oh yes, he's good. I just wish he could remember exactly what happened to him. For some strange reason, he remembers absolutely nothing. I had the doctor run a test to see if he had been drinking or doing any drugs that would cause him to forget, but it takes a few days to get the results back. Once I get that, I should be able to determine more, but in the meantime, we're at a standstill. There's this one girl named Vanessa we spoke with whom remembered something one hour, but then couldn't remember even talking to us or other students the next hour. It all seems suspicious to me, especially since there's no one else who heard or saw anything. Asked the RA about him coming to your building yesterday and she said she was so into her homework, that she didn't look up to see who all she was allowing to enter. I initially felt that she needed her job taken away for that shit, but then I remembered how it was when I was in college, so I decided not to report her. Plus, it's the start of the school year, so everyone will be in and out and not everyone has keys; at least that's what she told us. You didn't see him coming or going in the hallways, did you?" He looks over his glass as he takes another sip.

"I saw him earlier that day hugged up in the corner with some chick, and he followed me to my car begging for forgiveness, but after that, no, I didn't see him anymore." I try my damnedest to remember what I'd told him and Detective Reed earlier that day. I know he's only asking again to catch me slipping.

"Oh, yes, that's right. Well, thank God he's still alive. I'm sure something or someone will slip up, so I'll just keep asking around until they do." He's so sure he'll get the job done.

The conversation goes on for another fifteen minutes before my phone rings. It's Carmen, and she's right on time. I pull my phone from my clutch. "Hello. Is everything okay? Calm down. I'll leave now. I should be there in less than ten minutes."

"Are you leaving?" Malik asks as I chug the rest of my beer and signal the waitress.

"Yes, sorry. One of my friends is in a situation, and she needs me to come quickly. I'll take care of the bill." I take money from my wallet as he places his hand on mine. The waitress comes and I ask for the check and a to-go box.

"Don't worry about the bill, I'll handle it. Do you need me to come with you?" He puts his credit card on the table.

"No, you don't have to come. I'm sure it's a woman thing. She is crying, so it's probably something with her sorry ass boyfriend. She may have found out his ass is gay or something. I've been telling her that all along." I put my hands over my mouth after I realize what I'd just said. I laugh on the inside at the facial expression Malik makes. Just as the waitress is placing the bill, along with everything else I requested on the table. She gives me a weird look and smiles hard because she too noticed his expression. She then rolls her eyes at him as she retrieves his credit card and the check and turns to walk away.

"Oh… um… wow… okay. I guess, let me know when you make it back to your room. I'll be seeing you around campus since I have to be there for the next few days." His voice trembles with nervousness as the waitress brings his receipt back, and he signs it.

I smile and stand, and so does Malik as he comes to my side of the table. *Gentleman my ass*, I think as I pick up my leftovers. We both thank the waitress as she comes to collect the receipt. She stands there as she notices he didn't leave her a tip, "Cheap ass, gay ass, bastard." I can't believe my ears. I look at him and then her, waiting on his comeback.

"You didn't leave her a tip?" I ask him.

"No, I didn't. I always leave her a great tip when I come in here. Not getting one from me this time shouldn't hurt her. Plus it's after seven, they charge a gratuity." He didn't defend the gay comment, so it must have some truth to it.

In my clutch, I pull ten dollars out and hand it to the waitress. "You never know what a person could go through. This job could be her livelihood. It could pay her way through college. Every penny counts. What would you do if the shoe were on the other foot? It's not about what you *usually* do. It's about what you're doing now." I turn to the waitress, "Have a good night."

Malik and I both leave the restaurant, and as I'm walking to my car, Skylar pulls up with a white girl. She sure gets around. I inspect inside the car and realize it's Casey, the white girl from my Financial Accounting class. Maybe that's why she gave me her number. Was she hitting on me on the low? "Well, I'll be damned," I yell out before it's too late to take back.

"Isn't that your roommate?" Malik asks.

"Yes, it is. How do you know?"

"I know everything."

I remember the conversation with the waitress and think to myself, *apparently you don't, dumb ass!* At my car, I try to hurry and get in before Skylar sees me. Malik stands, waiting for me to let my window down, so I do. I tell him I have to hurry and get going because I don't want to leave my friend waiting. He leans in and kisses me. It was a respectful kiss, but nowhere near as good as Carmen's. As he pulls away, an image of him dancing with a man forms in my mind. YUCK! I'm disgusted!

I guess my facial expression told on me because he asks, "That bad, huh?"

"No, sorry, I just remembered I have class first thing in the morning, and I haven't prepared for it. The thought just boggled me. That's all." I shrug.

With him not defending the gay comment made by the waitress, I wonder if I should mention it. Maybe I'll talk to Carmen about the situation when I get back and see if she knows anything about him since she *is* gay. It's a bold move, talking to her about a guy I went on a date with, but who cares. She and I are not dating.

"Okay. Well, I'll let you go. Drive safe and let me know when you make it back to campus." He walks away backwards as I start my engine.

I pull out of the parking lot and turn on Cicero. I make a call to Carmen, letting her know I'm on my way back. She tells me she's out on the lawn talking with some of her classmates, and she'll stay out until I get there. I hang up and turn on V103 and jam the scant distance to campus.

It takes ten minutes to get back. Carmen sees me as I'm walking to the dorm, so she joins me. I wait until we're in the room before I probe her about Malik and his gayness. "You're talking about the detective guy? He's gay. I've seen him a few times at some gay hangouts up on the North side. Is *that* who you were with?" It was obvious she was holding her laugh in.

Chapter 12

7:47am

When I returned last night and vented to Carmen about Malik, she started acting weird and shit, like she hadn't just made me cum hours before, or like I was a groupie or something. She woke me up early this morning, telling me she was leaving for class, and to lock the door. After she left, things felt unfamiliar. It could've been me being sleeping that made me feel this way, but who knows? I'm glad I don't have class until twelve, but I can't to go back to sleep. I wonder about how she feels about me. Not sure why it would matter since I'm not gay. Or am I since she made me cum? I can't believe Malik is gay. Why does he do that to women? That should be a crime, and his ass should get locked up for it. I remember reading something about a gay man that had aids and was dating straight women just to transmit the disease. He was eventually found out and sent to jail. Why would anyone intentionally give someone aids? Understanding the whole 'down low' thing will now make me look at men differently. I wonder if Jarmaine is on the 'down low'. Hm, that's surely something to think about.

I can't believe Skylar either. I will have to get the juice from Casey while we're in class, or maybe I'll invite her for drinks just to find out what she and Skylar has going on. Maybe she needs friends? Who knows? I'll see if she wants to hang out this weekend while I'm downtown. Oh shit, I forgot to text Malik last night and let him know when I made it home. I don't care, anyway. Fuck him! His ass is gay! I should at least try to talk to him about it and see if he'll confess it to me. I don't see how anyone could hide who they are. That shit would drive me crazy; not being able to live my life to the fullest or how I choose. It's so much going on around here. Serenity is what I could use to clear my mind.

It's only day two of school, and it seems like I've been here for months. Thanksgiving break can't come fast enough. Miami, here I come. My mom will go crazy if I tell her I kissed two girls and liked it. As evil and hypocritical as she is, she would go straight to the Bible on me. I know it. What I don't understand is how so many individuals can judge a person's lifestyle and call it a sin when judging is a sin itself. If she comes at me sideways, I'll tell her just that. I think I'll keep my lesbian escapades to myself and the person I have them with. Are they escapades or is it something that just happened? I will have to find out what's wrong with Carmen. So much is going on that not even a beer can fix all this shit.

Skylar just came in the room, and I view her differently since I've seen her with so many women.

MM

As I close my journal, Skylar comes out of the bathroom and says, "Aye yo, I saw you at Hooters last night with that detective dude. What up with that?"

"I saw you pulling in the lot with Casey. What's up with that?" I ignore her initial question and answer her with a question.

"Really Melody? Is this the game you want to play? Just answer the damn question." She sounds frustrated.

"Why are you all in my business? What does it matter to you, anyway?" I become just as frustrated at her as she is at me because she's all up in my business.

"It doesn't matter to me, but it should matter to your ass,

considering the fact that he is a damn down-low ass creep." She laughs out loud.

"It wasn't anything like that. I went to have a beer, and he was there. Yes, he was hitting on me, but no way am I interested. Now, you answer my question," I reply evenly and get up to get my clothes for the day.

"Good, cause I would have drove your ass if it's more than that. Casey, she's nobody. Somebody I fuck so she can help me with a little tutoring... another one of my victim's basically." Skylar bucks her chest out in confidence.

"You are such the whore, Skylar," I say in disgust.

"I ain't no hoe; I just fuck a lot and let these chicks do whatever they want for me. You can call me the head doctor, baby. Got a problem? I got a cure for that ass. You should know, or maybe not!" Her laugh is louder.

She's so stupid. "Nobody has time for your foolishness, Skylar." I push past her and go shower.

She yanks me from behind and says, "But you like it though," while humping me and laughing.

"A fucking lie." I elbow her in her stomach.

She grabs her stomach in pain and says, "Aye, you gone keep your fuckin' hands off me. That shit be hurting."

"And you will keep your hands off me. PERIOD!" I lock the bathroom door after I slam it in her face.

Once I'm out of the shower and dressed, I notice the message indicator on my phone. It's a message from Carmen: *Have a magnificent day, Beautiful.* I guess that answers my question, or maybe it doesn't. Either way, it sure put a smile on my face. Damn! There are ten missed calls from Malik and five texts, all saying the same thing: *Did you make it home?* I ignore his messages, get dressed and leave the room.

Walking down the hallway, the gossiping talk about Jarmaine fills my ears; nothing new though, just the same gossip Vanessa started. The RA waves when I pass her. We've gotten acquainted over time because she's the same RA that's been in every dorm hall I've lived in. Heading to the cafeteria for breakfast, disgust comes over me when I notice Malik and Detective Reed. I avoid eye contact as I continue walking with a faster pace. He told me he would be on campus for a few more days.

As soon as I get to the table and set my food down, Malik walks in without the Reed lady. Or maybe I should refer to her as his 'cover-up'. "Hello, Melody," he says.

"Oh, hey, Malik." I pretend he startled me.

"I've been texting and calling you, trying to make sure you got home safe. Did I do something wrong?"

"Sorry about that, Malik. I got so busy with my friend, time seemed to have gotten the best of me, and I haven't checked my phone today."

"Oh, okay. I'm glad you made it home safe. Would you like to hook up later today?"

"I have classes all day, so I cannot. Maybe we can hook up sometime next week."

"You're telling me I have to wait all the way until next week to see you?"

"I'm swamped with classes and assignments, and I'm going away for the weekend, so it must be next week." This dude sounds and come off like a damn creep.

"I see. Next week is cool. Just hit me up and let me know the exact time and date." He makes a sad face and I ignore it.

"I'll do that," I say with a fake smile. When he turns to walk away, I spot Skylar looking at me and smirking. Maybe I should say something to him about the rumor I keep hearing. I don't know if he will tell me the truth or not, but asking wouldn't hurt. Well, it wouldn't hurt me... at least.

Both classes were boring as hell, but while I sat in them, Malik texted me twenty-two times. He was telling me how badly he needs and wants to see me before next week, and how there's something about me he can't resist. Maybe I need to come out and tell him or ask him, about the accusations.

When I get back to the dorm room, there are three dozen roses sitting on my desk: purple, white, and yellow. I read the card, assuming they're for Skylar, but come to find out, they're for me from Malik. The card reads: *Please see me this weekend. Malik* Now I'm feeling uncomfortable. Not sure what I should do with the flowers, I remove the card and sit them on Skylar's desk so she can think they came for her. I don't want them talking shit to me or about me and this interesting Malik.

My phone goes off just as I sit on my bed, and it's a text message from Malik. The phone then rings and it's Malik. I ignore the call and he calls again... and again. This dude is showing clear signs of craziness. He sends another text: *I hope you like the flowers since purple and white are two of your favorite colors.* What in the fuck! How does he know that? I throw my phone on my desk and look out the window to see if he's stalking me. After confirming that the coast is clear, I turn my ring-er on silent and lie back, staring at the ceiling.

~

I've slept the entire day away, and I wake up to several more text messages from Malik, and one from Carmen. I disregard Malik's text, but read the message Carman sent: *Came by to give you a hug, but didn't get an answer. We should hang out this weekend, away from campus.* Her message makes me smile from within. Why do I feel this way about this *woman*? Am I a lesbian that's just now realizing it? She sure makes me feel some kind of way. I can invite her to the condo on Saturday. I text back and say: *Saturday is cool. I'll be downtown at my parent's condo. We can hang out then. Let me know and I'll text you the information.* I send the message and hug the phone in my chest.

Another message from Malik comes in: *I can't stop thinking about you. Please text me back or call. I sat outside your dorm hall most of the evening, hoping you would have to leave and I could see you. I want to see you before next week. I know I've said that already, but I can't help how you make me feel. No one has ever made me feel this way before.* I look at my phone and turn it off, because this guy has officially scared me.

The leftover Hooters is the first thing I've eaten today. Skylar is not here, but I can tell she's been here because of the tornado that's on her bed; stuff that wasn't there before I fell asleep. As I'm eating, I vent in my journal.

Thursday, August 28, 2006

9:20pm

It's late, and I sure hope this food puts me back to sleep so I won't be up all night. Malik has been texting me all day, and it's creeping me out. Maybe I should tell someone about his weirdness before he tries something. He is a detective and probably knows how to get away with many crimes. I watch those shows on the Investigation Discovery channel and see how crooked a cop can be. I wouldn't put anything past him.

I wish my mother and I had a closer relationship so I could have someone to share my feelings with. I wish my sister was alive too. Lucia is always so busy, that when I talk to her, it's only for a brief period. I'm not sure if I'm even ready to tell her about my feelings for another woman. I've heard that talking about things sometimes helps you figure them out easier than keeping them confined. I have no friends and Skylar will only laugh and have something negative to say, and Carmen... well, let's just say I can't and don't want to talk to her about her. I've already talked to her about Malik, so maybe I can tell her how he makes me feel awkward with his stalking. If it wasn't so late, I would call her right now. Writing my thoughts down helps a little, but you, journal, can't give me the advice I need.

MM

I place my journal under my pillow, and clean my dishes. I hop in the shower to relax, and someone enters the room just as I'm rinsing off. I assume it's Skylar, since she's the only one with a key.

The shower does exactly what I wanted it to do, calms me. As much as I hate sleeping in shorts, I put some on until I get in bed because I don't want to give Skylar any bright ideas. My stomach cringes when I leave the bathroom and notice Malik sitting on my bed.

"What are you doing here? How did you get in here?" I ask, frightened.

"I'm sorry, Melody. I just had to see you. You've been ignoring me, and I thought maybe I did something wrong. I see you got my roses. I let myself in. Please don't be upset with me for picking the lock. I really need to talk to you about something." He stands and walks closer to me.

"I can't believe you! Are you crazy?" I'm speechless, but get those words out.

"Yes, I'm crazy about you! I can't stop thinking about you. Why don't you want to see me?" His pleading is scaring me more.

I bite the bullet and have a conversation with him about the accusations. I swallow hard and say, "I heard you were gay and that you use women as cover-ups. You're more on the down-low… they say."

"That Hooters bitch told you that, didn't she? I will fuck her entire life up." His actions clarify that he's fuming.

I lie and say, "No, I heard it from other people around campus."

"Look, I'm not gay at all. I just like certain things that men can do for me. That doesn't make me gay. I love women. I don't need them to cover up anything that I do. Men are better than women at one thing in particular."

How disgusting! "So, you think *that* doesn't make you gay, or bisexual?"

"No, it doesn't make me either. I don't do it all the time. I have my moments when I need some magnificent head. Like I said, women don't know how to deliver that."

I can't believe my ears. "Well, Malik, I'm not sure if I'm okay with dealing with someone who is not comfortable enough with themselves to be up front with women." I fold my arms in front of me.

There's a lengthy pause before he replies, "I know you were the last person to see Jarmaine before his injury. I know what your friends did to him. I know this because I've been watching you since I saw you at the beach. I fell in love with you as soon as I saw you. I felt determined to know more about you." As he continues, I redial Carmen's number in my phone without him noticing. He's still talking, "When I followed you here to campus, and that happened to Jarmaine, I requested to work the case so I could be near you. I picked the lock tonight because I needed to tell you I know and I promise I won't tell anyone else, nor will I arrest you for conspiracy of assault and arrest your friends for attempted murder, assault, *and* battery."

"So you're blackmailing me? Really? Well, little do you know, I'd rather you lock me up right now than deal with you in any way. You're a disgrace to mankind. As soon as you lock me up, your ass will get fired from the police department and everyone will know you're a gay ass liar." I try to remain calm but can't.

"And how will they know that?" he asks as he walks close to me.

"Because, as soon as I saw that you had broken in here, I speed dialed my friend and she heard everything, and if she hasn't, it's all on her voicemail." I hold my phone up to show him I'd dialed Carmen. I put it on speakerphone because honestly, I don't know if she answered or not. "Carmen?" I ask, praying she isn't because I want the conversation saved.

"I am, and I've recorded all of this shit." She sounds pissed.

"Now see, Malik, women can do just as much as men, better than men. I would appreciate it if you found your way to the door." I step aside so he can exit.

Fear comes over me once I notice the rage in his eyes. He walks towards me and as soon as he reaches to snatch me, Carmen comes bursting through the door. She's still on my phone. I end the call. "She said to leave, now please do as she asked before shit gets ugly." Carmen holds up the metal bat and lays it on her shoulder. Malik looks at me and leaves.

Wow! Another woman saves the day. She is every bit of amazing! I don't know how I'll ever repay her.

Chapter 13

I made it to Friday! It's late in the evening when I exit the elevator and toss my backpack on the all-white expensive sofa. I walk to the balcony that faces the lake and observe the many families out on the beach. It's a beautiful day in downtown Chicago as the breeze from Lake Michigan blows my hair. My phone alerts from inside. It's a text message from Carmen: *I hope you made it safe. Text me when you get settled.* I invited her to hang out with me since she's been so kind and saved me from that creep Malik. I have had no more problems out of him since that night.

I'm still having a hard time processing his actions from the situation, though. He fits the definition of a crooked detective who uses his badge and title to get away with shit the average person wouldn't get away with.

I reply with a simple okay. I go through the fridge and find one of my favorite meals cooked by the housekeeper: steamed shrimp, roasted asparagus, and creamed corn. While my food is warming, I open all the windows so the breeze from the lake can flow in. I get myself a beer and bottled water to go with my dinner.

Sitting down to enjoy my meal, images of Carmen cloud my thoughts. She's been the sweetest person to me and I've become fond of her, even with my trust issues. The feelings she gives me allows me to feel free. In some ways, she puts me in the mind of my sister, so caring and gentle. She's thoughtful, and her charm is overwhelming. My mom would have a fit if she knew I thought of a woman in this way.

I finish my dinner and gather my things for a warm bath. I text Carmen afterwards to let her know she can be on her way. She has the information already because I gave it to her before leaving campus.

Vaseline beads and bubbles add a soothing feeling to the scalding water in the enormous garden tub. They filled the linen closet with freshly washed towels. So I take a few and place one on the toilet to dry off with, one on the floor to step on, and throw one in the tub to wash with. Some pleasant tunes will be perfect to help me relax, but my mother interrupts my mission to turn them on.

"Hello, Mother." I exhale.

"Hello, did you make it to the condo?"

"Yes, I did. I was preparing for a bath," I respond, hoping she gets the hit and ends the conversation.

"You must've had a long week." She ignores my efforts.

"No, I just want to take a bath since there's only a shower in the dorms." I emphasize my urgency to bathe.

"That's understandable. I received another letter from your father today, have you thought about going to visit him?"

She couldn't be serious right now. Is she trying to have a conversation about my father with me right now? "Yes, I have. I will go before I come home for Thanksgiving."

"Have you called or go see Jarmaine?"

"No, not yet, mother. I'll go see him one day next week," I tell her as I go in the bathroom to turn the water from hot to cold so it'll be nice and warm.

"I'm not interrupting your bath, am I?" It's obvious she doesn't care.

"Goodnight, Mother," I say, answering her question with my overt actions of ridding her with a farewell.

"Goodnight."

After I end the call, I select my "Wind-down Music" playlist. The first song that plays as I undress is "Officially Missing You" by Tamia. My body sinks in the water and embraces the softness that the Vaseline beads provide. The tub pillow catches my head and my eyes close as Tamia's lyrics take me directly into thinking mode. I am officially missing her, and I can't figure out why. Is Carmen my definition of genuine love? She's clarified that sex is not what she wants from me. Well, it's not *all* she wants from me. She told me she wants to love me, and I love her, unconditionally. What is unconditional love? There are so many thoughts that swarm my brain since she has come into my life. I fear hurt. I fear being used. I fear… fear. Having true love would be nice, but I sometimes wonder if I deserve it? I'm just now learning how to love myself unconditionally and I fear sharing it, but I find myself open with sharing it with her. Will I be able to handle a relationship with another woman? I don't know. The music and my thoughts take me away like Calgon for God knows how long. I open my eyes to run more hot water and Carmen stands in the doorway watching me. My throat sits in my stomach, preventing me to speak. Instead, I freeze in mid reach, staring at her with my jaw dropped.

"Did I frighten you?" She slowly walks closer and kneels down on the side of the tub. She closes my mouth and kisses my neck gently. "I wanted to surprise you. You don't think *I'm* a creep, do you?" she questions, mocking what I said about Malik.

Finally able to speak, I clear my throat and reply, "How can I think you're that when I gave you all the information you needed to get in?" I was so absorbed in my thoughts, I didn't hear her come in.

Was that a question or were you being disrespectful? She asks as she undresses and joins me in the tub. She then straddles me in an awkward position; knees levered up, hips joined to mine, and feet flat at the bottom of the tub.

"You never cease to amaze me." I unwittingly wrap my arms around her neck. Why is it so easy for me to attach to her?

"Is that good?" She moves her lips closer to mine.

"It's all bad," I say, not knowing if I'm joking or not. She gently kisses me with so much passion, I immediately melt into her. There goes that electric shock. I mirror her kisses. Her lips are soft against mine. It causes me to let out an adoring moan in her mouth. She doesn't stop. Her kisses grow even more sensual as her body gets closer. She pulls me up some so we are breast to breast. She's still straddling me, and I can feel her vagina on mine. Our buttons connect when she reaches down and spread my lips apart. My body weakens. A moan transfers from my mouth to hers. She moves in the water, taking my body with her like the waves in the ocean. I let out another moan and this time she returns one. Our bodies speed up. My body explodes, and she throws her head back and lets out a loud moan as if hers exploded with mine. We slow down. She kisses me again.

Carmen cups my breast with each hand, while circling my nipples with her forefinger each time our buttons unite. The moaning begins again. She stops kissing me and whispers my name slowly in my ear. My body fills with desire. She says my name again. My body fills up more. She says my name again, this time breathing gently in my ear after every syllable. I explode as she squeezes my breast and says my name louder. I mutter the words, "I… am… cum… ing."

Our tongues wrestle for a minute or two. Carmen then stands and reaches down for my hand, helping me up. She knows I'm weak. She steps out and supports me as I try to keep my balance. We walk into the bedroom, and there are purple rose petals all over the bed and on the floor. I smile deeply. When did she do all of this, I wonder? I must've really been in my thoughts and lost track of time. Is she trying to make me fall in love with her? Why can't men treat me this way? Why do they try to take what is so sacred, when all they have to do is treat me like a beautiful woman, and I would gladly share my temple with them? She lightly picks me up and lays me down on the bed, lies beside me, and turns facing me while resting her head on her propped up hand. She looks me in the eyes and stares at me for I don't know how long, because I get lost in her eyes. Even in the dark, the beauty beyond them shines through.

I eventually break the stare and ask, "Why are you staring at me?" It's the only thing I can think to say without sounding stupid.

"I'm not staring at you; I'm admiring your beauty." She runs her fingers gently across my lips.

"The beauty of my eyes?" My question is tender.

"No, the beauty of your soul." Carmen leans down and plants delicate kisses on my lips.

"What... are... you... try... ing... to... do... to... me...?" I ask, pronouncing every word slowly and softly between each kiss she plants.

"Love you."

I put my hand up to stop her. "But why me?" I question her before going any further.

"I've been saving myself; saving myself for someone like you. I've been a lesbian for as far back as I can remember. I've had no type of abuse from a man; not mentally, physically, sexually, or emotionally. I just never had a desire to be with one. I told myself I wanted to learn the concept of love before I jumped in a relationship with a woman. I didn't want to jump in the game pussy first. I wanted to love me. Truly, wholeheartedly, and unconditionally before trying to love someone else. I seek companionship, and not a relationship. After I fulfilled these aspects, I saw you and I said to me, 'self, that woman will be my wife for she is my soul mate.' I felt your spirit when I first saw you; which was two years ago walking across campus."

"Why didn't you say anything? I could've used a friend," I whisper.

"I wasn't ready to say anything to you then. I had two classes with you last year and made it a priority to stay out of your view. This year, when I saw you in class and later found out you were Skylar's roommate, I wanted to save you. Everyone needs saving, and I felt it was my duty to save you from pain and hurt, and then capture you by love; unconditional love. Now that I know you're not gay, I find it unbelievable that I've fallen so hard for a straight woman. Who would've known that being around a person, or seeing them for the first time, would affect me how it has? I never believed in love at first sight until I saw you. You have a sensitivity about yourself that's hidden behind a tough shell. I want to be the one to bring that out of you. I want to be the one to make you smile for absolutely no reason at all. Your smile brightens the sun on the dreariest days. I always have marvellous days, but seeing you make them even better. I hate to say it, but I see why everyone finds it hard to let you go. If it's too much for you, tell me, and I'll understand." After saying all of that, her gaze remains absorbed into mine.

"I barely know how to love me, let alone someone else. I don't know you." I pause and lower my head in shame, and then sigh, "But here I am making out with you in ways I've never done with anyone else."

She lifts my chin until her eyes hook and reel mines in. "I can show you how to love." She kisses me softly.

"I don't know." I'm not sure if I'm lying or telling the truth.

Carmen says nothing else, but reaches on the nightstand, picks up the Aveeno lavender lotion, and smooths it all over my naked body, from head to toe and front and back. As I lay on my stomach, she sets the lotion down and picks up peppermint and lemon scented oil. It immediately opens all my senses and pores. I can hear her rubbing her hands together and then feel her message over my shoulders, moving down to my mid-back. The oil is warm, and the scent is relaxing.

She slowly massages me everywhere, including my feet. Squatted down at the foot of the bed, she asks me to reposition myself to my back. Once done, she tickles me… literally, when she slowly sucks my toes. It tickles, but it feels so damn good too. Surprised, I arch my spine and grip the sheet with both fists as her fingers caress my body and her tongue follows. I'm mind blown and caught in her rapture. I try to speak, but whines ooze from my lips instead. Her name then follows. She spreads my legs as she reaches for my cookie. Opening my jar, she licks slowly below my button while allowing her nose to tickle it. I wince in pleasure as she repeats the steps. Her tongue moves in and out of my jar gradually. I lock my fingers in her hair until she takes one hand and intertwine her fingers with mine.

Carmen stops with her episode of teasing my button and places my other hand where her nose once tickled. She moves my forefinger to my opening to retrieve more juices and then sucks the same finger seductively. She uses her finger as a guide to navigate rounded motions on my button. Each time I attempt to move, she pulls my hand that's intertwined with hers tighter. After a few tries, she eventually lets go. With my free hand, I reach for her face and pull her up to kiss her lips. She's surprised when I don't move my other hand from my button, not even when she moves hers. "You like how you make yourself feel?" Her whispers in my ear turn me on more.

"Yes," I mumble softly as I turn my hips to match my circular motions. My dough rises as I speed up. She then whirls my hand.

"No," she rejects, "don't cum yet. I want to cum with you and then hold you in my arms while you fall asleep." She lies down to the right of me, takes my right hand, and places it on her button as she places her left hand on my now stimulated clit. She is wetter than Raging River and turned on is an understatement for what I am right now. With my right hand on her and her left hand on me, she takes her free hand and once again, guides me to move it the way she likes, which is the same way I enjoy pleasure; slow and gentle until I reach my climax. She turns her head towards me and kisses my shoulder. Moans proceed as I change my hips to the rhythm of her finger's rotation. She does the same, and we are both moaning and moving to the same beat. We elevate the more our bodies move with ecstasy. I speed up. She speeds up. I speed up more. She speeds

up more. I breathe harder. She breathes harder. We both then clinch
our legs together at the same time as we orgasm, calling out each
other's names. I'm left disoriented as she turns on her side, pulls me
as close as close can be, lifts my head so it lies on one of her arms
while she wraps the other arm around me, and holds tight.

~

The smell of food wakes me the following morning. Carmen isn't
in bed when I reach for her. My body immediately sits up, afraid
she's left. She sees me from the kitchen and comes in with a plate of
bacon, eggs, rice, smothered potatoes, orange juice, and yogurt on a
tray. A smile from me to her is my way of thanking her.

"You enjoy this, and I will go for my morning run." She kisses
me on the forehead and gets dressed. Not the ultimate forehead kiss.

"How long will you be?"

"Maybe an hour. I have to keep this sexy body of mine in shape,"
she says, lifting her shirt and rubbing her abs.

My food was so good, it was all gone before I could taste it. I
guess that's what a night full of sexcapades do; make you hungry. I
take my plate to the kitchen and place it in the sink as the shower
calls my name. The bath tub remains filled with water and memories
of the night before swarm my head. My entire body tingles, especially between my legs. I let the old water out, shower, lotion, and
slip into a pair of Victoria Secret yoga pants and T-shirt. A glow on
my face radiates through the mirror as I pull my hair up into a bun.
Is this what wonderful sex does? Or is it, love? I ignore my thoughts
as I brush my teeth. Once I'm done, I slide into my thong sandals,
and search the refrigerator for a bottle of water. On my way to the
balcony, I pick up my journal and pen. From where I'm sitting, I can
see Carmen stretching. "What am I doing?," I ask myself out loud
as I open my journal to the next empty page.

Saturday, August 30, 2006

9:48am

I had the time of my life last night with Carmen. It's not just the sex that I enjoyed. I also enjoyed the pillow talk. She opened up to me and revealed things that I would never have guessed, like her not dating anyone. I just knew she was a player that crushed a lot, like Skylar's ass. No, Skylar is a flat out whore. There's something different about Carmen. Something different about the way she treats me, touches me, and talks to me. She listens to every word I say and is exceptionally observant. She knows what to say, what to do, when to say it, and when to do it. She makes me smile from my soul. Am I in love? Is this what love is? It sure feels like love. How do I even know what love feels like since I've never experienced it? This is that textbook love; the kind you only read about. Can I love her the same way she loves me? I don't know if I'll be able to answer these questions soon, but I know I have to figure this entire situation out before I go home for Thanksgiving. Depending on where Carmen and my relationship go, I want to tell my mother. It's only been a week of school and so much has happened, but it's only been two days for she and I. Can you love someone that fast? She says she's loved me since she laid eyes on me two years ago. Is there such a thing as love at first sight? I think we view love in two distinct ways. I see love through her eyes, but I don't see them through my own eyes. Maybe I'll eventually fall in love with her as she has with me. Wait, that makes me wonder... am I a lesbian?

Has she turned me out? Is this what I want? Is this what I need? There are so many questions I have to ask myself, and I must answer them before I'll know if I love her. She's everything I could ask for, but she's a woman providing all the things I would expect a man to provide. How does that work? That's so not fair. Not only do I have to figure this lesbian thing out but also if my heart is ready for something so deep.

MM

2nd Phase

Chapter 14

My flight lands earlier than scheduled in Miami at 1:26 pm the day before Thanksgiving. Since it's the holiday, travelers flood the airplane and airports. It took me forever to walk to baggage claim and fetch my luggage. I need preparation before facing my mother with the news I plan to share, so I take the extra hour and get food instead of calling the driver. I walk to Terminal D East to my favorite restaurant, Islander Bar & Grill, for beer and food. As much as I hate airplane food, not eating before leaving Chicago or on the airplane was not the best idea because I'm starving and can feel a hunger headache. I arrive at the restaurant just-in-time because the headache makes me weak. The nearest empty seat is facing the entering passengers, so I make my way to it, sit, and pull out my journal.

Wednesday, November 22, 2006

1:42pm

I spent some time with Jarmaine before I left. He remembers nothing from his attempt to take my cookie, to him getting his ass whooped. It only makes it easier for me to forgive him. It took him about eight weeks to recover enough to go home. There was an inconsistent swelling on his brain that prolonged his discharge date. The doctor said the trauma to his head causes his thoughts to freeze, or he forgets all together. I'm grateful that he's doing better, but sad that one stupid mistake on his part caused permanent damage. I guess it's true when they say, "You reap what you sow."

Things have been going great for Carmen and me these past few months, but individually, things haven't been going the way I would like. I'm failing out of all of my classes, and I no longer have a desire for school. I only attended school in the first place because of my mother. I don't care about anything pertaining to managing a business. Writing is more my thing. That's something I wouldn't dare tell my mother, though. Barely making it to class and trying to focus when I'm not there mentally is not good for my health. My mind just wasn't there. I'm smart by nature, but with the distraction of Carmen, I've stopped caring. Our relationship has me so off track, that I stopped writing in my journal, praying, and everything else. She's doing great in her classes, and for that reason, I refuse to share my failing grades. I appreciate how she's able to focus on her studies and love me. She and I have stayed involved ever since that sensual weekend in August. The only problem I'm having with all of this is that I haven't been honest with her. I told her I was from St. Louis and that's where I was going for the holidays. I'm not sure if it's because I'm afraid to trust her completely or if I'm afraid of trusting myself. Whether I'm in love with her puzzles my brain often. She's told me she's in love with me, but I don't know if I trust that. We've kept our relationship a secret from everyone, even Skylar. To keep the gossip down and everyone out of our business, we don't hang out at school like normal couples do. I don't want to mess anybody up, and I don't want her to have to mess anybody up for having our names in their mouths. Our business isn't everybody else's business anyway...

"Ma'am can I start you off with a beverage," the waiter interrupts.

"Yes. Heineken draft with lemon, please?" My eyes remain focused on my journal.

"I'm sorry, but we no longer have Heineken on tap. Would you like it in a bottle?"

"Yes, that'll be fine." I continue writing.

...Skylar suspects nothing between Carmen and me, but if she does and is just not saying anything, I don't care. Skylar is still whoring. Well, at least she was when I left this morning. Her changing her whorish ways would shock me. I think it's just in her nature. She may need some counseling for it. As much as Carmen is in the room with me, I don't see how Skylar wouldn't suspect something. She found out about the situation of Malik breaking in my room, and told me as a friend, she would never let me stay there alone, but then she never had her ass there.

Malik stopped working on the case, and they threw it out since no one remembered anything and they couldn't get any leads. I haven't heard from him since that creepy night. The rest of Skylar's crew of hoodlums never enrolled to St. Xavier. Come to find out, they were there all the time just hanging out and fucking everybody. Nasty ass chicks. The entire damn crew is just plain nasty. I'm so glad Carmen isn't like that. Or is she? See, these are the things I don't trust. I don't know if I can believe anything she's told me. Do I love her sexually? I do. She makes me feel good mentally and emotionally too... I think. Is it lust that has me thinking it's love? Shit, I don't know. Figuring it all out is what I have yet to do. What I am positive about is that she has my world turned upside down, whether it's defined as sex, love, or lust. Maybe coming home was an outstanding idea. It'll be good to escape the things going on in Chicago and figure them out. My mind is all over the place. I don't know if I'm coming or going, or if I should stay here or go back. Maybe I won't return to school... since I'm already failing and officially on academic probation. How will I tell Carmen all of this? Will she understand? Returning the favor of giving her all of me, the way she gives me all of her, would be great, but I question if she's given me ALL of her and if that's what she wants. I need time. There are so many questions I have about me, about her, and about us and what we're doing. Staying here and figuring this out will take the time I need. I now just have to figure out how to tell Carmen my decision.

"Here's your beer with lemons, ma'am, and I brought you a chilled glass. Would you like me to pour it for you?" He lifts the beer and glass and attempts to pour until I stop him. I close my journal, using the pen to save the page.

"No, thank you, I don't need the glass, but can you bring another beer. Thanks." I squeeze a lemon into the bottle.

"Okay. Are you ready to order, or do you need more time?"

"No, I know what I want." I sip some of my beer. "I would like the Coconut Shrimp Platter, and a Green Reef Salad with whatever vinaigrette you have today." I take another sip as he takes the menu.

"Would that be all?"

"Yes, thank you." I open my journal.

...The sex is the best sex I've ever had in my life, or thought about having, but she also makes my heart feel a certain way. Being humble and accepting everything she does is difficult, because I don't know what to do with it. She makes me contradict myself in so many ways, as if I'm bipolar. It's weird because she gives me the comfort I've always wanted from my mother. She gives me the attention I've always needed from my mother and my father, not to mention the love I've always earned from the both, together.

Speaking of my father, I went to visit him, and I left feeling the same way I did before the visit. There were no feelings. It was a cordial interaction where told him I forgive him and that I love him. I dislike admitting my love for him, but I love him. I just can't seem to erase all the pain and turmoil he's caused my family. Money was the only reason my mother stayed with him after the incident with my sister. That's her problem, she thinks I'm supposed to do the same thing. She called me, asking why I won't consider getting back with Jarmaine. The way she ignores me is the same way I ignored her. She'll most likely address it again when I'm in her presence, so I'll cross that bridge once I get to it. It won't be as easy to escape the conversation while in her presence.

"Shrimp platter," the waiter says as he sets my food, another beer, and more lemons on the table. "The gentlemen over there has paid your bill for you." He points to a tall, fine ass man. I smile and mouthed, "Thank you," and then thank the waiter. He rushes off, and I put my journal down. I infuse my beer and shrimp with lemons, lay the napkin across my lap, and place the silverware on my plate. When I look up, "Mr. Fine" is staring at me and smiling. I choose to not return the smile because I'm reminded of Malik the creep. I'm distracted by my phone. It's a message from my mother's driver letting me know he's pulling up in front of baggage claim. I already have my luggage, but I don't tell him that. Instead, I reply informing him I'll be there. I gobble down most of my shrimp and chug the rest of my beer. Waving the waiter down, I place a ten-dollar tip on the table and I put my journal back in my carryon. I'm surprised when "Mr. Fine" approaches the table.

"In a rush?" he asks, showing off his Colgate smile and wearing cologne that is penetrating my senses.

"Uh, yes. My driver is outside waiting for me. Thanks for lunch." The waiter comes to clear my table. Saved by the waiter!

"Here's my card. I would like to take you out sometime if you don't mind." He puts his card down on the table. I pick it up as I'm standing and throw it in the first trashcan I pass. I know it's rude.

I hurry through the airport and make it outside to notice the driver standing outside the car. I speak and leave my luggage waiting at the curb as I climb in the back seat. He closes the door behind me and spruce my things in the trunk.

The ride is silent. I stare out the window and take in the scenery I've missed. The beaches remain beautiful, and the weather is amazing for November. Not too hot, but just right. I've always had a thing for palm trees, and they're blowing in the opposite direction as we're driving. It's such a beautiful sight to see. The fresh smell from the ocean seeps in when I crack the window open. Missing Carmen takes effect as I lay my head back on the seat. I wish she was here with me. If there was a way that I could be honest with her, I would, but the fear of her reaction causes me to remain private.

My phone alerts, and it's Carmen: *I hope you made it safe. Call me when you get settled. Love you much. XOXO.* The message makes me smile and sends that electrical excitement through my soul, causing my cookie to please. I reply letting her know my status and I'll call her when I get a chance. I put my phone down just to have to pick it back up because it's going off again. Her reply is a simple, "Okay." She's so patient.

We turn on my mother's street, and all of my nerves jump to my throat. I don't know if I'm returning to school or not, so why am I so nervous. I said I wasn't going back, but the way I change my mind, who knows what may happen. Maybe I should wait until my mind settles before I think about telling her about Carmen and I. Will I be running from love if I stay and not return?

As we approach the gate, both beers sit at the pit of my bladder ready to release. Phil, the driver, creeps around the long driveway, passing the front door, and pulls beside one of my mother's six cars that line up along the garage. Before he could put the car in park, I jump out the back seat and ask if he could take my luggage to my personal space inside the pool house. I rush into the house. Lucia is in the kitchen whipping up something that smells so delicious, it makes my stomach talk as if I hadn't just eaten. I speak while running past her, then into the restroom to release my bladder.

My heart skips a beat when I hear someone approaching the bathroom door. "The Misses say she be late for dinner." Thank goodness it's just Lucia.

"Okay. Thanks, Lucia." I stand to flush. That sure calmed my nerves, but I know hearing my baby's voice would calm them even more.

"You want snack to hold you til then?"

"No, ma'am. I had food at the airport." I turn the water on to wash my hands. "Is there any beer, Lucia?" Since my mother will be late, I'll get drunk before she gets here and pass out.

"Yes, Melly Baby. You want with lemon?"

"Yes, that would be fabulous. Can you take some to the pool house also? I will go out on the dock and make a phone call." I dry my hands, open the door, give her an enormous hug and kiss on the cheek, and walk towards the kitchen.

Lucia is short and looks like she's worked out every day of her life. She keeps her long, jet black mane that touches her butt wrapped in a tight bun. She has skin that is so flawless and ageless that people find it hard to believe she's in her late fifties. Lucia follows behind me, speaking in her Cuban accent that hasn't changed from the day I first met her. "Me will do that and cut you lemons up."

"Thanks, Lucia, you're the best." I remember my phone is in my bag, so I take a beer that Lucia has placed on the counter, walk over to the pool house and fumble through my luggage. I use the bottle opener on my key chain to open my beer. Through the French doors, I take the walkway that leads to the dock. I dial Carmen along the way.

"Hey, love. I see you made it." She answers on the first ring with a voice full of excitement.

"Yes, I did."

"How was your flight?" She asks.

"I slept the entire time."

"Hmm. Still tired from an endless night, I see." I'm flattered by her sarcasm.

"Just a little." I smile hard and reflect on the episode of the night before.

"I wonder why?"

"Oh, you know why."

"Tell me." She's speaking in her midnight love-making voice.

I change the subject, "I miss you already."

"Not as much as I miss you. I miss *her*. Touch her for me." She says referring to my cookie. Boy, does *she* miss her touch.

"I can't right now. Too many people are watching." There's not a single person paying attention to me. They're too busy enjoying the beautiful water.

"Will you touch her for me later?" She sounds so sweet and innocent.

"I will. Will you?"

"Anything for you," she replies. Those words make me reconsider the thought of not going back to Chicago.

"How was your last day of class?" I make another attempt at changing the subject, because I become horny and there's nothing I can do about it right now.

"Class was excellent. You know I was at the U of I today, and my medical classes are much longer than the classes I have here on campus. Other than being long and drawn out, they were good. I can't wait for you to come back. I have something special for you. I think you will love it. I *know* you will love it, just like you love me."

"I can't wait either. I'll admit that I enjoy being home, but after a day or two, it's as if I'm living in a psyche ward. My mom can be crazy sometimes, but I have missed her. Thanks for taking me to see my father before I left. I don't know what I would've done if you weren't there after my visit." I have become confused by not only what I say, but what I do. She has me contradicting every thought within my brain.

"You don't have to thank me for anything. You deserve the world, and I want to be the one to give it to you. You know I'll do anything for you. Have I not shown that?" Her voice is no longer midnight love-making, but a lot more serious.

"You have. I've never disputed that, but I need to thank you. That's just who I am. I like to show gratitude."

"Melody Moore!" I hear my mother screaming. "Melody! Fucking Moore!" she screams again.

"I have to go. I'll call after I have this conversation with my mother." My nervousness takes over me. I take a long swig of my beer to prepare for war. Mother sounds upset.

"Okay, Baby Love. Calm down, everything will be okay. Just be honest with her and tell her how you truly feel. Make sure you drink all of that beer before you talk to her, though." I'm confused at her attempt to comfort me when she giggles.

"Thanks Babe. Later." I chuckle and drink the rest of my beer.

"Okay. I love you."

"Me too." How can I say something when I'm in denial of what it means? I don't know if this is the last time I'll talk to her or not, but if it is, I *should* tell her I love her. Too late now.

My mother is fuming as she stomps towards me. Here goes war... The closer she gets to me, the more nervous I become. She reaches me and says, "What the fuck is this!?" She holds up a picture of me laying on top of Carmen, on the patio at the condo in Chicago. Saliva gets stuck in the pit of my throat when I try to swallow. The beer bottle falls from my numb fingers and shatters.

Chapter 15

While screaming at the top of her lungs, my mother presses a picture into my chest. She stands five-feet-seven inches and her Bob hairstyle cuts right at her chin. Her physique has a perfect structure that looks good on her. For her to be in her beginning years of her prime, —forty— her yellow skin complexion is flawless and wrinkle free. Her perfect teeth, arranged within her smile, reveals a softer side of what and who she pretends to be.

"What is this?!" I lower my head with shame when I take the picture and see that it's me and Carmen. "Answer me, dammit!"

"I don't know what it is." This is not how I wanted her to find out. I wanted to be the one to share this news with her.

"I know what it is. It's you laid up on my fucking balcony with another woman. Are you a lesbian now? Or is this what you've always been?" I can feel her rage.

"I don't know."

"You *don't know*? Well then, tell me what you know!"

"I don't know," are the only words I can think to say.

"You want to be lying around with some dyke, when school is your primary focus! You will NOT see her again! I mean, you WILL NOT! I will do everything in my might to change this. *You* should be with a *man*, not a woman. What can she possibly do for you that a man can't do? Huh, Melody?! Tell me that! What can she do for you? What *does* she do for you? Not shit! A man can do so much more! Do you think I pay your tuition so you can sleep around with women? Huh? Do you think I bust my ass for you so can you do this? That money your father left ran out a long time ago. I'm the reason your tuition gets paid. I'm the reason you don't have bills to pay. I'm the reason you have credit cards that you don't have to pay. I'm the reason, Melody! I work hard to assure you live a grand lifestyle and this is the thanks I get. What is it you have to say for yourself? Who's the man in this relationship? You are her?" She stands with her hands on her hips.

"There is no man in the relationship. We're both women and we know we're women. I appreciate everything you've done and continue to do for me, but she gives me love. Love in so many ways. No man has ever made me feel the way she makes me feel. I'm sorry, Mother, but I think I love her." I look into her eyes when I speak, so she understands my feelings.

"Love her? Ha! You're barely twenty-one. You don't know how to spell love, let alone feel it! You haven't even experienced life and you say *love* her. You're a disgrace!" Although I don't know if she's being sarcastic or serious, because she's yelling and laughing at me to my face, her words cut deep, and they hurt.

"Why, because *you* never showed me the meaning of love?" I surprise myself when I say the words. And as soon as I do, she smacks me, hard. I rub my face and look at her. "I hate you, Mother." I shove her out of my way and stomp to the pool house.

She catches up with me and grabs me by the arm and swings me around, "You hate *me*? The person who's taken care of you for your entire life. You hate *me*? The person who's provided for you when your father left. You hate *me*, but you think you *love her*."

"I would like to go now," I say, ignoring her ignorance.

"Go where? Where are you going, Melody? To your dyke bitch?" She asks as she holds my arm tight.

I try to wiggle free and say, "Mother, you're hurting me."

"I'm hurting you? I'm hurting you? Do you not understand how much this hurts me? To find out my daughter is fucking another woman." She asks.

"I'm sorry, Mother." Tears fall.

She releases my arm and walks away. "This is far from over, young lady," she informs me before approaching the French doors. She then turns and walks back towards me. When she reaches me, she sticks her hand out, "Your phone. Give it to me NOW!"

"What? Why do I have to give you my phone?" I ask, completely baffled. What is she planning to do, sabotage me?

"Give me the phone." Her voice is stern and intimidating.

"But Mom." I cry harder.

"But Mom nothing."

I give her my phone; she snatches it and walks away. She turns again and tells me she's going out, and to be ready for dinner by six. My body is unmoving. It feels as though my entire world has fallen apart. My knees hit the wood surface as the tears pour. I'm feeling empty. As I kneel sobbing, I think to myself that maybe this is best for me. Everything happens for a reason, right? At least that's what the saying is. I'd already had intentions on not going back, so maybe this is the confirmation I need. But I love her. Love has caused me to run away. I'm not sure if it's love or the fear of love. I slowly pick myself up and walk into the pool house. Lucia has brought my beer and placed them in the refrigerator. I get one, put a lemon in it, and take it to the bathroom with me.

Viewing myself in the mirror, red eyes with tears dropping, my thoughts take off. *I'll apologize to my mother and tell her about my failing grades, and about how I plan not to return to school. I know that'll make her happy. I'll tell her how she's right, but in the meantime, what will I do with this empty feeling that's inside me? What will I do about Carmen? How will I tell her? Maybe I won't say anything to her. Maybe I'll just give her the impression that I disappeared off the face of the earth. This isn't right. I have to say something to her. I don't want her to worry. No, I won't say anything. Because of her, I've flunked out*

of college. Because of her, I'm completely confused about my sexuality.
Maybe I should go to counseling and try to forget about her. But how?
Maybe I'll change my name so she won't be able to locate me. She thinks
I'm in St. Louis, so I know that's where she'll look. I lied to her about
who I am and where I'm from. Maybe this is the reason. Should I tell my
mother about these plans and ask for her help? In her eyes, I'm searching
for love in all the wrong places; maybe she's right. As much as I hate to
say that, it could be true. I will contact no one in Chicago. Am I wrong
for doing this? Does it matter? I don't think it does. I have to do what
I have to do for my own well-being. Although I don't like school, or my
major, flunking out is not a pleasant look and it'll forever affect me.
What's more important, being loved or my education? If I could have the
benefit of experiencing both and knew how to handle them, that would
be picture perfect. Unfortunately, there's no such thing as picture perfect.

Distracted by Lucia's voice, I turn to discover her standing in the
doorway with another beer for me and one for herself. "Okay, my
sweet Melody?" Her tone is always soft and sensitive, and it comforts
me during my times of need.

"I'll be okay, Lucia. Thank you so much for always being here
for me." I take the beer from her hand. I'm knocking them back like
a drunken old man. My thoughts took over so fast and so hard, that
I didn't realize I'd drunk the entire first beer while standing in the
mirror. She takes my free hand and leads me to the bay window, and
we both sit. This is where our talks have always taken place. I can
never talk to my mother, but I can always to talk to Lucia when I'm
home. She knows just about everything.

"You know how you mother is, my sweet darling. I try to calm
her before her came outside, but her rushed past, fast. That damn
Malik. Him always just wanted she money, but her fucking he makes
worst only," she says in her broken English. Then she continues in
Spanish, "Sólo espero que él muere en su sueño (I just hope he dies
in he sleep)."

Confused, I clarify, "Did you say Malik?"

"Yes, Malik. He come to follow you like her paid he to. He no real detective, him just private investigator. Her make it seem like it random. Her knew all the time, just wait for you come home. Her extra ass." She looks at me and laughs because I taught her to call my mother "extra" years ago and told her what it means.

I let out a snicker but feel sick to my stomach at this disgusting news. "Does she know that he allows men to give him oral sex?"

"Her know. Him was round for years. Him used to do a threesome with you father and she. Him was kept away from you kids, so no suspicions." My mouth waters. I jump up and dart to the bathroom, and all the beer and food I ate immediately comes up. Lucia comes with me and rubs my back as I continue releasing all that was in me. "Let out, baby, let all out," she says to me. Once I'm done, she puts her arm around my waist to keep me stable, and walks me back to the window.

"How do you know all of this, Lucia?" I ask in between sobs.

"Honey, Lucia be round for long time. Me know everyting." She goes to the kitchen and returns with a cold wet towel, and wipes my mouth and forehead.

I feel sick. I'm more confused now than I was earlier. "What will I do, Lucia?"

"Baby, you love she or you *think* you love she? You confused. Take time for Melly Baby. Figure out you. Then go from there. If her love you, her will be there. Tell she what is going on and why you leave and don't go back." She pauses and takes a long swig of her beer. I look at her and giggle at her jacked up English, while still crying. "What funny?" she asks seriously.

"No matter how much I've tried to teach you proper English over the years, it's still fucked up."

"You know what me mean though, right?."

"Yes, Lucia, I know exactly what you mean and I always know what you're *trying* to say." I bury my head in her lap. As a child, whenever I would hurt myself or became sleepy, I would climb in

Lucia's lap and lie there until I fell asleep. As I got older and bigger, I would just lay my head there.

She rubs my hair like she always does and says, "Be all right, my child. Be alllll right." She leans down and kisses me on my head.

"Thank you, Lucia," I respond as the tears fall.

"Welcome, baby. Anyting for me sweet Melody."

I lay with my mind full, allowing everything to sink in. "How dare she react the way she did, and she was having sex with a man who likes to get his dick sucked *and* sucks dick?" The sobbing continues.

"That's prolly why, sweetie, cause her know how that lifestyle work. Can't tell you why for sure, but you not worry bout that, try to get rest." She wipes my tears with a Kleenex and I follow her instructions and cry myself to sleep.

<hr />

When I wake up, Lucia has left me. She usually does once I pass out. My eyes blink a few times to adjust to the clock, only to notice that it's almost five. My body feels like it's been sleep for days. I slowly get up and go to the bathroom to shower. The mirror reflection reveals how I look and feel. My eyes are baggy and I could use a facial. With no tunes, I shower quickly and get dressed. My pink capris and blue T-shirt will suffice for the moment as I throw my hair in a ponytail and slide on my Sperry's.

Not caring how I look, I walk to the house, hoping my mother doesn't have a thousand and one questions for me. I will go in here and quickly apologize and tell her how right she is so she can leave it alone. Her boyfriend Sam's Bentley sits in the driveway. Damn, why does he have to be here? I'll beat around the bush with my apology, not revealing what I'm apologizing for. I'm sure he already knows since she can't keep anything from him.

In the house, I walk in the dining room to see my mother, her boyfriend, and the same guy from the airport all sitting around the table. I can't help but wonder if she has people watching me everywhere. I mean mug my mother as I take the seat closest to her.

"Darling, this is Victor White. He's an AR for Lyrical Records. Victor, this is my daughter Serenity. Your stepfather invited him to dinner to discuss business." She speaks as if nothing has happened between her and me, and who is this Serenity person she just called me. And Sam is not my damn stepfather!

"What a coincidence," he says as he stands until I'm seated.

"You two know each other," my mother asks.

"We crossed paths at the airport." I don't care about who he is or his purpose for being here, but I care about Serenity, whoever that is.

"Yes, I bought her a beer, and she threw my card away earlier today while I was waiting to get picked up." He allows his beautiful smile to smite me.

My mother looks at me in disbelief, "You did no such thing, did you? How rude of you?" She returns her look to Victor. "Well, I guess it's a small world." She looks at me and suspiciously sips her wine.

Chapter 16

After dinner, Mother insists that I get Victor's contact information. I do so just to shut her up. Once he finally leaves, in the kitchen I fix a plate of food from the left-overs to take back to the pool house with me, and my mother stands at the counter watching with a glass of wine in hand. I talk to her and get it over with. Here goes nothing.

"I've decided not to return to school," I blurt out as I close the refrigerator.

"Good, because you weren't going back there on my dime, anyway. You can enroll in school here."

"You can't keep me sheltered forever, you know?" I question as I wrap my plate of food.

"I'm not trying to keep you sheltered. I'm trying to assure that you don't make stupid decisions." She fixes herself a plate.

"Do you not understand that I have to make mistakes to learn, Mother? Do you understand that learning is the only way to grow? Do you understand that to live I must grow? I don't think you do, because if you did, you wouldn't be so adamant about keeping me under your wing *or* having me followed." Before I realize it, I share information I'm not sure I'm supposed to share. I don't want to get Lucia in any trouble.

"What makes you think I had you followed?" She looks puzzled.

"How else would you get pictures of me? I have common sense.

But you wouldn't know that because you swear I'm only book smart."
I place the containers of leftovers back in the refrigerator.

"Watch your mouth, Missy."

"While we're putting everything on the table, I guess I should let
you know that I'm flunking out of college and they have placed me
on academic suspension. And since you insist on me not returning,
it doesn't matter what the options are after suspension. Maybe you
were right about me not knowing what love is. Maybe it *is* best I stay
away from Carmen."

"Is she the reason your grades have made such a drastic drop? I
knew about you failing when you first failed. Is she the reason?" My
mother pours herself another glass of wine.

"Would you like for me to lie to you or tell you the truth?" I
pour myself a glass of wine.

"I would always prefer the truth," she advises me as she raises
her glass to cheers.

"Yes, she is the reason, and therefore I think it's best I don't go
back. You were right; I don't need any distractions from my studies.
To be honest with you, I'm not sure if I want to return to any school
at all. I think I'd rather find a job and go from there."

"You don't want to finish school. You get to the very end and give
it all up? Well, that's your choice, since you say I don't allow you to
live. I'll help you get a job and after that, you're on your own. You
can live in the pool house until you can afford a place for yourself,"
she states as she opens another bottle of wine. She sure is drinking
a lot, and awfully fast.

"Mother," I say to her in a calm tone.

"Yes, child."

"Who is Serenity?"

"That's you!" She exclaims. "That's your name, so that girl
doesn't come looking for you and find you. I've changed your name
and any other traceable information. There's an envelope on your
dresser that has all your fresh information, and a new driver's license.

You have no other choice but to accept it. I did all of this before you came home," she breaks to take a long gulp and continues, "It also contains a new cell phone. If you contact her and give her this information, you'll must leave this house and I'll disown you. I will have no child of mines fucking someone of the same sex as long as I'm living. Do you know how that can ruin *my* reputation? But I don't have to worry about that since you've vowed to not contact her. Aren't you grateful I've taken care of all this for you?" She sits and sips.

"I'm very grateful, Mother. I like the name Serenity. It means peaceful. I can sure use a little peace in my life right about now. I don't think contacting her would be the best idea. I just want to move on with my life, or my fresh life, and that's that. I don't want to fight with you about it, and I don't want it to be a continuous discussion. Can you give me your therapist's information?" I rub my temples.

"There's a card in the envelope," she slurs. I can tell she's drunk now because of the way she's knocking back those glasses of wine like someone will take them from her.

"Are you okay?" I question.

"I'm excellent! Why do you ask that?"

"Well, the way you're drinking, I thought something may be wrong." I pause and look around. "Where's Sam?" I pour myself another glass.

"He had to leave. Said it was business," she mumbles. Based on her response, whatever is wrong with her relates to him.

"Is he coming back?" I ask, leaning on the counter.

"I don't know. If he does, I'll be sound asleep," she utters. Just as she attempts to pour herself another glass of wine, she misses the glass completely and pours it all over the counter. I walk to the sink and get the dish towel to wipe it up, but she stops me and shouts, "NO! I will clean it up!"

This lady is beyond drunk. I attempt to clean her mess again, and she allows the help. She then falls to the floor crying. Not knowing what I'm supposed to do, I stand frozen, staring down at her. The thought of what I would want done if the shoe were on the other foot enters my mind, so I kneel beside her and place my hand on her shoulder, "Is it something you want to talk about, Mother?"

"I wish so hard I had your strength," she sobs.

"What does that mean?"

"I don't know what it means. It means… I'm weak."

I sit beside her, puzzled as she lets it out. I lay her head on my shoulder to comfort her, but it doesn't work because she nudges me away and continues to cry. After what seems like an eternity, we stand and I lead her up the stairs to her master suite. I remove her shoes as she sits on the side of the bed. Once undressed, she lies down on her side in the fetal position. She's continues to sob as I pull the covers over her.

"You know, I'm only trying to protect you from yourself." Her statement paralyzes me as I'm exiting.

"I know, Mother." My back faces her so she can't see my face. "I know it's all for my good." I force my body to move as I depart, close her bedroom door and go back to the kitchen to get my food. Lucia is standing at the sink washing the dishes that my mother just dirtied up.

"Her had her drunken pity party, me see." Lucia doesn't look up.

"Yes. How do you know?"

"Her do it all time. Me think she drinks to cover fact that she boyfriend married and just have baby."

I stand in the middle of the kitchen trying to piece together the last hour. I finally get it together enough to walk over to the other sink and begin rinsing and drying the dishes that Lucia has placed in the other drain. "What?" I say in complete shock.

"Yes, me thought her tell you. Her has so many secrets but punish you for you honesty." Lucia hands me a plate to rinse and dry. "Her not better than you."

"How long has this been going on? Her drinking, that is."

"Long time. Couple years. Her try keep it secret, but you know Lucia know everyting. He stay some nights, some nights he go. Say it business. He don't think her know anyting, but her had Malik follow he too. That's why her drink like her do. When he stay, her don't drink like that, but when he leave, her get real drunk," Lucia informs me.

"Wow! Why won't she say anything to him?" I ask her as if she knows the answer. She's Lucia, and she knows "everyting", so she just might.

"Me don't know. Me guess cause her don't want to lose he. Her no good for she self," she chuckles. I chuckle too because I completely agree.

We finish the dishes and say our goodnights. I get my plate of food and head to the pool house. The closer I get, the more I can make out the conversation that's being held. It's Sam; he didn't hear me coming. He's sitting near the dock talking on his phone. I tiptoe lightly, being sure I remain discreet. The door to the pool house is open, so I listen in on the conversation before going in.

"Are you sure about this?" I hear him ask the person on the other end. "So how much did she pay you and how much information have you given her?" He's silent for a minute or two; I guess getting a response from the person on the other end. "Why are you telling me this now? What do you want from me and why didn't you say anything sooner?" Silence again. "Let's keep this between the two of us. No one, I mean *no one*, should know about this. I have to figure out a way to fix this before she tries to leave me. I hope that damn daughter of hers doesn't find out, because if she does, she'll be the one to convince her to leave. Then I wouldn't know what to do about my finances. She's a significant asset to me, and I want to keep it that way until I open my business. After that, I don't care what she knows or what she does about it." I cannot believe my ears. "Keep doing what she's paying you to do and make sure you keep me posted on anything else she requests. In the meantime, I'll see if I can rush this business proposal with my partner. I don't know. Tell her you made a mistake, got a hold of my DNA, had the test ran, and the child isn't mine. See what that does, and I'll figure out a way to discredit the information she has on my marital status. I can guarantee that I'm not leaving my wife; not for her. I just don't think she's worth it. My wife has been by my side for over twelve years. She just can't help me financially right now. Susan is a beautiful woman, I'm just turned off since she's given birth. Any way, that ain't none of your business. I understand she's paying you well, but if you keep this between the two of us, I can give you double that."

I creep into the pool house figuring I've heard enough, put my food in the refrigerator, and lie down. My brain works overtime as it remembers the envelope on the dresser, so I'm forced to get back up. Sam sticks his head in the open door just as my hand reaches for the envelope.

"Hey, Mel... I mean Serenity. I thought you were still at the main house," he says, looking apprehensive.

"I was. I came to lie down about two minutes ago."

"Oh okay. Well, I'm going to bed now, just thought I'd get some fresh air before I turned in." He walks away but then turns back around, "You should give Victor a call, he's a righteous guy, and *very* successful."

"I'll think about it. I have to find a job before I think about calling anybody," I say to him as I close one of the French doors. My mother's condition jogs my memory, so I inquire, "Mom got pretty wasted tonight. Any idea what that's about?"

"She's been doing that a lot lately and when I ask her about it, she tells me that her work has gotten stressful. She wasn't too bad, was she? I know sometimes she gets so drunk that I have to carry her to bed when I get here. Hey, Mel, can I ask you why your mother referred to you as Serenity when she introduced you to Victor?" Now he's being nosey.

"Yeah, she was that drunk tonight. Her calling me Serenity is a lengthy story that I don't feel like getting into. Let's just say that it's my name from here on out." We laugh it off and he leaves. I really don't like him or trust him; I tolerate him.

I open the envelop and the driver's license hits the floor. I pick it up. It's the same picture of me I have on my current license. I retrieve the cell phone next, and there's a message from an unfamiliar number. It's placed on top of the dresser and a business card is the next thing item. Dr. Veronica Young, MD Counseling and Meditation Management / 1395 Brickell Ave Suite 863, Miami, FL 3313 / (305) 756-0148. The new birth certificate and social security card are the last items in the envelope. I pick the phone back up to check the message. It's from Victor. *I'm here for you if you want to hang out or talk.* How does he have this phone number already?

I ignore the message and undress to my bra and panties and lie down in bed. My mind immediately drifts to Carmen. Maybe I should call her. Maybe I should text her to let her know I'm okay. I'm instantly turned on by the thought of her. My body becomes warm and an electric shock runs from my brain to my vagina. I feel my river flow when I fondle down below. My body weakens as I press play on my button and move the way I did when Carmen would be down there making soft circular motions with her tongue. Repeating steps from when I'm with her, my mouth sucks my finger, tasting my juices. Wet and ready, my finger goes back to my button and continues in rotation, causing my body to speed up. The electricity builds up in the pit of my stomach. I'm about to cum, but I'm not ready yet, so I stop to let myself calm down. My heart rate quickens. Just as I place my finger back on my clit, I hear someone open the door. I open my eyes and it's Sam. I quickly pull the covers to my chin.

"I thought you might want this," Sam says as he shows me my old cell phone.

"Where did you get that?" I ask out of curiosity.

"It was on your mother's vanity."

"I don't need it. I have the new one. You can throw that one away." I remember the text and ask Sam, "How did Victor get my number? Did you know that my mother did all of this identity changing?"

"Yes, I knew. I'm the one who got the extra phone for her. She didn't tell me what she needed it for. She just asked me to do it and I made it happen. After I got it, I insisted that she tell me who it was for. I heard your old one ring, and I figured you'd want to check it. I'm not trying to get all up in your business or anything, but you have a lot of messages from someone named Carmen. She appears worried."

"Why did you make it seem like you didn't know who Serenity was when you were just in here? You know what, don't bother answering that. I'll contact her from this phone. You can trash that one." I hold back the tears that are forming. Why am I running from her? I love her. Or I'm not sure. It *could* be love since I'm having a hard time getting her out of my head. Sam notices my change of mood and comes to sit on the bed.

"Is everything all right?" he asks.

"Everything is fine." He makes me feel uncomfortable, so I move as far away from him as I can without falling off the bed.

"If everything is fine, why are you crying, Mel, I mean Serenity?"

I didn't realize the tears are flowing. I wipe my eyes and say, "I just miss being in Chicago, that's all."

"You may not know this, but I'm aware of *everything* that's going on with you and the girl at your school." He stands and looks down at me.

"I don't care about that. I don't care who knows. I have to move on with my life." I give him attitude because I wanted to tell him I know about his wife and the damn baby. I also want to advise him I know about the scheme he's pulling on my mother, but I'm too pissed right now to give a damn about my mother and her feelings, or what happens with her and this dead beat. She deserves to hurt the way she hurts everyone else. She thinks her money is her power. Well, little does she know, her money is what will cause her pain. And why in the hell does he continue to act like he knows nothing when it's obvious, he knows everything.

"But you're still crying?"

"I'm crying because I want this to be over. I wish none of it ever happened." I turn away from him, hoping he leaves.

"I think you should give Victor a call. Hanging out with him could be something to take your mind off all the madness that's going on. What could it hurt?"

"I'll take that into consideration," I respond. He gets up and walks to the door.

"Have a good night, Serenity."

The door closes. My body turns on its back to finish what I'd started before he walked his nosey ass in here. I touch down there and I'm no longer wet so I say fuck it and close my eyes and cry myself to sleep. Maybe giving this Victor guy a call won't be such a terrible idea since there's nothing else for me to do. Or maybe it will. What can he possibly do for me that my Carmen can't do?

Chapter 17

The smell of bacon wakes me the following morning. My eyes open to see that Lucia has placed a small feast on the stove. All for me. My long arms and yawns equal each other as I stretch. Realization sets in when my legs swing from under the cover and my feet hit floor. My toes embrace the plush and tan carpet as I walk to the stove. Lucia has made my favorite; bacon, eggs with cheese, smothered potatoes, hash browns, and buttermilk biscuits with strawberry jelly. She knows exactly how to spoil me.

I take my warm breakfast to the table where she has orange juice poured and covered. As I sit and eat, I remember the text message from Victor and go fetch the cell phone. Lying next to it is the card for the therapist, so I pick it up. Back at the table and eating, I read Victor's message again: *I'm here for you if you want to hang out or talk.* My thoughts can't help but wonder why this guy is so nice and willing to be a shoulder. He doesn't know me and I sure as hell don't know him. Carmen needs erasing from my memory, so maybe he can help me with that, either him or this therapist lady. I put the phone down and finish my breakfast.

When I'm done eating, I make the call to the therapist. I hang up on the first ring and then dial again. I hang up again, unsure of *why* I need to call her. I remember I need to get Carmen out of my head, so I dial the number again, but hang up on the first ring and for the second time, consider using Victor to get over her. *Nah! Nice thought, though.* All of my other issues cross my mind and I notice how writing them in my journal have not and do not resolve them. I dial the number one last time and let it ring more than once without hanging up. "You have reached the office of Dr. Veronica Young. Our office will be closed on Thursday and Friday of this week for the Thanksgiving Holiday. Normal business hours will resume on Monday. If this is an emergency, please hang up and dial 911. Thank you and Happy Holidays." A long beep follows. That's right! Today is Thanksgiving. I completely forgot.

I hang up the phone, clean my plate and go on a mission to find Lucia. I must tell her about all the shit that went down last night, especially about the phone conversation between Sam and Malik. It's a strong possibility she knows about it, because whenever I tell her anything, she has the same response, "Me know everyting."

Sam is sitting at the breakfast table on the phone when I walk through the kitchen. He appears to be so engaged in whatever conversation he's having, that he doesn't hear me come in and close the door; let alone stop and listen for a few minutes. "I promise I'll be home in two days, baby. This was a trip I had to take to get the promotion I want. As soon as I get back, I'll make it up to you. I hate being away from you and the kids for not only a day, but for the holidays too."

Lying ass bastard! His lies are universal, I see! There's no need for me to say anything to my mother because she already knows his situation, and if she wants to be the milked cow, that's all on her. I would hope she's smarter than what she's portraying to be with this clown. If I tell her he will leave her once his business opens, maybe that'll light the fire under her and she'll leave him alone. His own damn wife doesn't even know he plans to open a business. Her dumb ass thinks he has a job and my mother knows the opposite. He seems to screw them both, three sixty and literally. That's funny, but fucked up at the same time. If the shit ever hits the fan, I hope it'll be a wake-up call for my mother and she stops buying love. I don't know, but I can only wait and see how all this plays out.

My stomach can no longer take his foolishness, so my quest to find Lucia continues. My mother startles me once I'm completely out of the kitchen. She's standing by the door listening to Sam. Alarmed, I ask her, "How long have you been standing there?"

"Long enough." She turns and walks up the massive double-sided, swirled stairway.

"Are you going back to bed, or are you going to help Lucia cook Thanksgiving dinner? Is there anything you need me to do? Speaking of Lucia, do you know where she is?"

"No. No. Grocery shopping. Send a bottle of wine up when she comes back," she tells me from the top of the stairs. I can tell through her dark brown, heavy eyes that she has had little sleep, but is about to drink the day away. I'm having a tough time trying to determine if I should feel sorry for her or not.

I take my mother a bottle of wine myself as I make my way back to the kitchen. Lucia has most of her ingredients for dinner spread across the counter. She and I always race to see who can cut the vegetables the fastest, so I get the celery and a knife, and place them on the table to get a head start after I come back from my mother's room.

Sam has ended his conversation and is now drinking coffee and reading the newspaper. He nods his head at me and says, "Serenity."

I nod back, "Sam." I smile. "Happy Turkey Day." I turn to go to my mother's suite and then instinctively turn back to Sam, "Tell the family Happy Turkey Day."

He rushes from his seat, charges to me and grips my arm, "What the fuck are you talking about?"

"Wasn't that your wife you were just on the phone lying to?" I stare at him without blinking to let him know how that he does not intimidate me.

"You listen here, you little brat, you better not mention a word of this to your mother. You hear me?" His grip tightens.

"I don't have—"

"Everyting right in here?" Lucia enters from the garage door.

Sam releases my arm and responds, "Everything is fine. Isn't it, Serenity? I will expose you to Victor," he whispers.

"I'm all good," I inform Lucia as I let out a smirk. He was two seconds away from getting cracked upside the head with this bottle. I don't care how much it cost. And I hope he doesn't think I care about him telling Victor a damn thing. Lucia shoots me a look to ensure I'm cool. I nod at her and turn to go up the steps.

"Are you going up to your mother's room?" Sam asks me.

"I sure am." I respond without looking back.

"I'll take that up. I was on my way up there, anyway." He takes two steps at a time to catch up. When he does, he grabs the bottle of wine and says, "Not a word," in a stern voice. I laugh and go back down the stairs. If only his dumb ass knew that, she's fully aware of all his wrongdoings.

Lucia is unpacking the groceries when I reenter. The celery needs to get rinsed off, so I take them from the table and go to the sink and Lucia joins me. She looks at me, nudges my shoulder with hers and says with a smirk, "You was gone crack him head, huh?" I laugh and ask her how does she know. "Lucia know everyting."

"No seriously, how do you know?"

"Me saw you grip bottle," she answers as her laugh continues.

"Oh, Lucia, I love you." I rinse the rest of the celery and go back to the table. She comes to join me with some onions, bell peppers, a cutting board, and a knife.

"After finish, tell mama dinner ready at doce y media," she speaks in Spanglish.

"Si, señora," I respond in Spanish.

"Gracias mi dulce bebé."

"You're welcome, Lucia." Our smiles echo each other.

Once all the vegetables get cut, I go to my mother's bedroom to tell her what time dinner will be ready. The closer I get to the room, the more noises I hear. Standing at the door, it's obvious that she's having sex. "Please don't stop," I hear her say.

"Is it good to you, baby?" I hear Sam ask.

"Yes, Daddy, please don't stop." I hear a smack. "Tell me you love me."

"I love you, baby."

"Tell me you'll never leave me."

"I promise I'll never leave you," she says, then a smack follows. "Please don't stop. I'm going to cum for you, Daddy. Please don't stop."

YUCK! That's probably why she won't let his ass go. She doesn't love him and he doesn't love her. They lust after each other. But she tells me *I* don't know what love is.

I go downstairs and tell Lucia what I just witnessed, and she already knows everything. I remember to tell her about the chain of events from last night, and she's aware of that too. I can only laugh at this woman and wonder what she doesn't know.

Lucia places the food on the table as we all gather around. My mother, Sam, Lucia's 13-year-old daughter, Bella, and me. Lucia sits in between Bella and me once she places the turkey tray in front of Mother, who prays, and we all pass the food around, fixing our plates.

"Everything smells delicious, Lucia." I nudge her.

"Tank you, my Sweet Melody." She leans in and kisses my cheek.

"Serenity," my mother corrects her.

"My sweet Serenity," Lucia says as she winks at me. My mother always has been jealous of our relationship.

"Yes, everything smells wonderful and looks good. You've

outdone yourself yet again. I'm very grateful that you've been a part of our family for so many years. I sometimes wonder what I would've done all these years if you hadn't been here. I'm also grateful for my wonderful baby. Sam, you've been my rock for the past four years and many more to come. You've been there for me when no one else has, and I'll always be grateful for you. Last, my daughter. I'm grateful for you being home."

Lucia and I look at each other and chuckle. I look at my mom and reply, "Thanks, Mother." She's been doing this every Thanksgiving since they have locked my father up; get drunk and want to give thanks to everybody but the right body. She says fuck me, and her boyfriend is the head of her life. She needs God in her life, I swear.

Everybody eats in silence and when we're all done, Lucia and I clear the table and my mother and Sam go back up to the room with another bottle of wine. "Is that all they do now days?"

"What that?" Lucia asks.

"Drink and have sex," I remind her.

"Ever since him want money, yes. Him use her for business, after that, him disappear. Her will see. Me can't tell she anyting, so me not try no more. Me think that's why she drinks more when him not round; cause her want he round," Lucia clarifies for me.

"I see! This is a sad situation. That explains her saying she wished she was as strong as me. She will never possess the strength that I have, because she never likes to be alone. It's like she yearns for attention from somebody. My grandmother was never like that and showed her nothing but love and attention when she was growing up. I just don't see where she gets it." I plop down in a seat at the kitchen counter and begin twirling my thumbs with my head down. "And all she's grateful for from me is being home. Huh! She has some nerve. I find all this so hard to believe, Lucia. It's so much to wrap around my tiny little brain. My mother had a private investigator following me and taking pictures while I was away at school by someone that she and my father were both fucking. She had my name changed, which I'm not too pissed about because I like it. Her boyfriend is playing her like Bozo the Clown. She's never made me a home-cooked meal. She's the same woman that allows a man to fuck her and not make love to her. I remember when my father was home, and I was younger, I would hear them having sex all the time. They would be so loud that I would have to come to your room. You remember that, Lucia?" I look at her for confirmation as she nods. "Whenever I have children, I'll never treat them the way my mother treats me, and I mean never. She's never been there for me. You've been there more than her. All she ever did and continues to do is shower me with gifts and money. When Sabrina was a baby girl, we would hug each other to get the love we desired from our parents. I sure miss her, Lucia. Can we go visit her grave tomorrow? I'd rather go vent to her than some damn therapist."

"It's okay my Sweet Serenity. Lucia make it all better for you," Lucia says as she wipes the tears that always seem to fall without me knowing. "We go see Sabrina tomorrow. Stay all day if you like." I hug her long and hard and thank her for always being there for me. "You no have to thank me, you me Sweet Melly baby. Me mean Serenity." She strokes my hair as she hugs me tight and close.

"Oh, you two break it up." My mother comes in, interrupting us and slurring in her drunken lingo.

Lucia and I release our embrace, and I wipe my tears away with the napkin she gives me. I look at my mother. She doesn't acknowledge the fact that I have tears in my eyes, and it makes me wonder if I'm invisible to her. Disregarding her drunken slurs, I go to the refrigerator and get Lucia and me a Heineken. I open both, squeeze a lemon in each, and we click bottles and both take a long sip. We signal each other to go to the bay window in the gigantic living room. Lucia walks past my mother first, and I follow. To my surprise, and I'm sure to Lucia's too, my mother turns and follows us.

"Do you guys know how much I love him? He's everything to me. There's nothing I wouldn't do for him. He loves every bit of me; inside and out. He's my soul mate. More than your father ever was," she says, snarling at me. Then she continues with her drunken rant, "He gives me everything I need and more. He makes me feel like I've never felt. Don't you wish *you* had a man like that?" My mother sits between Lucia and me and rubs my hair. "Don't you wish you had a man to love you the way Sam loves me. You'll have it one day. Just hang in there."

"No mother. I'm sorry, but I don't want anyone to love me the way Sam loves you," I pause and then continue, "I want an unconventional love."

"What, you want love from some dyke bitch?" she asks as she leans so close, she showers me with her saliva. "You think that's love? If you do, you don't know a damn thing about love! As long as you like dykes, you will never know what love is!" Her words are piercing and insulting.

"You say Sam loves you. You say he does all of this and that for you. Then if this is the case, why do you drink so much?"

"Because I can." She speaks in slow motion, blowing her stank breath in my face.

"Are you even happy?" I bag my head back, giving her the shit face, trying to avoid the stomachache her breath is causing.

"As happy as I'll ever be." She stands and stumbles so badly that Lucia has to rush to catch her. We both look at each other and shake our heads.

I allow her last statement to ride as Lucia helps her to the bottom of the stairs and then calls for Sam to come and get her. She looks pitiful as she lays side-way on three steps waiting for him. "I will *never* be like her," I tell Lucia when she returns and sits next to me.

"Me know, child. Me will make sure. Me not worried though."

"I'm not worried either, Lucia, and never worry about me. I'll do everything I can to prevent from ending up like her... lonely and sad. I like to drink, but I know when to say when, and I don't drink every day to get drunk. I drink because I like to enjoy a beer now and then. She drinks to get entirely wasted, and to numb the pain she allows

Sam to cause her. This is the reason I don't feel sorry for her. I know she's my mother and I love her, but I find it hard to respect someone that doesn't respect themselves. How does she expect anyone else to accept her for who she is when she doesn't accept herself, or she doesn't know her own worth? What is her value? I bet she knows nothing about being valuable, and I'm not referring to sex. If she knows something about it, I bet you any amount of money it has a dollar sign with a damn number. That's what's wrong with females. They don't know their own value. They don't value themselves but expect others to. I'll admit, I have a hard time loving people and being loved, Lucia, which causes me to question the relationship I had with Carmen." I pause for air because her names causes me to lose my breath. "I don't know if she truly loved me or if I truly loved her because I don't even know what love is, *and* because it's so easy for me to walk away from that situation and start over. Does it hurt? It does, but life is pain right?"

"Not all time, but some time." We raise our bottles, clink them, and take another sip.

"Would you like another one? Maybe with tequila shot this time?" I ask while standing.

"Oh child! Bring lemons and salt," she tells me, as if I don't already know what to bring. She must've forgotten she taught me how to drink tequila on my twentieth birthday.

In the kitchen, I go to the pantry and get a bottle of Gran Patrón Platinum, two beers out of the fridge, cut up a few lemons, and salt. On my way through the foyer, the sounds from my mother and Sam having sex again meets me at the bottom of the steps. She has no respect for the other people in this house. I guess she figured she paid for it, so she can do whatever she wants.

In the living room, the only thing Lucia does is look and laugh at my expression, which intends to speak for itself. We sit in the window until nightfall. Like the old days, we both fall asleep in the window, my head in her lap, and before we know it, the sun is coming up.

Chapter 18

I lay awake in bed thinking. The weekend was so long that it seemed as if Monday would never get here. My mother got fucked and wasted the entire weekend, in no particular order. Lucia took me to visit Sabrina's grave and then we had dinner. Not being in much of a writing mood, I allowed myself to catch up with Lucia, dance, and listen to music all weekend.

Important phone calls will take up most of my day. I made the ultimate decision to walk away from the Carmen situation and redirected my focus on myself. Not saying anything to her at all is my best bet, because I know it'll hurt her to the core and she'll come looking for me. Me knowing her; I know she's questioned why I haven't called her back. I just hope she'll someday be able to get over me and move on, rather sooner than later. *Will me not telling her hurt just as badly?* I question myself and then shake it off. A morning jog will help me get my mind off things; something I haven't done in what seems like forever.

After I'm dressed, I go through the main house to let Lucia know I'm headed out. She's cooking breakfast when I enter. "Up early, me see," she says standing over a skillet of bacon. "Misses say call she at work when you wake up."

"I'm on my way out for a run. I will when I get back." I pick up a water and head towards the front door. Sam is sitting on the sofa on his phone. He sees me and ends his conversation. "No work today?" I ask him sarcastically.

"Yes, I'll be going in later," he explains as he stands to walk towards me.

Before he gets too close, I say, "Oh well, have a wonderful day," and walk straight out the door. He calls my name, but I ignore him and start jogging to the end of the street to take the path to the beach. The sound of nature is the replacement of music since I've yet downloaded any on this new phone. When I get to the end of the street and turn down the path, I notice how there are very few joggers out, which is abnormal for a Monday morning. The few people give me an eerie feeling that I ignore and take off jogging, anyway. A runner passes every so often, leaving me on the beach alone, mostly. I keep the same pace the entire time as I reflect on being home. *I sure miss this scenery.* Living in the city is cool, but I like to enjoy the beach all year round. In Chicago, the beach is only fun for two months during the summer. After that, the breeze from the lake froze the hell out of me. I wonder what everybody is up to back at school. I wonder if Carmen has tried to reach me. She's probably moved on. If she really loved me like she say she did, she would find me. Is it weird that I don't want to reach out to her, but I want her to look for me? Maybe I should just let even the thought of her go all together... which is so much easier said than done. I wonder if Skylar is still being the whore she is. Once a whore, always a whore because you can never turn a whore into a housewife.

Another jogger passes, and I'm distracted by the familiarity of the individual. Gosh, that guy sure looks like someone I know. He looked like Malik. Only difference is this guy has facial hair. Malik doesn't have facial hair. Hell, he looks like he hasn't even hit puberty yet. My assumptions cause me to believe that my mind is playing tricks on me until I'm being grabbed from behind and told not to say a word. The person leads me to a beach house not even fifty feet from the beach with their hand covering my mouth. Once in, they put tape over it, tie my hands behind my back, sit me on the couch, and again tell me not to think about getting up. I still don't know who it is. Every time I try to look back, they push my head forward. Finally, they come around to the front of me and it's Malik. *I knew I wasn't fucking crazy*; I think to myself as I kick the shit out of him. "Mm! Mm!" I try yelling through the tape.

"Listen, I will not hurt you. I need to talk to you and this is the only way I know you'll listen. I tried telling you everything back in Chicago, but your *girlfriend* came to your rescue. Yes, I can admit the way I went about things were wrong, but I was only doing what they paid me to do. Now it seems as if things are getting way out of hand, and it's no longer worth the money. I'll start from the beginning. Once I'm done, I'll untie you and take the tape off, but not a minute before, because you talk too damn much and I need to say what it is I have to say." He places a chair in front of me, sits, and crosses his legs. "Years ago, your mother hired me to spy on your father, and you father hired me to spy on your mother. Your father thought your mother was cheating and your mother thought your father was not only cheating too, but was gay. Well, they both turned out to be right, but what your mother didn't know is that your father and I were lovers well before she hired me. Your mother then became attracted to me, but your father didn't know this. For their anniversary, your father wanted to see how she would react to a threesome and I was… let's say 'the chosen one'. That one night led to a relationship that your mother, father, and myself had for many years, until he went to prison for the incident with your sister. Even though your father is away, we still have a relationship, but I do what I want until he comes home. For a while, you mother and I continued having sex, but that ran out fast because it was no longer fun for her considering she wanted the best of both worlds; your father *and* the infamous me. Now she just hires me to do her dirty work, like be a spy on you. Once she found out about you and Carmen, she wanted me, first try to convince you to fall in love with me, but when that didn't work she wanted me to harm her to the point of no return." Malik stands and walks behind me and loosens the knot on my hands. My eyes follow his every move.

He comes back to sit and continues, "Now, her boyfriend Sam… he's another story. He and I have had a none sexual relationship, but he initially hired me to spy on your mother. Now he wants me to harm you. He says you know too much. He then realized he wouldn't get his business off the ground without her. So, he's now playing the waiting game and wants me to hold on to the money. At some point, my job is to do what he paid me to do, which is get rid of her… for good." He stops talking, walks to the other end of the sofa, and picks up a briefcase. When he opens it, it's full of money. "I have spent not one penny. I have no intentions on harming you or your mother, but it wouldn't surprise me if he doesn't hire some-one else to. I'm only telling you all of this now because your father wants me to put a stop to it before it goes any further than it already has. He says you're the only one who's smart enough to put all this madness to an end without the disarray He's aware that your mother has become a complete drunk who's never in her right mind. I will take the tape off now and allow you to talk, but first, promise me you won't scream." I nod up and down. "I'll untie you once we're done. I don't want you to run, Melody. Can you promise you won't run?"

Blown away by everything he just said to me, I shake my head yes. When he snatches the tape off, I yelp in agony. "Did you have to snatch it off like that?"

"I'm sorry. I only did it fast so it wouldn't hurt as bad."

"Ugh! Anyway, who is Victor? Is he in on all of this too?" I ask him, unsure why that's the first question to come out of my mouth.

"No, not at all. I've checked him out on your father's behalf. He's a cool dude and really is about his business. He and Sam are friends from school. Sam wants him as an investor in his upcoming business; nothing illegal, but he doesn't know that Sam's a crook," he explains.

Completely confused and not knowing who to trust, I ask him, "So what do you think I should do?"

"Your father has given me small instructions on what *he* thinks you should do, but you can handle it however you feel. His primary concern was making sure you got the details of everything that's been going on."

"Why are you doing all of this? What's in it for you?"

"I owe it to your father. He did a few favors for me when I had nowhere else to turn," he answers.

"Then why take on so many jobs from my mother? You may not have any intentions to harm me physically, but you've already harmed my emotions and a part of my mind by spying on me for so long. I don't trust *you* or anybody else. And let's not forget about all the creepy shit you was doing in Chicago. The story about your mother living with you, was that true, or was that some shit you made up?"

"Everything I told you in Chicago was a lie. I did and said whatever so I didn't blow my cover. I fucked up by hanging out in the gay clubs and being seen by that petty bitch from Hooters. It was always about the money, especially after your father left. Your father took excellent care of me before he went away. Once he left, your mother only paid me for jobs. How else was I supposed to make a living for myself?"

"No, it wasn't a question, but this isn't about me. Well, in a way it is. I'm the common denominator to this whole equation. I don't want you to think I'm a terrible person. Until your father gets out of prison, I'm only doing what I'm paid to do so I can make it out here in this world. I don't want anybody's blood on my hands. This is another reason I've taken the time to fill you in on so many details."

"How do I know I can trust you? I heard Sam on the phone with you the other night. You know... when you informed him about my mother knowing all his business. Why did you tell him she knew? That's what made him want to harm her. I'm not worried about me.

And I'm really not worried about her, either. I just want to know why? Why are you telling me all of this now? I get my father told you to nip this shit in the bud, but you can let him know that I'm much smarter than he thinks. Now, I've listened to you, so can you listen to me and untie my damn hands?" I turn sideways and show him the rope he has my hands tied with.

"I'm not asking you to trust me. I'm asking you to trust yourself. You know good and damn well Sam is up to no good. If I wanted to do something to you, I could've been and done it; like the night when you first got here, and you were in your damn bed masturbating. I could've taken you out then, but I didn't because like I said, I don't want no damn blood on my hands. Not only that, but the respect I have for your father, and the love he has for you and your mother, I could but would do nothing to harm either of you. Now you can believe me or you can't. I frankly don't give a damn; but I'm only trying to help you, not hurt you. And you're right… you are much smarter than your father thinks you are." Malik unties my hands.

"I'm very grateful for you sparing our lives. I just think this whole situation is fucked up and I don't know who to trust. I don't even know if I can trust myself. I've taken in everything you've said and I have to go figure out how to fix it." I stand to leave.

"If you need help with anything, will you let me know?" He jumps in front of the door before I reach it.

"I'll think about it," I respond as I push past him.

I walk out the door and go the opposite direction I ran in. How am I going to deal with this? Shit, I don't even know how I will approach this damn situation, let alone deal with it. I hope my father doesn't think this is a way to get close to me. Maybe Lucia will know what to do and how to do it. My nerves are so shot behind all of this foolishness. It's like every day it's something new. If it isn't my mother, it's her damn boyfriend. If it isn't her boyfriend, it's me. When does it all end? My father was right about one thing though,

I can do this and it not be so messy; so I have to figure out a master plan before it's too late.

I arrive back at the house to find my mother standing in the kitchen with Lucia and stuffing her face with a sub-sandwich and potato chips. Lucia sees me come in and sits a plate at the table for me. "Run good?"

"Yes, it was a wonderful run." I have a habit of correcting her English when I answer or respond, even though I know she'll never understand my corrections. She hasn't in all these years.

"Must been. Gone long time." Her accent is as heavy as it was the day I met her.

"It's therapeutic, plus, you know how running causes me to lose track of time." I wash my hands and take a seat at the table.

"Time waits for no one," Lucia and I both say in unison followed by a laugh.

"You jinx me." She holds up her pinky finger.

"You've picked up too many things from me over the years, Lucia," I smile as I take a bite from my perfectly made sandwich. I never have to tell her what I want to eat or how I want to eat it. There's not too much of anything that I have to tell her about me; now my mother, she knows very little. Sometimes I wonder if I'm adopted.

"No, no, no. Me teach *you* well." She shakes her forefinger at me and laughs.

"Oh, enough with you two already. Do you ever tire from all the damn mushiness? Are you two fucking? That's probably where she got the gay shit from to begin with." My mother takes a sip of whatever she has in her glass, which I'm almost positive is wine.

Lucia looks at her and says a few words with a lot of meaning, "*Never* insult me again." She then turns to me and says, "Eat up so can shower."

I sometimes wonder if I would still live if Lucia had not been around to keep me grounded and sane. I look at my mother as she finishes the beverage in her glass, and then I do something out of the ordinary by asking, "How has your day been so far?"

Her chestnut brown eyes peek over the brim of the glass. She pauses before finishing the remaining with one gulp and then replies, "It's been good. I spoke with my friend at Bank of America and she's looking for an executive personal banker. If you're interested, you can start this week. I know it's not geared towards what your major was, but it pays very well; one hundred thousand the first year, plus incentives. Benefits included and you'll have your own office and personal assistant. You make your own schedule as long as you meet the required hours every month." She sips. "I figured it could be a noble way to start over. I left her contact information on my vanity. If you're not interested, you must find something on your own and it must be soon. You won't need any training because the job is common sense, which you think you have plenty of." Her expression confirms her statement. "The only things you're required to do is to assist and support clients with their financial needs. You may not have much personal experience in monitoring your own finances, but I'm sure you're aware of what it takes. I wrote your father a letter telling him how you've fucked up." She pours herself another glass of wine, finishes it fast, grabs her briefcase off the chair next to me and leaves without saying another word. What a way to end a conversation.

"Will you at home for dinner time?" Lucia yells behind her.

"Those are the plans, if not, put me a plate in the microwave." The front door closes.

After checking to make sure she's gone, I turn back towards the kitchen to gossip with Lucia. "Some shit happened while I was away, and I need your help on how to figure everything out." I fill her in on the information Malik shared and ask what she thinks I should do. She tells me that the first thing is to make sure my mother's will leaves nothing to Sam. *That's the simple part,* I think to myself. She then tells that she will figure the rest out, and for me not to worry about it. She says we have time. I don't see how though, unless she knows something I don't know.

After finishing my lunch and promising Lucia that I would take the job at the bank to start a financial establishment for myself, I leave the kitchen and go to my mother's room to retrieve the number from her vanity. It's lying right on top. Under it is an envelope addressed from our OBGYN. Inquiring minds would like to know, so I pick it up and open it. As I'm reading, I can't believe my eyes. No wonder she's been drinking like a fish under water and won't leave Sam alone. She's pregnant; 7 weeks, to be exact. Is it even his? Does Lucia know about any of this? Does she plan on keeping it? I look at the date and it's dated for November 1, 2006. That was three weeks ago. Is she still pregnant? How do I get the answers to all these questions without being found out? Just as I finish reading and put the letter back in the envelope, I hear my mother's voice telling Lucia that she forgot the file she's working on. I hurry and place the letter just how I found it and make my way into the hallway.

When she sees me, she asks, "Did you get the number?"

"Sure did! It was just where you said it would be. Thanks! I'll call her right away." I show her the card and hurry back downstairs, jumping two steps at a time. Once in the kitchen, I immediately take Lucia's hand and drag her into the pantry, out of ear's listening. "Did you know she was or *is* pregnant?" Lucia's "what the fuck" response confirms she had no clue.

My hand covers her mouth. "*We* have to figure out a way to find out if she still is. How do we do that?"

I uncover her mouth to let her answer, "Pay Malik."

"Yes! Why didn't I think of that? Come on." I pull her out of the pantry, leading her to the back door.

"Me must finish dishes. Go and me come shortly." Lucia pushes me out the door.

I hear my mother coming down the stairs behind me, so I hurry off. In the pool house, I plop down on the sofa and extend my legs to the ottoman. While waiting, I call my mother's friend at the bank and seal the job.

Felicia answers on the second ring and we talk for about five minutes before our conversation ends. She gave the same information my mother provided and I start on Wednesday. That gives me another day to clear my mind from all the fuckery. Lucia eventually comes in with a beer for me, and a beer for her.

She sits down beside me on the sofa, ready for the chatter. "Her pregnant?"

"Apparently. That's what the doctor's letter read. Said she was seven weeks, but that was three weeks ago." I get comfortable by propping a pillow behind my back and sitting Indian-style. "So, you think we should hire Malik to find out if she's still pregnant or not?" I ask her for reassurance.

"Him must be good. Everybody else hire he."

"But he'll tell my father. Do you think it's okay that my father knows, or do you think he'll say something to my mother?" I question her.

"Him might tell father unless we pay him not to. Him so devoted to you father that him will still spill beans, probably," she answers.

"I'll find out. We have the same doctor. I'll make a doctor's appointment and bring it up to Dr. Ivanovsky as though my mother has already told me. Oh wait, Raven is the receptionist there. She's been there since our senior year of high school. I can get anything out of her because she's *always* up in someone else's business since she has none of her own," I inform Lucia, then chug over half my beer. She takes her last sip and leaves to prepare dinner.

I dial the therapist. We've agreed to meet tomorrow at four. There's a feeling that I just might like her. Our conversation puts me in a thinking mood about how to deal with all the situations that surround me. First things first; I have to deal with my mother and a new baby, if there is a new baby. Let me call and make my doctor's appointment while that's still fresh on my mind.

The phone rings three times before the receptionist finally answers. "Hi Raven, it's Melody. Can I make an appointment for as soon as possible?"

"Hi Melody! We haven't heard from you in a while. Are you home from school? Is everything okay? How soon would you like to come in?" I don't know if she's excited or just doing her job.

"Whoa! Slow down there, Raven. You must really be excited to hear from me? Yes, I'm home from school. Actually, I'm here for good... or until I leave. It'll definitely be on *my* terms, though. Everything is perfectly fine. I just need to come in for my usual check-up. Do you have an opening for tomorrow?" I know I'm pushing it by requesting to come in so soon, but I'm willing to take my chances.

"I have nine-thirty and eleven."

"I'll take the eleven."

"Okay, I have you down. See you tomorrow and come a little early so we can catch up a little. It's been a while and I miss my friend." She's giggling.

"See you then, Raven." I giggle back. I know she's the only person I'll be able to get the information I need from. Not only is she nosey, but she talks too damn much. Therefore, I only share information that I want her to know, and I'm okay with her repeating. I can only imagine how interesting the conversation will go. Raven and I haven't seen each other since we graduated almost four years ago, and we both mistakenly had our parties on the same day. We fought about it at first, but then wound up joining them together. She was one of the few friends I had in high school. We attended school together from Pre-K to twelfth grade. Her parents are just as wealthy as mine are. Her father is the chief of police and has been since I can remember, and her mother owns three of Miami's hottest salons; not just beauty shops, but salons where you can get everything done, from hair to massages. She caters to men and women, and her clientele ranges from local celebrities to Donatella Versace.

We hang up and I go to the house to see if Lucia can reserve me a car for tomorrow. She arranges for me to get picked up at nine-thirty and goes back to her duties.

Chapter 19

I parade into Dr. Ivanovsky's office with my long, white flair, Versace maxi dress, my blue Versace sling-back flats, a yellow Louis Vuitton Murakami bag, and my favorite Prada shades. I wrapped my hair into a tight bun at the crown of my head.

I remove my shades once I reach the desk. Raven jumps up, runs around it and gives me an enormous hug saying, "Girl, I didn't know who you were walking in here looking like a million bucks. For a second there, I thought you could've passed for being Mrs. Moore."

"Well, hello to you too, Raven. It *has* been a while. I have changed a little, or have I?" I break our embrace and spin around.

"Girl, you look good, and your skin is flawless! What do you use on it? I wish my skin looked as good."

"Nothing a little shea butter and Dove body bar can't fix." I turn the attention to her. "You're looking good yourself. What have you been up to?" A little small talk won't hurt. I figured this is the only way I'll *easily* get the information I need. It'll be rude to go right into the conversation asking questions about my mother. Raven is nosey as hell, but she's far from stupid, and we agreed to catch up when I spoke with her yesterday. That was the point of coming in early.

Raven twirls her five-feet-three-inch body around mimicking me and replies, "I haven't been up to anything besides working out and trying to get this plump body of mine together." She isn't lying about the plump part. She used to be much bigger in high school, but I can tell she's been working out. Raven is short with a light-skin complexion. Her perfect teeth compliment her beautiful smile that can brighten a dark alley. It appears she's cut her sandy red hair into the new Rhianna hairstyle everyone is ranting about and wearing, which is nothing but a modern-day Toni Braxton cut. It looks good on her. She's dressed in a long green maxi skirt with a purple, yellow, green and white dotted scrub top. It's funny to see how her top hugs her cleavage to play peek-a-boo. From what I recall, Raven wasn't a fan of revealing her body parts. I guess I'm not the only one that's growing up.

She looks at me with her green eyes—inherited from her Caucasian mother—and leans in close enough for only me to hear, "Girl, how's your mother doing?"

Good, she's getting right to it, I think as I chuckle and answer, "She's fine, mostly. Has she been back since her... you know... situation?" I have to make her think I know more about the pregnancy than I do.

Raven takes my arm and pulls me to the break area. Catching the one patient that's waiting roll her eyes, I smile as we pass her. "Oh wow! I don't see how she does it. I know if it were me in her predicament, I would've tried to kill myself after the first abortion to prevent having two more and then this miscarriage. When she came in two weeks ago after she left the hospital, she looked horrible and reeked of alcohol. She was past drunk. She even fell asleep on the exam table while doc was examining her. I mean, sleeping so well. Doc didn't even wake her once she finished. She slept for about a good two hours. When she *did* finally wake up, all she did was cry and talk about how she wanted to keep this one. I guess God works in mysterious ways, huh?"

"Yes, I guess so." All this news catches me so off guard, Raven catches me dazing. It's like I'm hearing her, but from a distance.

"You okay? You look like you will be sick, or you just seen a ghost." She grabs my hand.

I immediately gather myself. "Yes, I'm fine. I just wish there was something I could do to make my mother feel better. Honestly, between you and me, she's been acting a little strange since the miscarriage."

"Although Mrs. Moore is almost is in her forties, her body can't bear another pregnancy. She asked doc to take blood work on her to see if she can get a more legitimate reason why not, and doc did. Now we're just waiting on all the results to come back."

"Can you tell me what they affirm once you get them?" She and I both know she's not supposed to do it, but I ask anyway.

"Now you know I'm not supposed to do that." Her answer is what I suspected it to be. She takes a deep breath and continues, "But I'll see what I can do. I'll call you once the doc figures everything out. You can't tell anyone I'm sharing this information with you, because you know it can cost me my job."

"Yes, I'm fully aware. Thank you so much." I stand and give her an excessive hug.

"No problem. That's what friends are for, right?"

"You know it!" We leave the break room and she goes behind the receptionist desk just as another patient walks in. I sit in one of the waiting chairs.

After shopping all day, a wasted trip to the therapist's office, taking a ride to the job, I'm now sitting in traffic for what's going on almost two hours. I can't help but replay my doctor's visit. *I didn't remember any of the process from when I was younger.* Maybe because I was so zoned out behind what my father had been doing to my sister, that I blocked everything and everybody out except for her. That day was a horrific day for me because my father was doing something I never imagined he would do, and for Sabrina to not tell ME of all people, made me wonder. I would always question where she would get so much money from, and her response was always the same, "Helping Daddy at the office." Once everything came out, she was helping him all right. He had her so fucked up in the head to where she no longer wanted to live. I wonder if she killed herself because of what he did to her or if she couldn't live without him. There's always so much to consider.

It's a little after seven when I finally make it back home. I'm just in time for dinner. I fill Lucia in on the events and information for the day as I stuff my face. She knows about the blood work, but says she didn't tell me because she didn't want me to worry before the results were back.

I eat the rest of my meal talking about my day, and place my plate in the sink just as someone enters through the front door. I go see who it is because I want to catch my mother before she slips upstairs, but it turns out to be Sam. He has a few suitcases with him that he drops at the door, walks past me, and into the kitchen. I follow behind him and when Lucia sees him; she looks at me in confusion and begins making him a plate. He sits at the table, Lucia places his plate in front of him, and he eats like a hog and doesn't say a word, not even to thank Lucia. I take my time drinking a beer because I want Sam to hurry and leave so Lucia and I can finish talking. It seems the longer I wait, the longer he takes. I'm the first to give in as I get up and throw the now empty bottle away. I tell Lucia I'll catch her later and pick up my shopping bags from the back door where I'd left them, and pretend to make my way to the pool house, but stand on the other side of the door snooping.

Out of eye's view, I listen. It appears Sam is moving into the house. To me, this means I have to put my plan into action much sooner than I thought. How dare he try to invade my mother's space? He already has control over her mind, body, and soul, now he wants to run her household. Maybe he's making his move because he knows I'm about to make a move. Maybe Malik is still giving him information and has told him I'm putting a plan together that'll stop him once and for all. I don't know who to trust. I wish I would call Malik for any help. I have to figure this out on my own. How does his wife feel about him moving out? Maybe he told her he had to go out of town on business again, but this time for much longer. Maybe! Maybe! Maybe! Does he know about the several pregnancies and miscarriage my mother had? Maybe she hasn't told him she's miscarried because she wants him to think she's still pregnant. That'll be her way of keeping him. Wait! Maybe SHE'S the pregnant woman that Malik found out about but didn't tell him. So, my mother thinks he has another child on the way and doesn't know that she's the woman that Malik is referring to. But why wouldn't he just tell her he knows she's with child. Maybe Malik doesn't know who the woman is. All of this shit has become too much and I think I just confused myself. I realize they've stopped talking, so I take a peek around the door. Sam's sitting alone at the table, so I leave him be.

~

I'm trying on the clothes I purchased today and dancing around the room when Lucia comes in with two beers. She goes directly to our spot in the bay window and starts talking before I can turn the music off, "So—"

She's cut off before she can get another word out, "Me already know," I say mocking her broken English.

"You know already what?"

"I already know that Sam is moving in the main house."

"How you know?" She looks confused.

"Sweet Serenity Baby know everyting." I sit next to her and place my hand on her shoulder. Then, we both burst into laughter.

Chapter 20

Wednesday came fast. I'm making my way to the office of Felicia Cook—my mother's friend who got me this job—and when I enter, there he sits. Chocolate skin tone and dark almond-shaped eyes that compliment his jet black, curly hair. It takes about a minute to scan his long and lean body from head to toe. He sits with one leg laid across the other and a cup of coffee in hand. His pores exhale a scent that's lingering through the office and raping my senses. I stand in the doorway admiring him before Felicia sees me and invites me in.

"Serenity, please come in. Have a seat. This here is your first client. Victor White meet Serenity; Serenity Moore, meet Victor." I enter the room and take the seat next to Victor as he stands until I sit. All of this Melody, Serenity bullshit will confuse the hell out of me. I guess it's just something I will have to get used to since that's what my *new* ID says.

"Ah… So we meet for the third time, I see. You know what they say; third times a charm." He extends his hand.

"You two know each other?" Felicia asks.

"Her step-father—"

"Mother's boyfriend," I cut him off with the correction.

"Her mother's *boyfriend* and I are doing business together. We've crossed paths twice, but she refuses to give me the time of day." He undresses me with his eyes and it causes me to twitch in my chair.

This is uncomfortable for me. Not sure if it's the conversation, this man, or both.

"Who, *Sam*? You? Doing business with Sam? You sure about that?" Felicia probes from the top of her glasses.

"Come on now, Felicia, you and I go too far back for you not to trust my decision making?"

"Yes, and we also go too far back for me to *trust* you doing business with *Sam*. I'll leave that conversation for later." She looks to me. "Serenity, I've scheduled for you and Victor to meet on Monday afternoon at one o'clock. Today, Fernando will show you your office and give you a tour of the building. Once you're done with all of that, come back by here and I'll give you a list of clients." Felicia picks up the phone and calls her assistant. When she hangs up, she continues, "Once your clientele picks up, it'll be your responsibility to find your own assistant. You *will* need one. In the meantime, Fernando will help you with everything you need."

Just as she finishes, a well-dressed youthful man appears in her doorway wearing gray Armani slacks, shoes and belt, a nice crisp purple button-up shirt that leaves a little peek-a-boo at the top, and a gray vest. His skin is perfectly tanned and flawless, and his hair has not a strand out of place. He looks like he could pass for Cuban or Puerto Rican, and as soon as he speaks; his heavy accent fills the room. His English isn't broken like Lucia's, but it is obvious. "I'll be ready in just a second. A girl has to go to the John and freshen up," he says, disappearing before anyone can respond. Oh my G! Did he just refer to himself as a *girl*?

"Please don't let Fernando rub off on you," Victor tells me as he stands to leave.

I stand as well and ignore his suggestion. Instead, I reply and say, "I'll see you on Monday, Victor." I turn to Felicia, "Can you direct me to the restroom, please. I too need to freshen up."

Felicia's phone rings just as I complete my sentence. She covers the mouthpiece of the receiver and asks Victor if he could show me to the restroom on his way out. As we leave her office, I try my damnedest not to fall flat on my face. As captivating as his swag may be, I avoid conversation by ignoring him. We turn the corner and Fernando comes out of the men's restroom.

"Looking for me, honey?" he asks as he approaches us. I don't know if he's talking to Victor or me.

"Ha! You *wish* either of us was looking for your extra flamboyant ass." Victor answers before I have time to open my mouth and respond. Fernando rolls his eyes and smacks his lips at Victor. I chuckle on the inside at the whole "extra" comment because that's the same thing Lucia and I say about my mother, with her extra ass. Fernando is extra, though.

"I would like to freshen up. It shouldn't take me long. I'll be out in just a second," I tell him as I walk towards the restroom.

The bathroom is marvelous. It's lavished from wall to wall with marble floors and fog glass separations for the stalls. Instead of paper towels, there are five fluffy and white hand towels stacked next to each of the four tempered-glass vessel sinks. The oval mirrors are squeaky clean with fancy light fixtures in between each one. They all provide the perfect amount of light for applying makeup. Off to the side of the four sinks and mirrors, there's a full body mirror that flows from the ceiling to the floor. I stand in front of it, viewing myself. *I look damn good today.*

Standing in my white Donna Karan knee length pencil skirt, light blue ruffled button up blouse, and my taupe Gucci stilettoes, I turn from side to side, checking out my fabulous figure. I originally pinned my hair up in a loose bun, complementing my outfit, but I take the few pins out and let it fall down my back. Reapplying my Magnetic Nude MAC lipstick makes my lips look kissable, although I don't plan on kissing anyone. I wash my hands using the luxury smelling soap. Romance by Ralph Lauren is my perfume choice for the day. I spray a little on each of my sensual spots: wrists, behind the ears, and hair. One more look-over as I exit the restroom.

"Love the hair, honey," Fernando winks and snaps in a circle.

"I too think it looks better down," Victor chimes in.

"Thanks, fellas. See you Monday, Victor," I walk past him and feel his eyes following behind me. Not knowing where I'm walking to, I walk back towards Felicia's office.

"Um, this way, Sweetie," Fernando stands pointing in the opposite direction. I turn to follow, switching harder than it seems.

"I was trying to hurry and get away from *him*. Sorry," I whisper to Fernando. I can see Victor out of my peripheral as we lock arms and walk past him. He chuckles and walks backwards toward the elevator.

"Girl, why are you running from Victor? If it were me, I'd be running *to* his fine ass." Fernando giggles.

"Yes, well, let's just say I'm really not interested."

"Bad break-up?"

"No, I just need time to figure me out."

"Mm hm. That's what they all say. You must have let some girl experiment with the kitty cat." He says as he opens a door that leads to the most beautiful space overlooking the most beautiful view I've ever seen in Miami. I've seen some beautiful views. "This is your office, Ms. Moore. I hope you like it. I'll let you put your things down and you can buzz me when you're ready for the tour. Just hit the assistant button on your phone and it'll come directly to me. Make sure it's before lunch, please." He turns and switches off while I smile to myself and shake my head.

I sit my purse in the mahogany, executive high back, pillow top leather chair and walk to the window to take in the view overlooking the white sands of Miami Beach. What a beautiful sight. There are no walls, but glass windows that surround the corner space, giving me a view of both the beach and the busy downtown streets. The chocolate L-shaped modular desk is bright enough for me to see my reflection. There's a chocolate ceiling-to-floor bookshelf that runs behind my desk and fills with books; some familiar, some not. A large walk-in closet with a vanity and bench takes over my vision when I enter the extra door. It's like something I've never seen before. Feeling a bit overwhelmed, I take a seat on the matching mahogany leather chaise lounge that sits opposite of the desk, and breath it all in. Fernando's statement replays in my head… "You must have let some girl experiment with the kitty cat." I wonder what that's supposed to mean?

"Ready Serenity?" Fernando's voice blasts through the intercom and alarms me, breaking my thoughts.

~

Fernando's tour took up most of the day. As I'm wrapping up to leave for the day, a familiar voice interrupts me.

"I thought I'd come and give you a ride home." My mother stands in the doorway looking like a million bucks in her all white Armani pants suit and crisp, white button-up blouse.

"How thoughtful of you." I try not to sound unenthused. "I'll be ready in just a second. There are a few things I need to finish up with Fernando." I pick up the receiver to the telephone and hit the assistant button. We confirm my agenda for tomorrow followed by me wishing him a great evening. Instead of coming in, my mother remains at the door, watching me as if she has something to say. I wouldn't be a surprise if she does.

"Seems like you've gotten the hang of it already, just as I thought you would." A puzzled look appears across my face when she walks to the window. "Marvelous view. Do you like it?" She walks back to the door, not taking a second to look *around* the office.

"Yes, I love it," I answer more energized.

"Well, that's good. At least someone likes what they do," I hear her mumble under her breath.

"What was that, Mother?"

"Oh nothing, dear. Are you ready to go? The driver is waiting." I knew she wouldn't repeat her statement.

"Yes, all ready." I pick up my purse from the desk and follow behind her as she goes to Felicia's office instead of the elevators. They chat for a minute or two and we say our goodnights and head to the elevator. Mother seems different today. Maybe she's gotten her blood work back from Dr. Ivanovsky? Maybe she knows Lucia and I know she was recently with child? Maybe she's not happy about Sam moving in? So much goes through my mind while we ride the elevator from the 35th floor to the lobby. She waves at the lady at the receptionist's desk on our way through the corridor. When we reach the door, she says goodnight to the doorman and calls him by his name. She knows everyone here.

We climb in the back seat and there's silence for the first twenty minutes of traffic. Mother is in deep thought as she gazes out the window without blinking. Instead of sparking a conversation that I know will be awkward, I pull out my cell phone to discover a missed call from Raven. *Maybe she got her test results back*, I wonder as she looks at me from her peripheral.

"Have you talked to your dyke girlfriend?" I ignore her statement, but think to myself, *with all the bullshit that's been going on, I've barely had enough time to talk to me, let alone her.* As if I didn't hear her the first time, she repeats herself. I ignore her again and turn my head towards the window. She continues with disrespectful comments saying, "She was no good for you, anyway. You knew nothing her. All she wanted was your money to begin with, but licking on your little vagina made you too gullible and naïve to see how she was only selling you a dream. She caused you to lose focus and now look at you. You have flunked out of school and you have failed your father and I both. Lucky for you, I know influential people in prominent positions and could get you this job. Let's just hope you don't fuck this up like you've fucked up everything else. If I hadn't sent Malik to follow you, who knows what type of mess you would've gotten yourself into." She goes on for another twenty minutes before my eyes meet hers and stand their ground.

After a minute long stare down, I speak, "Is this why you wanted to give me a ride home from work? To hear you not only disrespect me, but belittle me? I'd rather walk home than deal with this. And to answer your question, no, I haven't spoken with *Carmen*, and if it makes *you* happy, I was just about over her until you brought her up. Now can you please decide? You either want me to get over her or you don't. I'm trying to move on. Either you will allow me to do that or you're not." That must have put her in her place because she says nothing else. Instead, she returns to her blank stare out the window.

As we pass the exit to our house, I don't bother asking where we're going. We take the fourth exit after to her attorney's office. "Why are we here?" I ask.

"Just come," she says in a much calmer voice than I'm used to.

We get out the car, walk in the building, and take the elevator to the 19th floor. My mother seems nervous as she fidgets with her purse strap. Her strides are slow and steady as we exit the elevator and walk to her attorney's office. When we finally enter, there sits Lucia and Bella. I shoot her a "what's going on" look and she shrugs. My mother's attorney, Michael, escorts us all to a compact conference room. In there is when we find out that my mother is creating an updated will, leaving everything to Lucia, Bella, and me. She allowed Sam to convince her to make him her beneficiary and Power of Attorney over her estates about two years ago, and now she's having second thoughts and wants to change it. As confused as Lucia and I both are, we sit and listen to the attorney as he run down a list of who will inherit what. Lucia will receive one hundred fifty thousand dollars and the pool house, and can live in it for as long as she likes. Bella will receive one hundred thousand dollars, which won't be available to her until she graduates college, and her tuition is paid in full. I'll receive her home and the six acres around it, her

boutique in downtown Miami Beach on Sunset Harbor Drive, all
of her jewelry, the safe and anything in it.

Looking at her makes me shiver. Maybe she got her test results
back, and its terrible news? Maybe she doesn't have that long to live?
I need to know what's going on. I can't just go walking around not
knowing. Maybe that'll be a conversation we can have on the way
home. Carmen... yes... I wonder how she's been. Has she found
someone else? I sure hope she has. No need of waiting for me because
I've thought about it... and realized I'm confused. My mother was
right. It was the sex that had me caught in a trance. It was wonderful
sex... but now that I know what to do I can please myself in the
same way and have the same reaction. When I don't think about her,
I focus better. Maybe she was no good for me, anyway?

"Did you get all of that, Ms. Moore?" Michael distracts my
thoughts.

I look at him, then Lucia, who nods her head. My mother is in a
daze herself and doesn't realize what's going on either. I reply, "Um,
yes. I got it." Lucia knows I wasn't paying attention, but I'm sure she
was, so I'll leave it to her to fill me in.

After my mother signs the updated will, I too sign because
she has made me the sole beneficiary and executor. She stands and
shakes her attorney's hand, and Lucia and I follow suit. Michael
leaves first and my mother tells Lucia that they'll ride back to the
house with us. We make our way to the elevator. Once in, my mother
puts her Versace shades on and says, "Not a word of this around
the house." Her tone is stern and demanding. *There goes getting any
answers out of her,* are my thoughts as the elevator reaches the lobby.
We get off, exit the building, and climb one by one into the back
seat of the waiting car.

"We're going to The Devise over on 41st Street," she informs the
driver. She then looks at Lucia, "You deserve a break today. You've
been cooking for me every day for many years and never complained.
It's the least I can do." Mother looks at me and says, "Never be

stupid for a man. Never allow a man to use you, your heart, your body, and most of all, your mind. I know you both are wondering what's going on and why. Let's just say I don't trust that bastard as far as I can throw him. I need to assure that the ones closest to me… are taken care of if anything happens. *He* suddenly wants to move in, and that just doesn't sit well with me. If something was to happen to me, know that it wasn't an accident and he's being held accountable. That mother fucker thinks I'm stupid." She looks at Lucia's daughter, who is more focused on her Nintendo Gameboy Advance than she is anything else, and who my mother thinks barely understands English, and continues, "He thinks he can just lay up with me every other night and then run home to that no good wife of his. Had she been doing her job to begin with, it wouldn't have been so easy for me to attract him. I have something for him, he just doesn't know it yet." Her eyes return to me. "Always fight fire with a fire extinguisher, never try to fight it with fire because it only makes the flames bigger and they last longer. With an extinguisher, you can put it out. Depending on how big the fire is, it may take some time, but I can guarantee you it'll go out, *completely*. He thinks he's moving into *my* house to run some shit. Well, he has another thing coming. I want you two to give him living hell every day he's there. If he so much as look like he wants to do something to either of you, make sure you let me know. I will fuck his world upside down." My mother is now looking out the window, but I can feel her rage as it radiates through her every word. I look at Lucia and I see her lower her eyes, which is a first. She must know something I don't know.

Bella sits between Lucia and me, while my mother is across from us. She puts her game down and whispers in my ear in Spanish, "¿Cómo te jodes mundo de alguien al revés?" which in translation means, "How do you fuck someone's world upside down?" I laugh because *I* know she understands, but my mother has no clue. Neither does her mother know she understands or speaks English as well as she does.

Lucia and my mother both shoot me a look as if they want me to disclose what Bella said. I roll my eyes at Lucia because she knows that's our sign for, "I'll tell you later because right now I'm about to lie." I do just that and lie to my mother telling her that Bella asked if I could help her get to the next level on her game. I take the game and pretend to push buttons like I know what I'm doing. I return the device to Bella and pull out my phone and text Raven to see why she called. She only wants to hang out, so I agree to meet up with her this weekend.

Apparently, my mother has already made reservations because when we arrive at the restaurant, we're immediately seated. The four of us follow the hostess to the round table, and the closer we get, the more I recognize Sam, already seated at the table. I nudge Lucia and nod toward the restroom. "Mother, we will take Bella to go potty."

"It doesn't take both of you. Sit," she demands. I go to sit and she mumbles, *"Normal,"* with a daunting emphasis. I take the seat to the right of the one she's taking, leaving two empty seats to the left of me for Lucia and Bella. Once seated, I send a text to Lucia: *Part of plan, so be normal.*

Chapter 21

10:00am

The past week has been interesting. So much has happened and left me inquisitive and confused all at the same time. I still haven't heard from Raven about my mother's test results, but we're hanging out today, so I hope she has information for me. The changing of my mother's will, her health, and her overall actions have been all I can seem to think about. The way she treats people and her evilness makes me question who she is as a person. Is she bitter? What is it? I'm afraid she may do something crazy if I ask her. Or she'll blow me off and not talk for some days. She's done that before and replaced drinking with talking. Maybe after I find out what her test results are, I'll say something to her. I know I must wait until Sam doesn't have his nosey, lurking ass around. Since he's moved in, she acts like she's afraid to move if he isn't in her presence. The other day at dinner, she disclosed timid actions. With her acting this way, it made Lucia and I question all the things she was saying while we were on our way to the restaurant. Maybe it was all a part of her plan... To make him think he's in control and she's under his spell. I'm not sure what her motive is, but I don't like it. It makes her look weak, and less of the women she is. I don't understand how a person can deal with something so much, that it drives them to drink the way she does. Drinking has become her all day, every day routine; come home for lunch and have a glass or two of wine, wine for dinner, wine before bed, and most days several glasses in between. She barely eats, and she's beginning to look sick.

Being driven to the state of incapacity is not an option for me. Carmen tried to cast me under whatever spell she had because I felt weak for her and everything she did. Unable to think about anything or anyone else besides her, makes me wonder if it was genuine love. Regardless of what it was, I'm kind of glad I got away from her spell. But am I away from her since I still think about her…

True enough, I desire genuine love, but I'd rather wait for it. I went to see Dr. Young, and we talked about a lot of things; my childhood, my sister, my mother, my father, and Carmen. I felt drained when I left. She wants me to start back writing in my journal at least twice a week. Dr. Young says she doesn't care if it's two or three words about how I'm feeling. I said I would try. Not sure how much of a success it'll be since I'm working an actual job now.

With all the events that have been taking place at my house, I've tried to consume myself and my thoughts in my work. I'll admit that I miss the sex with Carmen. Masturbating isn't getting it the way she used to get it… not like I thought it would. I sometimes wonder if that's the only reason she attracted me to begin with, especially after my mother said all the things she did about me not knowing what love really is and so on. She even had me believing sex is all Carmen, and I had, until I remembered how gentle and kind she was with and to me, how attentive she was, how she showed her admiration, how she stared at me and told me she loved me and everything about me. I could go on and on about the way she 'loved' me, but I can't because it's causing me to want her. Want her sexually and not mentally or emotionally.

Dr. Young says a relationship is no good if sex is all you desire from a person. What good is a relationship without companionship? I do not understand what companionship is because I've never seen it. I don't know if my mother and father even had companionship, especially considering how he was taking my little sister's innocence. If they had companionship, then maybe he wouldn't have had to look elsewhere for what he could get from his wife and vice versa. Speaking of his wife, I know I say all the time that I blame my mother for not knowing what love is, but the truth is the truth. She's never shown me love. I can't recall her ever telling me she loves me. A person can tell me something repeatedly, but until they show it, their words mean nothing. What's the saying, "actions speak louder than words"? That's the realest thing I can relate to. But wait; does that make me a hypocrite? Has Carmen shown me she loves me? I don't know! How can I know what something is if I've never experienced it? I will ask Dr. Young if there's a book or something that tells you what genuine love is. Or do I really want to know?

My mother says she thinks Sam truly loves her. He just doesn't know how to show it. How in the hell can this fool possibly love her when he has an entire family somewhere else, and she knows he's using her for her money? That's all I thought about when I heard her tell Lucia that bullshit. Well, at least she was smart enough to change her will before it was too late. It's been weird with him living here. He creeps around the house acting suspiciously like he's looking for something. He makes everyone here uncomfortable except for my mother. We don't know what he has up his sleeve. He may be off the hook with my mother, but not with Lucia and me. I'm not even sure if my mother really has a plan, besides changing the will. I question her strength to not allow that bastard to get in her head. She makes me resent her. She makes me look at her in a certain way, and it's not positive. She and he both give me a query feeling. I don't know what to think about her. I'm even at a point to where I don't even know how to take her, her actions, or what she says. Thank God I have Lucia in my life.

Lucia loves me! I know she loves me. Is that what love feels like? Maybe it is! She's the one person I trust more than anyone else. Actually, she's the only person I trust. I didn't have time to speak to Dr. Young about her, but I must remember to mention her in our next session.

My phone rings, disturbing my writing. It's Raven. I look at the clock and it's 11:12am. Damn! Where did the time go? "Hey, Rave, what's up?"

"Hey, Mel! I was just calling to confirm our plans for today." Her voice is gloomy, and she doesn't sound like her normal hyper self.

"Yes, five o'clock right?" I confirm.

"Yes, ma'am, five is right."

"Is everything all right, Raven? You sound like... like something's bothering you."

"Um, I really can't talk about it right now because I'm at work, but I'll talk to you about it when we meet up."

"Okay. Is it that no-good boyfriend of yours?"

"Eh... something like that." Her voice sounds sad, but I think she's lying.

"Well, all right. I'll see you later and don't allow him to ruin your day. Especially since you're hanging out with me. We can't have you down, I need some of that positive energy." I hear Dr. Ivanovsky in the background, so I end the call quickly.

"Okay, I'll see you later," I hear her say as I'm hanging up.

~

It's five o'clock already and I'm dressed down in a green cotton maxi dress and yellow thong sandals, sitting at The Clevelander Bar on Ocean Drive. I have my Heineken on draft with lemons and water with no ice with lemons. From what I remember, Raven doesn't drink beer, so I ordered her a frozen margarita. Just as the waiter returns with our drinks, I see Raven from a distance, striding through the sand. She's dressed in a blue skirt, white tank-top, and it looks like white flip-flops. The closer she gets, the more I notice her looking like she lost her best friend. She and I aren't as close as we once were, but she knows she can always call on me if she ever needs to talk, at least I hope she knows that. When she reaches me, she takes her seat and stares without saying a word. I say nothing either, giving her time to get herself together. Through her straw, she takes a long sip of her drink and then asks how my day is going.

"My day is magnificent! I think I should ask *you* about *your* day." My response is bubbly, hoping my energy spreads to her like hers normally does to everyone else.

"I'm sorry. I've had a long day. You would think by today being Saturday, it would've been easy at the office, but I guess that's what I get for thinking, huh? It just wasn't my usual Saturday." Her depressing mood is draining me.

"Well, Raven, you can't allow things to get the best of you. Whatever you're going through, just know that it gets better. Sometimes it takes something drastic to happen to us before we realize how strong we are. It can be something so simple that brings reality to the forefront." Raven stares at me as I continue on with my words of encouragement.

She takes another sip of her margarita, sits it on the table, and cuts me off in mid-sentence. "Mel."

"Yes, Raven? What's up? Are you okay? You're not in the mood to be here. This isn't like you not to have *anything* to say. Usually, you're the one rambling on about something, but today it's me. I sure hope you get over this funk you're in because honestly, you're slowly draining my strength. It's like I'm sitting here trying hard to uplift you and nothing is working." I've become frustrated.

"Mel," is all she says.

"What's up? Why are you continuously saying my name like something is wrong? What's up?"

"Your mother is HIV positive. We got the results back yesterday, and I was trying to figure out a way to tell you. Doc and I have both been trying to reach her, but she has returned none of our calls. We wanted her to know before I told you. I know I told you I would contact you as soon as the results were in, but I wanted to give her a chance to tell you first. There's no way I would've been able to come here and not say something to you, and I didn't want to cancel. I hope you're not mad at me." I sit speechless. I asked for the information. Now, I don't know how to take it. The tables have turned and I'm the one sitting here staring in disbelief. Surprised and sadness are the feelings that confuse me, and the confusion overwhelms me.

"Melody, please say something. Promise me you won't say anything to your mother. If you do, I'll lose my job. Let doc be the one to tell her first. Are you going to keep your composure until she says something to you herself? Please say something to me." She crosses her arms and plop back in her chair. "I knew I shouldn't have told you." Raven whispers under her breath in disappointment.

"I won't say anything. I have to go." I pick my things up, put my sunglasses on, stand, and walk to the waiting car without paying or saying another word.

After a car ride that seems like forever, I make it back home and walk through the foyer and into the kitchen feeling like a zombie. Lucia has dinner prepared and is sitting at the kitchenette eating with Bella. She sees me and asks, "Everyting all right, Dear?" There's no response. Instead, I go to the refrigerator, get a beer, and take the seat next to Lucia. "Tome su comida a su habitación para terminar. Shoo! Shoo!" she tells Bella. I'm glad she's sending her off because I'm not sure if I can hold these emotions together any longer.

Bella gets up from the table and leaves the kitchen. Once she's out of our view, Lucia looks at me and asks again if everything is okay. She tells me I look flushed, which is exactly how I feel. Like someone has drained every ounce of blood out of me. I take a sip of my beer. Lucia knows me well, so she doesn't pressure me to talk; instead, she gets up to get herself a beer and sits back down.

Finally, after a few gulps, my mind relaxes. I look at Lucia and say, "I have something very important to tell you, and you must say nothing to anyone. Agreed?"

"Si," she says in Spanish.

"Mother is HIV positive." My head hangs low as I utter the words.

After about a minute of silence, I look up to find Lucia staring at me as her eyes fill with tears. She looks pale with a stiffened body, similar to my current emotions. I use my napkin to wipe her tears. She closes her eyes and says, "Me should know. With everybody sexing everybody, me should know. Maybe father have it too. Maybe Sam have it too but don't know yet. Just nasty. Nasty mess, I tell ya."

"I agree, but we can't say anything until she says something to us. I don't know all the details, but I know she's in the dark because she hasn't answered or returned any of Dr. Ivanovsky or Raven's calls."

"They both call today a couple times. They leave messages over there." Lucia points to the message board next to the phone. "Mrs. Moore not home since early. Her not answer me call either to see what her like for dinner. Phone just ring and ring."

I retrieve the messages from the board because I don't want Sam's nosey ass to see them before my mother does. There are two messages from Dr. Ivanovsky and one from Raven. I take all three messages back to the table. I dial my mother, but there's no answer. As I'm hanging up, someone comes in the door. Lucia and I both dart to the foyer. It's just Sam. Without acknowledging him, we both turn and make our way back to the kitchen in disappointment.

I stop in mid-stride and face him, "Have you seen my mother today?"

"Yes, she's in the car. She said she'll be in soon." Sam walks up the stairs without saying another word. He seems to be distraught about something.

Lucia is back at the table, sitting. I stand next to her and say, "He says mother is sitting outside in the car. Do you think I should go check on her or do you think I should wait until she comes in?"

"Wait."

"Okay. Clean your face and take the messages and sit them next to the phone. When she comes in, tell her she has messages."

"Got it," Lucia gets up from the table and follows the instructions.

By the time my mother finally comes in, Lucia and I are both sitting at the table. Five minutes of waiting seemed like an eternity. She goes straight to the wine closet and gets a bottle of white wine. She can't reach the wine glass, so Lucia gets up, gets the stepladder, and retrieve them for her. After she sits the glasses on the counter, Lucia informs my mother of her messages. She picks them up and tosses them in her purse without looking over them. It's too late for her to return the call to the doctor, so she has to wait until Monday morning to find out she's sick.

As my mother fills her glass with wine, she looks at us and I ask, "How was your day? Lucia and I have been trying to contact you all day, but couldn't get through."

"Sam kept my phone with him when he dropped me off at the mall. I wanted to do a little shopping to clear my mind from the long and stressful work week. I'll check my messages when I get upstairs. He never told me you guys called. Maybe he didn't look at the phone either. You know him." Lucia and I both look at each other and then at her like the fool she's being right now.

It seems like Sam has radar ears because no soon as she could speak his name; he appears. "What's up, ladies? What are you up to?"

"On nothing, honey." My mother opens the bottle of wine, pours them both a glass, takes a sip, and then kisses Sam. To me, it's like she has to numb herself with alcohol to deal with him, anyone, or anything.

"That's what's up. I just came down to see what's taking you so long to bring that bottle of wine back up. You know we have to celebrate and then—," he leans in and whispers something in her ear, and she melts right into it. He then smacks my mother's perfectly round butt and turns to walk away.

When he's clear of my view, I look at her inquisitively, "*Celebration? What's that about? What are we celebrating, Mother?*" There's emphasis on every word.

"Yes, you heard him. *We* are celebrating. We made the down payment for the building to our business today." Her eyes light up.

"Oh! What happened to the things you were saying when we were in the car on the way from your attorney's office?" I ask her as I try to figure out if this was all a part of her plan.

"He had upset me when I said those things. I don't remember what it was I said." She picks up the opened bottle of wine and wine glasses, goes to the closet to take another bottle, and leaves the kitchen.

"Gone off meds," Lucia says to me once she no longer sees my mother's back.

"She is…" I pause. "Wait! What meds are you talking about?"

"Her got the bipolar. Thought you know. Been on meds since father left. One day her this way, the next, her that way." She throws her hands in the air, then proceeds, "Her say her tell you."

"Oh wow! So that explains it. I thought she was just a bitch with a capital B."

"Her that too!" We both laugh.

"You sure know how to lighten the mood. I guess we now have to take this situation one day at a time. Allow her to enjoy her *celebration* with a man she *knows* is using her and wait to see how her behavior changes when she calls the doctor on Monday. I still can't believe she got that place for him. How can she trust someone like him?" I whisper to Lucia.

"Me don't know, but her fool," Lucia replies.

"As much as I hate to admit that, I agree."

We finish our beers, say our goodnights, and go our separate ways. Today has been an interminable day and we both have made plans to sleep in tomorrow.

Chapter 22

12:26pm

Mother is HIV positive and I would like to know where she got it from. I don't know if it's Malik, my father, or Sam who transmitted it. Maybe they ALL have it, but who did it originate from? I'm not sure how her life will change. I'm not even sure if she will tell me. I don't even know how I feel about all of this. The fact that she allowed her husband to have sex with her and another man at the same time is disgusting to me, but who am I to judge? If she tells me, I will be as positive as I always am. She'll need my support more than anything. What I can't do is criticize her the way she did me for my sexuality choice.'

I hope she gets the proper treatment so she can LIVE. That's one thing about HIV that some people who are positive forget. They automatically think their life is over, when they have a choice on whether they live or die. And that choice is treatment. Although it may not take the disease away, it helps them understand, cope, and sustain it. It also prevents the disease from getting worse, so imagine what happens when an individual chooses not to get the treatment. I just pray my mother's choice is the right one. If she doesn't make the right choice, I don't know what I'll do. She can afford the treatment, so I hope she gets it. I wonder how she'll react once she finds out. I wonder if she'll say something to Sam. I hope she puts his ass out. Why must she be so gullible? I wonder why I'm not like that... or am I? Grandmother did the best she could to raise my mother properly. I'm not sure where she went wrong. My grandmother was a single mother with my mother being her only child. She had me at sixteen and immediately married my father. Could that be the reason we're all so fucked up? Could that be the reason we don't know how to love or be loved? Could it be because my mother never soared her royal oaths and only married because she was pregnant? I wonder if she ever loved my father, or if he ever loved her.

What is love? Is it just a four-letter word that people use without knowing and/or understanding the meaning of it? I feel Lucia loves me... I think. I wonder what it is she has to tell me. With everything that's happened over the past two weeks, nothing will surprise me. I'm really becoming tired of it all; it seems to be draining me. I plan to get my place downtown and closer to my work as soon as possible. I want to prove to my mother that I'm independent, responsible, and I can hold my own grounds. Her disbelief in me is my motivation in life.

MM

Chapter 23

My alarm scares me out of my sleep early Monday morning. I smack the snooze button. Fifteen minutes later, it goes off again, but this time, instead of hitting snooze, I turn it off. Lying still and mentally getting dressed causes me to drift for another five minutes. The alarm rings on my phone. I turn it off and jump up and go to the shower.

Afterwards, my body is fully refreshed and wide awake. My bathrobe clings to my smooth skin as I make my way to the closet. The meeting with Victor is today, so I plan to wear something as less sexy as possible. There's no need in him getting any bright ideas.

Standing in the walk-in closet, I skim the many pants suits until the white double breasted, slim fit Express suit catches my eye. I pull a hot pink blouse out to add a splash of color, along with my most comfortable pair of shoes; a black pair of Manolo Blahnik pumps.

Once dressed, I go into the main house for breakfast. Upon my arrival, my mother and Sam are finishing up their food. I place my purse and briefcase in a chair at the table and make myself a plate of food. Lucia has cooked eggs, waffles, bacon, sausage, grits, fresh fruit, and oatmeal. A piece of bacon, some eggs, and fruit is all my stomach needs to make it until lunch.

Taking a seat, my mother looks me up and down a few times and says, "You look nice. Simple, but classy and nice." I thank her and ask Lucia if she could call and have a car pulled out front for me. I continue eating eat my breakfast without uttering another word.

"So you're driving yourself today, huh?" my mother asks as she cleans her and Sam's plates from the table.

"Yes. I know where I'm going, so no need in being *lazy*." My reply is sarcastic.

Lucia adds her input from the other side of the kitchen. "Well, make sure you careful,"

"Always." We glance at each other and both wink.

"Here you two go." My mother rolls her eyes in the back of her head. "I promise you two make me wonder. Well, we already *know* about you, Serenity," she adds.

She has some nerve. How dare she judge me with all the secrets she has in her closet? And not only that, but she isn't and apparently hasn't been being careful while doing it. She may be in her prime and want to have fun, but whatever happened to using precautions while doing so.

Bravery comes over me after my thoughts, and before I know it, I open my mouth and allow the truth to come out, "Well, at least she's the *only*—"

"Car ready, Serenity." Lucia interrupts. She knew I was about to tear my mother a new asshole.

My mother comes so close it makes me uncomfortable. "What is it you were about to say?"

My immediate instinct is to ignore her as I pop a grape in my mouth, pick up my briefcase and purse, and make my way out of the kitchen. My shoulder brushes against her. "Have a wonderful day, Mother."

Her and her ignorance will not drain all of my pleasant mood this early in the morning. She's not worth it because she'll end up with hurt feelings. On my way out, Lucia stops me and hands me a lunch bag and kisses me on the cheek, just like she did when I would leave for school as an adolescent girl. The black 2006 Mercedes-Benz e320 awaits me when I exit the front door. The driver's seat embraces me, and my purse, briefcase, and lunch bag fill the front passenger seat.

The morning has gone by quickly and I've lost track of time. A knock at the door forces me to look up. It's Fernando, standing with Victor behind him. "Did you forget about your one o'clock meeting, Serenity?" Fernando asks.

"Um, no. Come in, Victor." I say standing and still writing. Once I complete my notes, I close my planner and walk to the door.

"Thanks, Fernando," Victor tells him as he enters my office.

"Afternoon, Serenity." Fernando stands in the doorway being nosy as usual. I've learned in just a few days to never tell him any business I don't want anyone else to know.

"*Thank you,* Fernando." Irony is used to shoo him off. I greet Victor, extending my hand. "Mr. White."

"Serenity." His handshake is firm and embracive.

"It's Mel—" I stop myself, remembering that he knows me by Serenity and *not* Melody, and take my seat.

"It's what?" Victor takes a seat across from me in his casual pants, V-neck t-shirt, and blazer.

"Um. Never mind."

"Never mind then. Have you looked over my accounts?" He gets right to business.

I'm upset I lost track of time because I'm starving and my stomach is speaking for me. I slide his file in front of me, open it and reply, "Yes, I have. After reviewing everything, I see you only have one investment, and that's with Sam's so-called business. Invest in a couple more companies for security. You always want to have options in everything you do, especially with finances. You should give a retirement plan some thought. Our bank offers—"

"Wow! You *are* good!"

His interruption confuses me. "Excuse me?"

"Felicia said you would be a good banker for me. She said you would be more *attentive* to my needs… as it relates to my accounts. Very impressive so far," he informs me.

"Why, thank you. I'm only doing my job. May I finish now?"

"Oh yes! I'm sorry. Finish." Before I can say another word verbally, my stomach speaks again. "Hungry?" he asks.

I reply, "No, I'm fine." My stomach growls again.

"Are you sure?"

Giving in, I respond by saying, "I lost track of time and didn't have time to eat my lunch. I'll grab a bite once we're done here."

"I could use a bite myself. You want to postpone this meeting for about an hour and we finish it over lunch? I won't hurt you. We can go get food and I'll bring you right back."

I *am* starving. "Food would be nice as long as you promise to *keep* it professional." I slide the file in the inside pocket of my briefcase. *I'm only going because I'm starving and I don't want the leftovers Lucia packed. I know that's what they are,* my thoughts convince me. A headache suddenly comes over me and I take it as a sign that I need food.

I stand and walk to my closet to retrieve my purse and he stands, "I always keep my meetings professional. Nice Manolo's," he points out.

What does he know about Manolo? "Thank you. I see someone knows their fashion."

"Well, when you have women that get with you for what you have, you learn quickly," he retorts back.

"Must be nice." His eyes follow my every stride as I walk to the door. "Ladies first."

As I pass him, I become captured by his scent. His sexiness is more revealing now than previous times. He's fine *and* sexy, and I did not understand. He stands about five to six inches over me and that alone is a turn on. Victor has jet black silky hair with big curls, and his skin is dark and flawless. They tapered his hair on the sides and back, and his sideburns connect to his goatee and mustache. His eyes are hypnotizing The color of them sucks you in like the watering of a rosebush.

A wave of electricity hits me. One that is familiar, but five times stronger. I flinch and damn near drop everything I have in my hands.

"Are you okay?" he asks as he places his hand on the small of my back to make sure I don't fall.

"I am. I think I shocked myself." We continue to the elevator.

He finally removes his hand from my back and pushes the down button. As we stand waiting, nosy ass Fernando suddenly appears. "Going somewhere, Serenity?"

"Yes, Fernando. I'm going to discuss Mr. White's accounts over lunch. Would you like to join us?" My question is serious, but only to test him, hoping he declines the invite.

"No, not today. Lucky for me I've eaten already," he says. He then continues with, "Keep your paws off her, Victor. You know you're known to have a reputation around here." Just as the elevator arrives, Fernando twirls on his heels and disappears.

Victor allows me to get on the elevator first before he joins me. He reaches across me to press the "L" button and his scent captures me again, taking me away like Calgon. The ride down is silent. It seems as if the elevator is stopping at every floor. Other workers get on, but then get off two floors after, leaving Victor and me alone, mostly. *Finally,* I think to myself as we reach the lobby. Victor, being the gentlemen he portrays to be, holds the open button to allow me off first. As we walk through the lobby of the bank, all eyes are on us. Noticing how some tellers are whispering to each other and then looking at us makes my stride sexier than normal. Since they want to talk, I'll give them something to talk about.

We reach the valet, and Victor's parked car sits ready and waiting. "Here are your keys, Mr. White. Enjoy the rest of your day."

"Thanks, my man! Did you take care of my number one girl?" Victor says to the youthful man that works for the valet.

"I did as best I could, Sir," he replies in a playful tone as Victor gives him a high five, passing him his tip.

He opens my door and I sit like a lady, and swing my legs around in the jet black Porsche, with leather interior and wood-grain dashboard. You can tell they have customized it to fit him because his long legs have the perfect amount of space between them and the stirring wheel. "Nice car," I say to him as stretches in on his side, turn the ignition, give it a little gas, brake, then hits the gas so hard, I jerk. He pulls from the front of the building onto 3rd Avenue. I reach for my seatbelt.

"Thank you. She's my favorite of all the vehicles I own." He switches into second gear.

"How many do you own," I inquire out of curiosity.

"Two sports cars, one sedan, one boat, and two motorcycles."

"Wow!" I'm amazed.

"Enough about me. What do you have a taste for?"

"I'll allow you to pick, as long as it's not sushi."

"Cool! Care for some music?"

"Sure! What do you have?"

"Just a little mixed CD one of my DJ buddies made for me." Victor presses play on his CD player. "Umbrella" by Rihanna seeps through the speakers, not too loud and not too low, but just right.

"Wonderful choice," I tell him and then mumble along with the lyrics. As we ride, my thoughts wonder... I sure hope he doesn't start asking questions about why I've rejected him so many times and keep this lunch date professional like he promised. He's fine *and* successful and to be honest, I don't know why I rejected both times. I'd already told myself that I needed a safe-haven from Carmen, and he would be the perfect heaven, I mean haven. I shake my head, clearing my thoughts. I must remember that my focus should be on me and not a piece of meat, because that's all he would be good for. But my goodness, is he a fine piece of meat!

We turn onto Lincoln Road and he pulls up at one of my favorite Italian restaurants; Quattro. "Good pick." I tell him.

"Are you referring to yourself or the restaurant?" I'm flattered by his flirting.

"Professional," I remind him.

"Indeed." He steps out the car, comes to my side, and opens the door.

"Thank you, Mr. White."

"Please, call me Victor. I think we're at that point since you've already dismissed me twice *and* not returned my phone calls or text messages."

"Professional, *Victor*," I remind him again.

We walk in and the host seats us immediately, which is a first for this high profile restaurant. They seat us at a square table close to the window, pour our waters, and fill our wine glasses with an expensive merlot: Graf de la Toure, Villa Russiz. I'm not a fan of merlot because of its bitterness, but I won't mention that to him. I ask the waitress for my usual glass of water with no ice and lemons, and she immediately returns with it.

"Have you been here before?" he asks me.

"Yes, it's my favorite Italian restaurant. My family used to come here often."

"So, you know what you want?"

"That I do. What about you?" The waitress remains and is ready to take our order.

Victor looks up from the menu, "I'll have the Inslata Di Bianco Di Pollo E Pomodorini Pachino Al Balsamico—oven roasted, diced chicken breast and mesolum greens, with cherry tomatoes, shaved parmesan and balsamic vinaigrette."

"I'll have the Insalata Di Granchio Mais Pomodorini Pachino E Soncino—jumbo lump crabmeat salad with corn, diced tomatoes and mocha greens—light on the corn please, and last, can you bring some balsamic vinaigrette and fresh torn basil on the side?" Victor's glare is making me hotter than a firecracker on the Fourth of July. The waitress takes our menus and leave.

While waiting for our food, we review his accounts and some other possible legitimate companies for investment. He pays close attention and compliments me in between phrases. I'd be lying if I said it doesn't make me feel some way—it may turn me on—but I'm trying my best to not make it so obvious. The only way I'll get some breathable air, and not *his* air, is to excuse myself to the restroom. I place his files back in my briefcase and slide it under the table. He comes around and pulls my chair out as I pick up my purse and walk off, trying not to look back to see if he's watching.

I go in the restroom and handle my business. Victor is leaning on the sink when I exit the stall. "You're the most beautiful woman I've ever laid eyes on. You've been on my mind since the day I saw you at the airport and you know what they say, 'Good things come in threes.' Seeing you in Felicia's office was the third time you'd crossed my path. I refuse to let you continuously walk out of my life."

"Professional," I remind him for the third time as I wash my hands at the sink next to him.

"You know you want me, Serenity," he says with a little more confidence than I like. He shouldn't be so bold.

"Let's not forget who the irresistible one is here, Victor," I respond with just as much confidence. "It's something I get from others often. The compliment of being irresistible that is."

He's now standing behind me and I can feel his penis pulsating through his pants. He feels so good; it paralyzes my body. He cups my breast, one in each hand, and caresses them aggressively. Aggression is not my thing, but I'm turned on by his. He then gently kisses the back of my neck and drifts to my ear. "Professional," I whisper out of breath. My heart rate speeds up and my knees buckle. He turns me around, takes my blazer off, undoes my shirt, then pants, and pulls them down. Victor sits me on the sink and falls to his knees like a lion as my cookie becomes his prey. His thick, wet tongue moves in and out, around and around, then in and out again. I moan, "Professional," as he continues to lick me down low. He grips my clit in between his lips and takes his forefinger and gently slides it into my now wet vagina. As he slowly penetrates me with his finger, my muscles tighten up in my stomach. I move to the beat of his drum and beg him not to stop. My body speeds up and just as I'm ready to cum, he stops. He slowly stands to his feet and sucks the finger he penetrated me with.

"Mm. Damn you taste good. Better than I expected," he tells me as he places that same finger in my mouth. "Taste," he says.

His finger feels my mouth with a sweet taste and I'm now turned on more. He undoes his pants and teases my button with the head of his penis. My eyes fall to his manhood… *Holy fuck!* Where does he think he's about to put that thing! It hangs beneath him like a horse's penis and I *know* I can't take all that! He must read my mind because I hear him say, "Relax, I won't hurt you." He teases me with the head again, making my cookie wetter than I can ever recall. No one has made me feel the way this man is making me feel, not even Carmen. He continues teasing me as he barely places the head in my vagina. He kisses me slow and passionate. His words are comforting as he pulls me to the edge of the sink. My body relaxes and he slowly and gently pushes his Mandingo inside me. I let out a moan so loud, I scare myself. "Relax," he says. My mind and body both relax. He stands straight up, still inside me, not moving, just staring into my eyes. "Gosh, you're so beautiful. You feel so good, I don't want to move."

"Please move," I beg.

"You want me to *remove* him or *move* him?" he teases.

"I want you to *move* him." I move my hips slowly back and forth. "Please move," I beg some more.

His movement matches my slow rhythm. He pulls my hips closer to him and leans my upper body back so that my head is resting on the mirror. My fingers run through his hair. It feels so good. "Stop moving," he says as he pulls all the way out slowly and then pushes all the way in even slower. With every complete entrance, his manhood reaches my stomach and causes me to let out a wail. It's not a painful feeling, but more like a pleasurable feeling. I can't help but move after he does that three times and he begs, "*PLEEAASSEE. Don't move.*" Disobeying his plea, my hips rotate in circular motions when he pushes all the way in. "Please stop. You will make me want to fuck you," he breathes in my ear.

"Fuck me, Victor," I whisper back.

"You're too beautiful to get fucked. Plus, I want to enjoy every second of this."

"Please fuck me." My body matches my plea as I pick up the pace.

"Please be still Serenity." I'm driving him crazy as he grips my hips trying to hold me still.

"Mr. White," I mumble in his mouth as he kisses me.

"Yes, Ms. Moore?"

"Please fuck me right… *now.*"

Victor then pulls all the way out, stops kissing me, stares at me while holding my hips in place, and then thrusts inside of me, catching me off guard and causing me to scream. He does it again… and again… and again until I beg him to stop. "Didn't you say you wanted me to *fuck* you?" He does it repeatedly. This time, when he does it, he stays inside of me and moves my hips back and forth in a fast pace while he remains still. My body tenses and then releases as I cum all around his Mandingo. He lets out a soft scream and says, "Damn, you can't be clinching my dick like that, woman. I'm not ready to cum yet." No sooner as he says that, there's a knock at the bathroom door. He pulls out and says, "Professional."

BOMP! BOMP! BOMP! My alarm buzzes so loud, not only does it wake me, but causes me to damn near pee my panties… or cum. I then realize it was only a dream. Why am I dreaming about him when I know nothing about him, except he's a fine piece of art with lots of money?

Chapter 24

Monday, December 11, 2006

8:23pm

Today's meeting with Victor was interesting because it turned me on from my dream. Every time he spoke to me or looked at me, it felt as though he was undressing me. His scent captivated me, just like it did in the dream. Maybe I should call him. He offered to take me to lunch afterwards, but I declined, afraid of what might happen. Not necessarily what he would do, but more of what I would do. The only other person I've felt such attraction towards is Carmen. I don't want to mix business with pleasure, but damn! How do I contain myself when he comes around? It's hard to believe that he'll be able to contain himself, considering how he looks at me. I saw him becoming bashful by some of my comments—nothing flirtatious—and he even made the statement that I flattered him.

Being so attracted and turned on by him makes me think of some statements my mother has made. Am I confused? He makes me feel the way Carmen did when she and I first met, and before we had sex. As bad as I want that dream to count, it doesn't. As bad as I need love I can't.

My mother... I wonder if she got her test results back; knowing her, she probably hasn't even returned doc's calls. I'll contact Raven tomorrow and check to see if she has. Am I a replica of her? Allowing sex—or the thought of it—to dictate what love is in my eyes? I had another appointment with Dr. Young today, and the session got more in depth compared to the last one. It felt like she was tearing me a new asshole. She says no relationship will work for me unless I face my underlying issues. What are my underlying issues? Do I even care to figure them out? These are questions I must answer first. She told me I'll gravitate towards physical, mental, emotional, and sexual abuse because those are the matters I witnessed growing up, and are the same things I'm witnessing now as an adult. How in the hell does she know? Could these be some situations she and my mother discuss? She told me in order for things to change; I have to make a conscious decision to break the cycle, especially if I want to raise children of my own. Apparently, I have a hard time trusting and committing one hundred percent to relationships because I'm not "mentally stimulated" by the people that try to have a relationship with me. It's so easy for me to walk away from Carmen because she didn't stimulate me mentally. Meaning, she didn't fuck me but made love to me, and she doesn't argue with me. She says that me running or not wanting anything to do with Carmen anymore is my version of love because that's what I'm used to and it's my foundation. She also told me it's my choice to decide what type of relationship I want to have. The last thing she said before our session ended was that I'm making the right mental choice to give Victor the run around, but not the right physical choice because I'm so attracted to him. I shouldn't have told her about last night's fantasy.

    I don't think it's a superb idea to see the same therapist as my mother. I've decided not to go to my next appointment and find my own therapists. Had I known what I know now, I wouldn't have gone to her. She gave me some brilliant advice, but I didn't find our conversations very therapeutic. She knows entirely too much information about my family, which for me only allowed her to form her opinion of me prior to our meeting. Maybe my mother wanted me to go to her so she could know all of my business, and maybe it was her way of keeping tabs on me when it relates to Carmen. Whatever her motive was or is, I will let her know tomorrow that I don't feel comfortable talking to Ms. Young, and since I'm working and can afford my therapist, I plan to find one and pay for it myself...

An alert from my cell phone distracts my writing. I wonder who this could be. No one has this number except for my mom, Lucia, and Raven. I put my journal down and fumble through my purse, retrieving my phone. It's a message from Victor: *You looked amazing today. I guess I must keep asking you out until you agree? Dinner Saturday?* I forgot he was the first person my mother and Sam gave this number to. Instead of responding, I place my phone on my nightstand and continue writing.

... Victor. I wonder how long I'll be able to ignore him on a personal level before giving up the cookie. If he's anything like my dream, he can munch on it any day. No matter how much I try to convince myself the opposite, that's one thing I can say I really miss about Carmen is the way she went downtown on me. She was definitely my little cookie monster. She knew exactly what to do and when to do it. Too bad I can't say the same about Jarmaine. Jarmaine. I wonder how he's doing. Maybe tomorrow I'll ask my mother if she's spoken to his mother lately. Christmas is coming up, maybe I'll even send him a Christmas card. Now that I think about it, if Carmen wanted to find me or contact me, he is the one person she could reach out to. Maybe she's moved on and forgotten about me in these past two weeks. With that thought in mind, I vow to forget about her too. Maybe I will take Victor up on his offers, and I might even fuck him, or let him taste my cookie.

From those written thoughts, I reach to the nightstand and grab my phone. I reply to Victor: *Thank you. Maybe.* I don't send it because I want him to beg, but then I second guess myself. If I make him beg for too long, maybe he'll find interest in someone else. The 'send' button is tempting. As I place my phone on the nightstand, another message comes through: *And YOU ARE!* I don't respond because I know that's his way of trying to get me to respond. *What the fuck is he talking about? I am what?* Instead of replying, I close my journal for night and turn the light off. Tomorrow is an early day.

Sitting at my desk and reviewing applications for a personal assistant, my office phone buzzes. I answer it on the first buzz, knowing it's nobody but that talkative ass Fernando. I don't see how Felicia can deal with him regularly. I must hurry and find my assistant. Sure enough, it's him. "Look up," he whispers on the phone. Victor stands in the doorway looking fine as fuck in a pair of nice fitting jeans, casual shoes, polo shirt and blazer. I say nothing as I hang the receiver up.

"So, you can't respond to a brother's messages." He invites himself in and takes a seat.

"Come in, have a seat," I say sarcastically.

"I already did." His smirk is sexy and charming.

"Clearly." I smirk back.

"Don't flatter yourself, Ms. Moore."

"Now why would I want to do that when I can… never mind." I catch myself.

"So, since you didn't respond last night, I thought I'd pay you a visit and get a direct answer from you today. And I plan to do so every time you ignore me." He crosses his long lanky legs one over the other.

"Thank you. Maybe. I'm what?" I respond to the text from last night.

"You're welcome. Maybe isn't an answer. Irresistible."

"Okay then, no. What do you mean by irresistible?" I'm confused because this seems like a conversation from my dream. How does he know about my dream?

"You'll say yes to allowing me to take you out one of these days. And come on, Ms. Moore, you know you're irresistible."

"We'll see about that. Thanks. Now, is that what you really came all the way across town for? To see why I didn't respond to your text messages?"

"No, I came all the way across town because you're irresistible and I wanted to see what you look like today."

"Please don't flatter *yourself,* Mr. White."

"Why flatter myself when I can flatter *you?*"

"Well, please don't flatter *me,* Mr. White. I have a client coming in about thirty minutes that I must prepare for. If you don't mind leaving, it's appreciated." A lie is told so I can escape to the restroom and dry my now moistened cookie.

He does as he's asked and stands to leave. When he reaches the door, he turns and says, "Please, call me Victor." Once he's out of sight, I retrieve my purse from my desk drawer and make my way to the restroom.

"What was that about?" Fernando questions.

"Oh nothing, we just needed to go over some numbers," I answer.

"Mm hm." He rolls his eyes in the back of his head.

"Wouldn't lie." My pace picks up, leaving him behind as I turn the corner.

Thank God no one else is in here. The thought of this man makes me want to have a mid-day masturbation session by myself. I walk into the stall and when I turn around to close the door, it's stopped.

"What the hell are you doing in here," I ask Victor.

"I knew I got your pussy wet." The closer he gets, the more I can smell his minty breath. It smells just like it did in my dreams.

"Actually—"

He places his finger over my mouth, leans me up against the wall of the stall, lifts my skirt, moves my panties to the side, and fumbles in my wetness. "How much longer will you continue to lie and deny?" he asks. "Don't answer that," he follows. For some strange reason, I don't stop him. He slowly slides his middle finger in and out as my juices overflow. His shoulder is where my head rests, and one foot steps on the toilet. He grabs the same leg and wraps it around his waist instead, causing me to stand on my toes with the other foot. He presses his body up against mine as he teases me with attempted kisses to the lips. Every time I attempt to kiss him back, he moves his head out of reach. Either this is turning me on, or I'm dreaming again. I bite down on my bottom lip as hard as I can to assure that it's not a dream and sure enough, it isn't because that shit hurt like hell. Still moving in a slow motion, I move with him.

"Why are you moving," he whispers to me as he stops with his gestures and presses his finger against my g-spot. This doesn't stop me from moving so he asks, "Why must you be so defiant, Ms. Moore?"

When I finally obey, his motions start back up. "Why do you ask so many questions," I mumble.

"The same reason you wish to ignore me," he replies.

Left speechless, I don't say another word. I allow him to do whatever until the muscles in my stomach, back, vagina, and thighs tighten up. I remove his finger, let my leg down, pull my skirt down, and exit the stall. As I leave the restroom, my juices run down my thighs.

I lock the door to my office before I enter the walk-in closet to catch my breath and change my pantyhose. What the fuck just happened… is the only thought I can arrange in my mind right now. An alert goes off in my purse. It's a message from Victor: *SHADY! SO SHADY! You taste just as good as I imagined.* I ignore the message as I finish changing and go back to my desk as if nothing happened. My door remains locked because I'm not in the mood for Fernando for the rest of the day.

Chapter 25

Friday, December 22, 2006

9:10am

Almost two weeks have gone by since mine and Victor's bathroom sex-capade, and I've been ignoring and avoiding him well. Although he's kept me turned on from every aspect, I like the mental game I'm playing with him much better. That'll teach his egotistical ass. I find it humorous how every time I ignore him; he shows up at my office, and when he does, I make it my business to be on my way out. Most of the time, I'm not going anywhere, but I find somewhere to go. He's been texting my phone like crazy and I must admit that I like it. I guess I am irresistible.

It's three days before Christmas and I have done none of my shopping, so instead of scheduling myself for any work this week, I shop. I even gave my new assistant, Savannah, the week off. The week off at the office, that is. She's so good in the office that I've hired her to be my personal assistant. Fernando didn't like that idea. Savannah doesn't invade my space the way Fernando does, or did. I'm glad Felicia moved him closer to her and gave him his own little mini office. This way, when Victor pop's up, he's unaware. Knowing him, he probably knows.

Lucia loves Savannah and mother tries to use her for herself. My clientele has picked up so much over the past week that I need her more so now than I did when I initially hired her two weeks ago. Mother didn't realize how much personal assistants came in handy until she saw how *much easier and organized Savannah has made my life. She also keeps my schedule busy—upon my request — to keep my mind occupied so that my thoughts don't consume of Carmen or Victor. I know, I know; I vowed to not think about Carmen at all, but I'm only human.*

Mother has said nothing about her test results to neither me nor Lucia, but we know she got them because Raven called me and told me she told her and the doc she's been aware of her disease for many years. She hasn't been acting any differently either. It makes me question if anything will ever change her, which is sad. You would think if an individual was going through something so life-threatening, it would make them want to do right. Not my mother, though. The only person she's been nice to, is Sam. I don't get it. The one person who treats her like shit is the one person she treats with the utmost respect. That confirms she doesn't have much respect for herself, let alone me or Lucia. We try not to get in her way because we want nothing to set her off. Our annual New Year's Eve All White Party is approaching, and I can only imagine how it will go since he's moved in. He'll probably invite all of his friends and brag on how he did everything, knowing good and damn well he will do nothing. I can't stand to hear his name some times… most of the time. I only respect him because I respect my mother, no matter how much she doesn't respect me, and he's her boyfriend. And the respect I have for her is dwindling because I see now how she doesn't respect herself.

"Breakfast ready, Serenity," I hear Lucia say over the intercom. I close my journal and make my way to the main house. When I get there, at the kitchen table is Savannah, my mother, Sam, and Victor. VICTOR! What the fuck! I can't let him see me like this! No wonder Lucia referred to me by name instead of baby or darling. I spin to go back to the pool house, but I get noticed before I make it all the way out the door.

"Serenity, darling," my mother calls out.

I turn around slowly to find all eyes, except for Lucia's, on me. "Yes, Mother."

"Come eat your breakfast before it gets cold."

Embarrassed, I walk to the table and take the only empty seat that has plating on it, which is next to Victor. I slide down in the chair with my yellow and white pajama pants and tank top on. "Good morning, everyone," I say out of respect and in a low tone.

"You remember Victor, don't you?" my mother asks.

"She does. She's my personal banker," he answers for me.

"Oh! You didn't tell me that," my mother teases.

"Yes, Mother," I say in frustration. *I don't recall telling you too much of anything now a day,* I think to myself as Lucia sits my plate of favorites in front of me: bacon, eggs, rice, potatoes, and a bagel.

I eat slowly and in silence as my mother, Sam, and Victor talk about their recent business venture. Once I'm done, I excuse myself, letting Savannah know I'll be dressed in about an hour and we can then leave for our day of shopping.

"Why don't you let Savannah have the week off and you and I do some shopping together?" my mother asks.

"Because that'll prevent me from getting the gifts I have for you, Mother."

"I can take you shopping," Victor chimes in.

"That'll be a magnificent idea," my mother says, clapping her hands. "Then maybe I can borrow Savannah for the day."

"No, I'm fine. You can borrow Savannah and I can go shopping alone." I'd rather go alone than go with Victor. Who knows what he has up his sleeve since I've been ignoring him.

"Nonsense! I will not have you out there alone doing any shopping. You know how crazy these fools get around the holidays. Victor will go with you and Savannah will help me for the day." She then looks at Lucia and requests that she calls a driver to pull around front.

"I can drive us, Mrs. Moore. No need to call for one of your drivers." Victor turns and winks.

⁓

He gets in his 2007 all white Range Rover and asks, "Where to?"

"Aventura Mall," I tell him.

"Aventura it is."

"Thanks," I mutter under my breath.

"Pleasure is all mine."

He gives his radio a little volume as we pull out the gate. "Good Life" by Kanye West flows through the speakers and I bob my head to the beat.

"What do you know about this music?" he chuckles.

"Who, Kanye? This is my jam!" I say as I sing some lyrics, "*The good life, it feel like Atlanta, it feels like L.A., it feel like Miami, it feel like N.Y., summertime Chi, ah, Now throw your hands up in the sky.*" I throw both hands up and Victor watches me, giggling. "What's so funny?" I ask him.

"You."

I put my hands down and stop singing. "Why are you laughing at me?"

"I'm not laughing *at you,* per se."

"Then what are you laughing at?"

"Nothing. I just think it's rather cute how a suburban girl knows this song and sounds good singing slash rapping it," he tells me. I turn to look out the window to hide my blush.

"Care to tell me why you've been ignoring me?" He turns the radio down.

"I haven't been ignoring you, I've been busy. If I were to ignore you, you wouldn't have your numbers. Right?"

"Well, I guess you have a valid point there. You know what I mean, though. Why have you been ignoring me on a personal level, not a business level?"

"I've been busy keeping your business intact," I answer.

"Let that be the reason."

"I will." I reach to turn the volume back up.

Victor reaches and turns the radio off completely and asks, "Why did you leave me hanging like that?"

"I don't know what you're talking about," I fib.

"I'm sure you do."

I chuckle and then turn the radio back on. We ride the rest of the way with the music playing only. I wonder what he's thinking. We reach the mall and it's packed with last-minute shoppers. The first stop is the Louis Vuitton store. Victor browses while I try on two dresses for New Year's Eve. I catch him watching me a few times, and my body becomes weak with the memory of the events from the bathroom stall two weeks ago. How does he have this effect on me? I ask myself as moisture forms between my legs.

Browsing through the dresses, Victor approaches me with one that's extraordinarily beautiful. He presses up against me so closely that I can feel his erection and taste the sweetness of his breath. "Try this on for me," he insists in a soft, sensual, deep, demanding voice. The dress is long-sleeved, long and white, with the entire back that drapes low and has a short tail. I take his pick, along with my two choices, and make my way to the dressing room. Victor follows behind, watching every stride.

I try my picks on first and eliminate them both, and then Victor's pick. The jersey material clings to every curve of my body, showing my flawless shape. I turn to look at the back of the dress in the mirror and he has excellent taste. I contemplate showing him when I hear him say, "What's taking you so long, woman? I want to see too." His mouth drops to the floor when I step out the dressing room. Silent, he walks up to me, lifts me up off my feet, and takes me back in the changing room. My back presses against the warm wall. He places me on my feet and caress my face gently with his long, soft, slim fingers. He moves in closer and closer, and his erection has grown. He kisses my lips so gently that it causes me to let out a soft whine. Thank God it's only us two in this fitting area. I resist his kisses because I want him to beg. The words that follow confirms that he read my mind, "I don't beg for what I want, but I will beg for what I need." He then turns me around and runs his fingers down my spine, causing the hairs on the back of my neck to stand, and then he stops at my waist. He bends my body and brings my butt into him. He grinds on me and my knees go weak. He leans me back up, kisses the back of my neck, and tells me to take the dress off. I undress slowly and seductively, allowing my breasts to fall freely. He stands against the wall observing and suddenly demands that I get dressed. He gathers the dress from my feet, says he'll take it to the cashier, and leaves the changing room.

"What the fuck!" I say to myself, standing in nothing but my G-string.

Once I'm dressed, I leave the changing room and go to the cashier to purchase the gown. As I'm approaching the register, she's bagging the dress. "How much do I owe you?" I ask her.

"Your total is two thousand five hundred dollars and twenty-eight cents. How will you be paying for this, Ms. Moore?"

"You can put it on my platinum account," I tell her.

"Ma'am, it appears they have already paid the dress. A... Mr. White. Mr. Victor White." She looks at the screen on the register again and confirms the purchase with her manager. My eyes search the store for Victor. He's walking towards me. I turn to the cashier, get the garment bag, and turn to leave. Victor's body stops me like a brick wall.

"Come with me," he says as he places his hand on the small of my back—just like he did in my dream—and leads me out of the store. Instead of going to another store or him even asking if I needed to go to another store, he leads me to the parking garage.

"Are we leaving?" I inquire.

"Live a little."

"*Live a little?* Well, have you know, living is what I do daily."

"If that's the case, stop asking so many damn questions and loosen up," he whispers in my ear.

We get to the garage and he leads me back to his Range Rover. He takes the bag from me and hangs it in the back seat on the driver's side. He then takes my hand and opens the back passenger door. "Get in," he says. I obey his order. "Scoot over," he demands. I do so, and he climbs in with me, and when he pulls his pants down, the size of his erection startles me. "Don't be afraid, I promise I won't hurt you," he says as he kisses my lips after each word. He then picks me up and places me on his lap while still kissing me fervently. Once on top of him, he pulls my skirt up to my waist and moves my G-string to the side. He massages my button with his thumb while penetrating me with his two fingers. He stops and pulls me close to him so I can feel his manhood against my cookie. "Is this what you want?" he asks me. I don't respond. He asks again and I don't respond. I want him to beg. I attempt to move from on top of him and he grabs my hips, holding me in place. I'm getting turned on by my teasing him and seeing him so adamant to have me. "I want you, Serenity. Please don't make me beg."

"No," I say to him in between me, trying to catch my breath.

"Are you telling me no?"

"No," is all I say.

Victor lifts me up and slowly place me on his Mandingo, easing it in inch-by-inch, second-by-second. I don't move. I allow him to do everything. Once he's all the way in me, my body stiffens as my cookie forms perfectly around his manhood. He holds me close while kissing my neck, then down to my collarbone. Each time I purposely tighten my muscles, he moans. My muscles tighten again. "Please don't do that," he begs. Both our hearts speed up. While squeezing my muscles, my body moves back and forth not allowing an inch of him to escape. "Oh, my God. This is better than my dream, he says. Please, Serenity," he whispers in my ear. He takes his hands and raises my shirt. Victor removes my bra and licks my nipples as if they're ice cream cones. My body is weakening and I can no longer hold my strength together. I release, and he grips each of my butt cheeks and slowly moves me up and down. "Oh, Ms. Moore," he moans. Both of our bodies move in sync and he speeds up. His kisses are becoming more passionate by the minute and my tendons tighten without intent.

"Please don't stop," I plead with him.

"Why not?" he asks in my mouth.

"Because I'm going to cum."

"Tell me before you do."

"I'm about to." As soon as I say the words, the unthinkable happens. He stops, lifts me off him, pulls his pants up, and gets out the vehicle. His erection plunges through his pants. Son of a bitch! What the fuck? Is this supposed to be payback for me leaving him hanging in the bathroom?

He stands holding the door open and inquires, "Where to next?"

Chapter 26

Sunday, December 31, 2006

12:27pm

It's been nine days since I've spoken with Victor and five since I've seen him. The way he left me hanging made me feel… empty in that moment. I haven't called him and he hasn't called me. Maybe this is the best thing to do, although I think about him more than I probably should. That day when we left the mall, we said nothing to each other on the ride home and when he came over to talk business with Sam the day after Christmas; we said nothing to each other.

I don't know what it is about him, or what he does to make me weak at the thought of him. No one has ever made me feel the way he does, not even Carmen. Yes, she made me feel good inside and out, but it's something different about Victor. Could it be the spontaneous sexcapades we have? Or could it be this game of cat and mouse we play? I don't know, but whatever it is, I like it. I like the way he holds me. I like the way he kisses me. I even like the way he talks aggressively to me during sex. It turns me on.

As much as I like him and the way he turns me on, I want so desperately to get him out of my head. Why can't I do that? If he wants to play, I'll play his game, but I aim to win. The next time he comes over to meet with Sam, I will do him like he did me. I will take him to a secluded place and seduce him until he's about to bust and then leave him hanging… again. But this time, I'll make sure he understands that I run this situation, and to never ignore me. Is that a double-standard? I don't care if it is! This is MY cookie; I can choose to not give it all to him if I want. That's how I see it, anyway.

There's a knock at my door. It's Savanna bringing my dress for today's New Year's Eve Party. "The makeup artist and hair stylist will be here in an hour. They're glamming your mother right now. Your schedule for tomorrow is clear, and I have emailed your client's list for the week. Your business cards came today and Lucia has lunch ready for you."

"Thanks, Savannah. Can you make sure my schedule is clear for Tuesday as well? I know I'll need the extra day to recoup." My journal goes in the safe I've recently had to purchase after I caught my mother snooping around my room.

Savannah hangs my gown in the closet and pulls out four pairs of shoes for me to choose from. The Victoria Secret joggers cling to my butt as I make my way to the main house. Lucia has outdone herself again with an enormous lunch spread. "What's the occasion?" I ask her.

"No occasion, some for party. Just getting out way right now so I drink with you," she informs me.

"Well, it is after twelve so pour up." I think before I continue. "Has Mother said anything to you about her test results? I know she has them because Raven told me. She said Mother has been aware of her disease for many years, and that she's considering going out of the city for treatment for about a month. The best thing is she's *willing* to get treatment. Do you think I should say something to her or wait until she says something to me?"

"Wait be better," Lucia tells me.

"But what if she says nothing?" I ask her.

"Still wait. Maybe her will."

"Wait it is," I raise my glass, Lucia raises hers and we toast to waiting.

While we're eating our lunch, my mother comes in with her hair and makeup looking flawless. "You look beautiful, Mother."

"Don't I!" she exclaims. She sits down and starts a conversation with Lucia about the event planner and how things are setup and decorated. "The guest will start arriving a little before seven, so make sure there's plenty of hor d'oeuvres prepared. I see you have the chilled finger foods ready. Make sure they're nice and refrigerated. When the planner gets here, can you show her how to set the food up? And, Serenity, can you ask Savannah to help with some decorations before she gets dressed?"

"I can do that," I respond. Lucia yes ma'am's to all the orders Mother gave her. I finish my lunch and my drink with Lucia before I go back to the pool house to get my hair done. The hairstylist is setting up. The shoe selection Savannah has set out waits for my approval. In need of a second opinion, she immediately comes when I call her. Putting on the dress reminds me of the episode of Victor and me in the changing room and in his SUV. I shake my head from side-to-side, removing the thoughts that are trying to take over my mind and body right now.

The silver GUCCI sling back heels are the first pair that I try on while standing in the mirror posing. Savannah shrugs her shoulders disapprovingly. The second pair is the all-white Sergio Rossi's with a platinum toe. These are more of a stiletto and give me at least five additional inches of height, going from five-feet-nine inches to six-feet-two inches. Savannah gives them two thumbs up. I try on the third pair; white Christian Louboutin's with diamonds covering the heel. Savannah says they're too much for the dress. Once I'm done, I hang my gown above the Sergio Rossi's. Savannah pairs the perfect clutch to match.

My feet slide into the Sergio's as the mirror display a stunning re-flection. Admiration overflows as I pose for myself. My makeup is immaculate, and my pinned-up curls are tightly tucked. Savannah walks in the room and she looks stunning as her silver gown grips to her tiny body, and her black stilettoes make her taller than what she really is. She pulled her hair into a long ponytail, revealing her perfect oval face. Her eye makeup brightens her light blue eyes but gives her pale skin a darker tint.

I pick up the silver clutch and we walk side-by-side to the party. It's almost nine o'clock and a lot of the guests have arrived. When we walk in, Lucia greets us both with a glass of champagne. She looks stunning too, in her long white dress and black heels. The three of us go into the enormous living room—where most of the guests are mingling—and make the table of hor d'oeuvres our first stop.

"Well, don't you ladies look nice," I hear my mother say.

She stands with Sam in a black halter dress that's cut right above her knees. She never wears white to the party. Sam has on an all-white tux and a black bowtie, I guess to match my mother's dress. "You guys look amazing," I tell them. Mother twirls around, showing off her dress.

"I try," she replies. "We will go mingle with our guests. You la-dies enjoy the night. And Happy New Year if I don't see you before then." Sam chuckles instead of saying thanks to the compliment.

"Same to you," we all say in unison.

"Enjoy." My mother and Sam both turn and walk away hand in hand.

I'm having a blast until I see Victor walk in with a gorgeous woman on his arm. I turn around and pretend I don't see him. Savannah calls him over. I nudge her aggressively. They greet each other and he introduces his date while I turn my back. Her name is Fame. He says she's one of his upcoming artists that he's been working with. "Well… don't you look spectacular?" I don't respond or turn around because I'm not sure if he's referring to me or Savannah. "Serenity," he says.

My head turns to him and he looks delicious in his white pants, white blazer, and white V-neck t-shirt. I'm trying to keep my composer when I reply, "Thank you, Mr. White. You don't look so bad yourself."

"I love the hair," he compliments.

"Thank you." I turn around fully and direct my attention to his date. "Hello, I'm Serenity. Thank you for coming." I slightly extend my fingers only.

"You're welcome. My Victor needed a date and I wouldn't dare let this art of a man come alone." She leans in and caresses his chest instead. *I wonder if he has sex with all his artists.*

"I hope you guys enjoy the night. I will go get myself a drink. Savannah, would you come with me, please?" I need another drink to calm my nerves and my jealousy.

At the bar I say to her, "Was it obvious that he turned me on?"

"Just as obvious as his flirting was. You better watch out. I've heard a thing or two about Mr. White. You know I used to be one of his partner's personal assistants."

"Yes, and don't remind me. *He* better watch out. Come on, let's go dance." I pull Savannah to the dance floor.

We dance to a few songs before my feet throb. I tell Savannah that I'm changing into some more comfortable shoes. "You need me to walk over there with you?" she asks.

"No. You stay here. Have a drink ready for me when I get back, and no champagne." The crowd is thick as I make my way through the living room and into the hallway. Lucia is in the kitchen giving orders to the servers, but she notices me coming in. "Everyting okay, Sweet Serenity?"

"Yes, Lucia. I'm going to change into some more comfortable shoes," I inform her.

"Don't be too long countdown soon," she reminds me.

"I won't."

Once in the pool house and in the closet, I kick the shoes off my feet and on top of another pair. The Alexander McQueen's go well and are just as cute and comfortable. Someone comes through the door, "Savannah, is that you? You better have me a drink if it is." When I exit the closet, I'm electrified on the inside to look up and see it's Victor and not Savannah.

"May I help you?" I play hard to get.

"You may," he says as he walks closer and begins kissing me. The feeling is too good to stop him. Instead, my arms find their way around his neck as I take every moment of his rapture in. "I haven't stopped thinking about you since that day." The kissing stops as he stares into my eyes and sways from side-to-side to no music.

"So you ignore me to show me that?" I question him.

"No, me ignoring you was to teach you a lesson. As bad as it hurt me, it was something I needed to do," he tells me.

"And what was the lesson?"

"Don't ever, I mean ever, leave me hanging the way you did," he advises me.

"How do we do this?"

"Business with benefits. You look beautiful in that dress. Now, can you take it off for a little while? I promise I won't be long. I've been holding all this in since that day and I know once I get in it… Take it off and let me show you."

The dress falls to the floor. He insists that the shoes stay on. He picks me up and lays me down on the bed. He tells me to wait a minute as he gets up to lock the door. When he returns, he removes his clothes and stands at my feet, staring down. Victor kneels at the foot of the bed and pulls me to the edge. He orders me to relax and I obey his request. Spreading my legs further apart, he kisses me, starting at my ankle, then up to my pelvis, one leg at a time. His nose rubs against my button and the friction causes me to jump and let out a sensual whine. He tells me to loosen up again, but my body wants him so badly it doesn't know what relaxation is. His soft, thick, wet tongue plays patty cake on my clit. My fingers run through his hair as he teases the opening of my vagina with his finger while still licking in circular motions. My movements mimic his. He demands me to stop. His actions repeat: lick gently and then suck. Lick gently and then suck. He does this until my body weakens and I'm craving him like a pregnant woman craving ice cream.

"Please don't stop," I manage to plea.

"I won't," he says as he stops licking and sucking and climbs on top of me. He continues to stroke me with his finger as he slightly licks and suck my nipples one by one, the same way he licked and sucked my "button". He stops penetrating me with his fingers and pushes both of my knees to my chest, placing the heel of my shoes on his rib cage. He gently eases inside of me. My vagina opens up to him. A loud moan escapes his lips when my muscles tighten around his Mandingo like a leather glove. I grip his waist, digging into his skin. He grunts louder and announces my name. My body tenses up as I explode all over him. He pulls out and tells me to turn over. I turn over, get on my knees and push my weak upper body up with my hands. "No," he says as he pulls my legs down and lays me flat on my stomach. I arch my perfectly round butt about five inches in the air. His hands are gentle as he caresses both butt cheeks. He plants wet and soft kisses on each cheek; going from left to right. He massages them, but stops kissing and starts licking; licking my cookie from the back. I collapse and he gently pulls me back into him. He takes his time, not being greedy, just enjoying the treat. His body slowly climbs on top of me and he opens me from behind. This time, when I collapse, he pulls me up on my knees as he remains inside. I push myself up with my hands, but he pushes my upper body back down, leaving only my butt hiked in the air. He orders me to grip the heels on my shoes and hold on tight. He thrusts as far inside as he can and begins moving in a circular rotation. I release the heel and crawl forward. He crawls with me. My body can't take what he's giving me. He slows down and continues to rotate. Going slow and steady, our moans fill the air with every gyration. He reaches under me and gently caresses my breast with one hand, while he massages my clit with the other. I move and he begs me to stop. I keep moving. He begs. I stop for a second and then move again in the same circular cycle, and he begs and pleads until I explode all over him again. He follows with three pushes inside of me and then pulls out. He falls on top of me from behind and whispers in my ear, "Happy New Year." I look at the clock and sure enough, it's twelve o'clock on the dot.

Victor's phone rings, but he doesn't budge. My phone then rings and it's too far for me to reach. Otherwise, I would've answered it. There's a knock at the door. Victor's body weight enables my ability to move. "They'll go away," he implies.

~

By the time Victor and I go another round and then head back to the party, it's almost 2am, and it's still packed; it usually is until sunrise. We enter at separate times through separate doors. No one questions my whereabouts, but Lucia and Savannah give me a look as if they already know where I've been. My mother and Sam are on the dance floor, grooving like it's their last dance. I'm sure they're both under the influence by now. I make my way to the open bar and order tequila on the rocks and a Heineken when Victor walks up behind me and asks if I'd like to dance. I turn to face him after getting my drinks and reply, "That's not a part of business, nor is it a part of the benefits, so no thank you." I walk away and join Savannah, who's sitting at a table talking to some guy. She looks like she needs a rescuing from the Big Bad Wolf, so my intrusion won't make a difference.

"Can you excuse me for a second… or two, please?" She says to him, then turns around and rolls her eyes in the back of her head and mouths, "Thank God."

The guy remains seated so I peek around her and say, "Actually, she'll come find you when we're done. It's a woman thing." He eventually gets up and walks away. A flood of questions about my whereabouts follow. I smile and shrug.

"Both of you were MIA. You're an adult, Ms. Moore; just make sure you're careful with him. He tends to—"

I cut her off, "I think he needs to be more careful with me than I need to be with him." I give a wink in confirmation that I know what I'm doing, and we both burst into laughter.

"You didn't!" she exclaims.

"Didn't what? Put it on him? I tried to in every way possible." A blush flashes across my face.

Lucia joins us as we continue in amusement. "Why so funny, you two? Sweet Melly Baby fucks fine man?" she asks as she takes the seat next to me.

"Sh! You mean *Serenity*."

"Me sorry. Me forget." She looks down.

"It's okay, Lucia." I squeeze her hand.

We continue our night sitting at the table talking, laughing, and enjoying each other for another two hours. Our drinks have set in and we're all feeling them, so we turn in. Savannah volunteers to walk Lucia to her wing of the house and says she'll have a driver take her to her downtown apartment, but Lucia insists that she stay in a bedroom on her side of the house. Savannah agrees.

After they leave, I go to the pool house, taking my shoes off as I walk across the path. When I flick the light switch on, only Victor is sitting on the bed. "More benefits?" he asks.

"Not tonight, I'm a little sore down there," I say while pointing to my cookie.

"Can cuddling be a part of our benefits deal?"

"Sure, it can."

We both undress and get in bed. He cuddles me from behind and his manhood rise to the occasion. That's all it took to turn me on as I toot my ass into his erection, which leads to more all-night sexcapades. How will I ever be able to work with this man regularly without wanting to have a piece of him?

Chapter 27

Saturday, January 13, 2007

1:47pm

The past couple of weeks have been great. Victor and I have an excellent "business with benefits" relationship. Whenever we want to hook up, we do. Not at all times do we have sex. Sometimes we use it as a getaway from our normal surroundings and just chill. It's a glorious escape from all the bullshit that goes on around here. He's my fresh form of therapy since I've yet gone back to Ms. Young. My mother still has told no one about her situation and walks around as if everything's okay. Sam is having his grand opening for his business tomorrow—thanks to my mother's money—and I doubt if I go. His dumb ass is opening up a men's boutique on a strip downtown, near South Beach, where there are a dozen other men boutiques. I know Victor will be there because he went against my advice and remained an investor in Sam's bullshit business, anyway.

Work has been going well. The requirements for my clientele have exceeded for the month, and Felicia commends me on my growth. I plan to get my place downtown next month. The pool house has become uncomfortable since Sam has moved in. Sometimes it feels as though someone is watching me and for that reason alone, I have to get a place of my own. The only people that'll have a key are Savannah and Lucia. My mother definitely won't. I know if I give her access, she'll be there every day trying to run my life. What she needs to do is try to fix her own life; in every aspect. I still to this day would like to know which one of those nasty men transmitted her with the disease. Everyone that she's screwing is screwing someone else, and who knows who that someone else is screwing.

What's so fucked up about it is my mother had the nerve to judge me and tell me how I was going to hell when she found out about Carmen. She has a lot of nerve. What makes her believe she wouldn't or can't go to hell for passing judgment. She's such a devil! Speaking of....

"Are you busy?" my mother interrupts as she barges through the door.

"Not really, just doing a little writing." I close my journal and place it under my pillow.

"You still writing in those damn diaries, I see." I won't argue with her today because it's Sunday.

"Um, yes. Since that's what you call it," I reply as I laugh at my thought of not entertaining her foolishness.

"Mind if we chat?" She sits at the bay window.

"Don't mind if we do." I get out of bed and join her in the window, sitting Indian-style. "What's on your mind, Mother?"

"I'll be going away soon." She grabs my hand.

"Is everything okay? Where are you going away to? How long will you be gone? Are you just doing this so I can stay in this house? Because if you are, it won't work. I still plan to move."

"Everything is okay. Where I'm going is, none of your business and I'm not sure how long I'll be gone, but I don't leave for two months. I know it'll be long enough to kick this drinking habit I've picked up. I'm not worried about you moving, little girl. You'll never be able to make it out in the actual world without the help of your mother."

I *know* she will not go to rehab for her drinking, but I go with it, anyway. And who in the hell is she referring to as *a little girl*. I laugh out loud at her series of bullshit. "Okay, Mother," is all I say. I just pray she's going to treatment for her disease and not just alcohol.

"Are you going to the grand opening tomorrow?"

What do you care? I think to myself before replying, "I didn't plan on it."

"Victor will be there," she teases.

"And your point is?" I ask sarcastically.

"Well, don't you want to see him?"

"I see him enough. I *am* his personal banker, or did you forget?"

"Oh yes, that's right. I forgot about that. Oh, well, I'm going shopping for something to wear to the opening. I'll see you later," Her weight loss is noticeable as she walks away.

"Later, Mother." I go to the refrigerator for a beer.

My mother stops and speaks with her back towards me, "While I'm gone, Sam will continue to stay here. I would appreciate it if you wouldn't be so... so... standoffish with him. Thank you." She exits, leaving the door open behind her.

She has to be joking with me. This dude uses her, moves in and uses her more, has a whole wife and family, and she expects me to act a certain way towards him. Fuck him. The lemon I squeeze in my beer squirts me in the face. I giggle it off. I wonder if Lucia knows about this mess.

A pair of joggers rest on the chair, so I put them on, grab another beer out of the refrigerator, and head to the main house with bottles in hand; one for me and one for Lucia. She's in her suite sprawled out on her sofa watching TV while Bella is on the other sofa chatting away on the phone. She swings her feet around and tells me to sit, but I take a seat on the floor.

"Did you know mother was leaving in two months?" I hand her a beer.

"Bella, to room go and talk on phone," she tells her daughter. When Bella leaves the room, she says to me, "Her for treatment go, right?"

"She *said* she will go to rehab for her drinking." I peel the label off the beer bottle.

"Her lie. Her go for treatment. Director of place call to confirm her admit date. Her say Sam stay here."

"Yes, and that's the part that creeps me out."

"Me too." Lucia squirms.

"I plan to have my place by then. You and Bella can stay with me whenever you want."

"Oh, Serenity, me kill he him try anyting." We both giggle and cheer to that.

Chapter 28

7:26pm

Time waits for no one. Two months have passed, and I've been able to get so much accomplished. Victor and I still have our casual sexcapades and it's getting more intense. Feelings are raising so much that I have to fall back and pull away from him. No one at either of our places of employment knows about us, and we both want to keep it that way. Fernando's extra ass is always snooping around and trying to pick Savannah for information. She and I both think it's entertaining, so she laughs at him just as hard as I do. I've established a steady client base and Felicia has promoted me to Executive Financial Planner. She has appointed me a few company accounts to handle, and they've been taking up most of my time. I appreciate the opportunity. That's why I work with no complaints. Valentine's Day came and went, causing me to miss the dinner plans Victor and I had. With things going the way they have been, I'm glad I worked through dinner because the position I'm in doesn't allow me to act on these feelings I'm gaining. I'd rather keep it as a sexual relationship and make him continue to beg for more. His persistence is a turn on but makes me question if it's the reason behind all these feelings floating around between the two of us. The best solution is to tame me. With Victor and work as distractions, I haven't thought about Carmen that much. Hardly at all. Though, I miss her warming energy at times.

Mother leaves tomorrow for her "vacation", and I'm still wondering if she will tell anyone the actual reason for her departure. She's beginning to look weird. She's thinning out more, and she has heavy bags under her eyes as if she hasn't slept in days. She has lesions forming on her face, but tries to cover them with make-up. Her increased drinking and lack of effort to go to work hasn't gone unnoticed. She can't go to work, but she can spend an enormous amount of time at Sam's boutique, which hasn't been doing well at all. I'm surprised it's lasted this long. Victor told me how Sam confided in him about the failure of the business. He even admitted that I was right about Sam and has made plans to take this investment as a loss.

Victor appreciates me being his personal banker and financial advisor because I take my time with his accounts, and I've yet steered him in the wrong direction. The company he works for is one of the many accounts I'm assigned to, and they're doing an outstanding job with their artists and how they manage their money. I've only been in the position for a month and they've taken all the advice I've offered, saying they trust my judgment. Felicia tried to give me Sam's account, but I refuse to see how much money my mother spent on nothing. It's not his fault because he can only do what my mother allows him to do.

I found a penthouse downtown, closer to my job. It has three bedrooms, three bathrooms, and a panoramic view of the ocean. That's more than enough for me, but I want to make sure there's enough room for Lucia and Bella if they ever need to move in. My plan is to move next week after my mother leaves. No one knows about me moving except for Savannah and Lucia. Victor doesn't know because I'm not sure if I want to tell him. To keep Sam's suspicion down, everything of mines that's here will remain here. While Sam is away one day, I'll take a few clothes, and that's all. My anxiety kicks in so often it makes me want to leave sooner.

My phone rings just as I'm finishing. I look at the caller ID and it's Victor. I decline his call, sending him straight to voicemail. I must get ready for our last dinner at the main house with my mother before her departure.

Lucia has prepared steak, lobster, shrimp, baked potatoes, two different salads, boiled corn, and my mother's favorite, peach cobbler, for dessert. We all sit around the table eating without conversation. Mother is picking over her food more than she's eating it. Sam looks at her and tells her to eat her food. I look over at Lucia and she winks her eye at me. That has always been her way of telling me not to say a word. She knows I desperately wanted to.

I obey Lucia's wink and look at my mother with disgust. She catches me and questions, "Is there something you'd like to say, Serenity?"

"No, Mother, I'm just going to miss you. That's all," I boldly lie.

"Well, you just make sure you take care of yourself while I'm away. I've transferred enough money into your account and it should last you until I return. I don't know how long that'll be, but you have more than enough," she tells me.

"No offense, but I don't need your money, Mother."

"Yes, you do," she says as she turns to Lucia. "I've paid your salary up and provided you with a little extra. You'll find it in a safe deposit box at the bank that Serenity works at." She pulls a small envelope from the pocket on her blouse and slides it to Lucia. "All the information along with the key is in this envelope."

"Gracias, ma'am." Lucia thanks her as she takes the envelope.

"Now, if you all will excuse me, I have an early flight." My mother gets up from her seat. I stand as well and go to hug her, but she rejects my embrace by putting her hands up.

"None of that. It's not like I'm dying." She slowly walks past me, then turns, "Sam, come." He gets up and follows on cue as they both climb the stairs to her master suite.

I sit, staring through my office window, recollecting the most recent events… It hasn't been three weeks since my mother left, and Sam's boutique closed down. He moved his wife and children into my mother's house. I moved out two days after she left, but Lucia has kept me in the loop. She came by and told me what was going on the day she saw him and his wife laid up in my mother's bed. Reaching out to my mother was a waste of time because her cell phone keeps going straight to voicemail. I wonder about her often and wish there was a way we could keep in touch. I called Raven to see if they'd heard from her and she told me the doctor has, but what they discussed is confidential. Raven is so afraid of losing her job, that she won't snoop in my mother's file and give me her location. My mother probably wouldn't care about Sam's actions, as long as he's still here. After all that's been going on at her house, I'm glad I left when I did, because my mouth can be brutal and Lord knows what I would've said to Sam, his wife, or one of his kids.

A reminder on my phone breaks my thoughts. Victor and I have lunch plans today, so I finish my work and meet him in front of the building. He's no longer allowed up to the office unless we're handling business. My rule.

When I get to the car, his driver comes around and opens the door, "Thanks, Aki." I slowly climb in the back seat.

"Serenity," Victor greets me.

"Mr. White," I reply.

"There's something you need to know." His voice is calm.

"What is it?"

"I'm in love with you."

I swallow hard and loud, damn near choking. "I'm flattered," I tell him. "We need to keep this professional."

"You really are."

"I am what?" I ask in confusion.

"Inevitable. I can't stop thinking about you. I yearn for your touch and your smell every day, all day. I can't get enough of you. I want to be around you every second of every minute of every day. What have you done to me? I can't look, let alone think about another woman. Can we go steady and see how it works?"

"Where's all this coming from?"

He orders Aki to drive. "I'm not sure. It's how I feel and you're making me feel weak as a man by questioning my feelings."

"Victor, I honestly don't think that's a splendid idea. There's so much I have to figure out about myself that I wouldn't be able to give you the attention you desire. That wouldn't be fair to you. You want to give me all of you, but I'm not ready to give *anyone* all of me. The feelings I have for you are deep, I'm just… a little confused about those feelings." The look in his eyes makes me regret rejecting him. He looks sad and lost. I want to be with him in every way, but as much as I want that, the words just don't come out.

"I understand, even though I don't want to, I do." Victor sadly turns and looks out the window.

We ride in silence. Once we arrive at Mr. Chow's, the conversation and mood has shifted. Victor seems to be a little distant now, and I'm not sure how I feel about that. That's an easy fix, so I remove one of my shoes from under the table, place my bare foot between his thighs, and fondle his Mandingo with my toes. My actions surprise him and he jumps. I wipe my tongue across my lips as his erection grows on my toes. "You sure know how to lighten the mood, don't you?"

"I don't know what you're talking about, Mr. White."

"Well, Ms. Moore, your little toes have found themselves in a place that could get them in trouble," he indicates.

I continue to play with his manhood until he declares that it's time to go. Our lunch remains on the table untouched as we make a dash for the exit. Once in the car, he tells Aki to drive to the shore. Victor takes me right there in the back seat, not caring that someone else is present. He licks me down low as if it's his first time. His hunger becomes apparent as his tongue penetrates my opening. Not caring that Aki can see us; I moan and squirm as my body reaches its highest heights. Victor removes his pants and sits me on top of him to ride his enormous erection as he sucks my breast.

Once we've gone a few rounds. Victor looks into my eyes, "You will be all mine one day. I will marry you and then I will remind you of this day. You *will* be Mrs. White."

Chapter 29

As I fill the garden tub with water and bubbles, my mind drifts to the statement Victor made the last time we were together, which was a little over a week ago, "You *will* be Mrs. White." I turn on the Jacuzzi, allowing the bubbles to relax my thoughts and body. No sooner than I lay my head back on the tub pillow, my phone rings. My first instinct is to let it go to voice mail, but I dry my hands to check and see who it is. It's Lucia.

"Come quick, Serenity. Trouble at the house. Come now," she says in a panic.

"Is everything okay, Lucia?"

"No! Come quick," she declares and then hangs up.

Half wet, I hurry to get dressed. I think to call Victor and ask him to meet me there, but I immediately have a change of mind. It takes no time for me to get to my car and down Collins Ave. Traffic is clear, so I jump on the highway hoping to get there faster. The tunes on the radio ease my thoughts of what could be wrong. Bow Wow's "Outta My System" is blasting through my speakers as I speed. This song makes me think about Victor. *"When I'm with somebody, all I think about is you."* That's the realist thing that little boy could've said in this song. It's true; all I think about *is* him. It makes me wonder, will I be Mrs. White one day?

I change the station. A love song plays, so I turn the radio completely off. Thoughts of my mother and her well-being cloud my head. I must contact her. Malik, I can have him locate her and see what type of facility she's in. How could I have forgotten about him? I make a mental note to call him first thing in the morning as I take the exit to my mother's house.

The gate automatically opens before I reach it. Lucia stands in the doorway and before I can get my entire body out of the car, she lunges at me and holds me tight.

"Lucia, what's wrong?" I ask her.

"Him touch her," she cries in my chest.

"Who touch who?"

"Sam! Him touch Bella! Me caught him pinned her against the wall!" she yells.

"What! Where is he? Where is Bella?" I question as I disconnect her embrace I run into the house.

Lucia has Sam tied to the banister at the bottom of the steps, bleeding badly from the head. I look around for Bella and she's nowhere in sight, but Malik is.

"You called Malik?" I ask.

"Yes, him know what to do!"

"Is he dead?" I probe as I angrily walk towards him.

"Not yet!" Malik says.

"Where's Bella?" I ask Lucia.

"In room. Him didn't get to go all way, cause me came in when me heard her scream. Me heard her and went running. Me hit him in back of head with gun and gun went off. When gun went off, bullet shot Bella. Her hurt. Me called Malik, him come and called doctor. Doctor with Bella trying to fix she. Me was only trying to stop he, not hurt me baby." Lucia falls to her knees, sobbing.

Malik stops me when I attempt to run to Lucia's suite, "Let the doctor finish. I know him personally and he'll never tell a soul about this. You don't have to worry about him or Bella. He'll take excellent care of her. In the meantime, what do you want me to do with this mutha fucka?" Malik points at Sam.

The spit from my mouth lands on his face, "You trifling bitch!" I slap Sam so hard, I hurt myself. Not bad enough to prevent me from picking up the vase next to the stairwell and breaking it over his head, though. After a few blows to the head, Malik grabs me and tries to calm me down.

"Let me take care of him." He holds my arms down to my side tightly to keep me still.

When he releases me, I bend over, take my shoe off, and throw it at Sam, hitting him in the head. "Fuck you!" I scream as I cry. "Fuck you! You sick bastard! I hope you die in your sleep!" Suddenly, I launch at him and Malik sweeps me off my feet and takes me in the kitchen.

"Let me handle this, Mel... Serenity. I'll take care of it. Trust me. No one can know about this. Not even your mother," he tells me.

"Where is his family that he moved in here?" I ask Malik.

"She moved out when she found out he'd been lying about everything."

BOOM! Me and Malik look at each other and run to the foyer. Lucia is standing in front of Sam with the gun in her hand and she aims at his head and pulls the trigger again, BOOM! Malik runs to her and removes the gun. Lucia stands frozen as she releases the 9mm. He goes to Sam and checks his pulse, "He's dead. Take Lucia to her wing of the house. I'll be back." Malik unties Sam in a hurry.

I run to Lucia and instead of taking her to her wing of the house, she's dragged to the pool house. "What the fuck, Lucia!"

"Me sorry to get you in this, Serenity. Me told you him dead if him touch me Bella," she cries with her face buried in her hands.

"Do you know what this means, Lucia? This means you must leave. Leave the country and go away. That's the only way you'll never get caught." I cry at the thought of being without her.

She looks me in the eyes. "Me can't leave you."

"You must! I'll be all right. Everything you've ever taught me, lives in here." I point to my head. "And all the love I have for you is here." I pat my heart. "But don't worry, because this won't be the last time you see me. I'll visit you as often as possible, wherever you go," I enlighten her.

Her eyes grow full of concern. "But what about the house?"

"You let me take care of that. We have to make sure Bella will be okay and then you must leave immediately. We have to talk to Malik to see if he can get you tickets to… Where will you go?"

"Me don't know. Maybe back home to Cuba. Me miss me familia."

"Cuba would be good. It's not too far," I imply.

"What you tell you mother?"

"Allow me and Malik to take care of everything. You know nothing and you must *never* mention it to anyone, *ever.* We must explain that to Bella."

"Me know her will never say anyting. Her too ashamed. You can't hear from this side of house to that side of house, so her may not hear shots. Her be unconscious still maybe."

"Let's go check on her." I take her hand and we walk through the yard to the other side of the house, instead of going through the house.

Lucia and I are sitting on each side of Bella when Malik returns three hours later. "You must leave, Lucia. I'll get you and Bella tickets to wherever you feel comfortable going, and you mustn't ever mention any of this to anyone. How's she doing?"

"We've already discussed that and she's doing fine. They will go back to Cuba. The bullet only grazed her shoulder, but it caused her to go into shock. That's why she passed out. The doctor said to call him first thing in the morning," I update to him.

"Good. Serenity, can I talk to you in the hallway for a second?" Malik immediately turns and walks towards the door. I tell Lucia I'll be back shortly and go to the hallway with Malik. "We'll tell your mother that Lucia had to return home because of a death in her family and stayed. You must hire a new housekeeper before she returns. I'll clean up the mess by morning and have everything arranged for them to leave. I hate to be so direct at a time like this, but get all your goodbyes in tonight. Even though I was loyal to your father, I'll never mention it to him. Speaking of your father, I have some other information for you. I don't know if your mother told you why she had to leave or not, but she's not too far from here at a treatment center in Ft. Lauderdale. She's HIV positive, and your father is the person who transmitted it. I don't have it. He was sleeping with other men and isn't sure who he got it from. There's something else that I need to tell you, but I need for you to brace yourself before I do. Your sister Sabrina was HIV positive. When she went to the hospital that night, the doctor did a rape kit and drew blood. This is the reason she committed suicide. You were too young to understand, so they kept everything from you." He walks towards the other side of the house. I stand in awe, not understanding why he told me so much at this very moment.

I feel like I'm sleepwalking, and can only imagine how I look as I follow behind him. "Sit," he says. While staring in space, I sit. "We have to work together now. I know you probably hate me for so many reasons, but we got to put all that aside."

"I don't trust anyone," I say. "Everything anyone has told me my entire life has been a lie. My mother, my father, you, and Lord knows who else. I need to make sure Lucia is okay."

Malik grabs my arm as I stand and prepare to leave the table. "Please say nothing to anyone. You're just as guilty as everyone else is."

I snatch my arm, "I may *look* dumb, but I'm far from it." Still, to this day Malik makes me feel queasy.

3rd Phase

Chapter 30

Bella has turned out to be a beautiful teenager, but after two years, I can hardly recognize my mother. That's how long it's been since I've seen either of them. As I stand in front of the mirror, looking at the woman standing behind me, I can't help but notice how horrible she looks. Tears fill the wells of my unmoving eyes as my thoughts reminisce on the things Malik told me. She turns me to face her and kisses me on the cheek. As I try to embrace her eyes, realization sets in that they are no longer the eyes of the woman I once knew as my mother. They are the eyes of a stranger. Someone I've never met before. They reveal pain, fear, and anger. She appears to be dying a slow death right before me, and that feeling alone breaks me down.

Instead of her comforting me like I needed and wanted at that very moment, she says, "I haven't heard from Sam since I left. When was the last time you heard from him?"

She never ceases to amaze me. I lower my head, feeling sadder. "I haven't. A few weeks after you left, the store closed, and he dropped off the face of the earth." I try not to look at Lucia and Bella as I wipe my tears away. My head raises, "I'm glad you could make it, Mother." Hoping the statement would shift the conversation from Sam back to me. After all, it is *my* wedding day.

She replies, "I wouldn't miss the most important day of your life for nothing. Besides, I had to bring you something borrowed." She reaches in her purse and pulls out a single diamond pendant necklace. "Your grandmother gave me this pendant the day your father and I married, and now I'm passing it on to you on your wedding day. Keep it close to your heart and one day, you'll give it to your daughter on her wedding day." Her hands are icy as she places one on each shoulder, takes a step back, and looks at me differently. A way she's never looked at me before. She then pulls me in with a hug and says, "I'm so proud of the woman you've become. And thank you for taking care of my home while I was away. I made it back just in time to see my baby marry the man of her dreams. You make me proud, my daughter."

"Thank you, Mother." I embrace her hug. She's so cold and her body is so frail. It makes me wonder if she was at treatment or not. It makes me wonder if it was too late and she now has full-blown AIDS. Now is not the time to worry about that. My man is waiting to marry me.

I break the grasp, turn to the mirror and examine the necklace. I tell my mother how beautiful it is and give her one last hug before going to Lucia and Bella, who are both standing and watching the two of us interact. Uncertain of my mother's appearance, I chose Lucia to give me away. We stayed in touch after she left, talking at least once a month. No one ever found out about Sam. His wife assumed they killed him because of his dangerous business habits. She said he was destined to scam the wrong person one day, and he's somewhere suffering the consequences. Allowing her to believe and think just that was the best option.

After everyone left—my mother, Lucia, and Bella—I had no one but Victor. Sex has been my scapegoat from everything that occurred the first few months of 2007. He's not the best person to talk to because he's so damn self-centered and wants to do all the talking, but I've gotten used to that. I've gotten used to him all together. Learning to love him for who he is over the past year wasn't easy, but the sex is more amazing than ever before. We haven't moved in together because we plan to do that when we come back from our honeymoon in Milan. We purchased a sixteen million-dollar, two story penthouse in downtown Miami, at The Setai, which is two buildings down from where I live now. Victor got the upper hand with picking a location, but I have the upper hand with the interior decorating. He did well with all the things I had on my must-have list: view of the ocean from the living room, master bedroom and kitchen, and my own personal office. For now, this is life as I know it.

~

The ceremony was beautiful. It was more than beautiful. Victor and I both had eyes full of tears as we exchanged our vows, and so did a lot of other people. It was just the two of us at the altar, no bridesmaids or groomsmen; just us two. This made the service short and sweet, although we have over two hundred guests. Most of them are Victor's friends, clients and their families, and artists and their families. My guests list is barely a hand full.

My plans to change into my receptions dress goes into play as I make my way through the crowded dance floor. Victor is somewhere doing what he does well, running his mouth. In the middle of the floor, I spot my mother getting down with one of Victor's co-workers. My smile warms me on the inside as I slide out of the ballroom with no one noticing. I get to the elevator, push "P", and step back. My head rests against the glass mirror as my eyes watch the elevator close. Before it closes completely, Lucia stops it with her foot, and it reopens.

"Not fast so, missy. Where you go?"

"I'm *going* to change into my other dress, Lucia." Her broken English always puts a smile on my face.

"I go with." She returns the smile and joins me.

We ride the elevator in silence and step into the penthouse at the same time. Lucia goes to the refrigerator and pulls out two beers as I step in the closet where my other dress hangs. She soon follows me and takes a seat on the bench next to the shoes. She reaches out with a beer in her hand; I take it and drink for what seems like forever.

"Thirsty, Serenity?"

"No, it's just refreshing." We both laugh.

"Me miss this. Me miss you." She lowers her eyes and hangs her head.

"Awe, Lucia. You know I miss you more. I've been working myself like crazy just to keep busy. You know I don't have many friends outside of Raven." I point to the back of my Vera Wang wedding gown and Lucia jumps up to help me unzip it.

"Me want to move back close to you," she says once she's done.

"Do you think it's safe to do that?" I ask her.

"Me don't know. Me can ask Malik."

"Do that, and if so, we can make it happen. That way, I won't have to sell my place and you and Bella can move in." The excitement that comes across her face is priceless. She places my robe over my shoulders and we both sit on the bench.

Lucia cups both my hands, "Me have something to tell you."

My initial thoughts are, *What now?* But I ask, "What is it. Lucia?"

"Come," she says as she extends her hand and leads me to a balcony that overlooks the ocean. "Sit." she demands and I obey.

"What is it already?" I impatiently ask.

"Mother was not in treatment for real. Mother is on drugs and is dying from disease. It worse now. Her told me everyting. Her didn't know you was gone marry. Her came home to say bye. She dying, her say."

"When did she tell you all of this?"

"In bathroom right after wedding. Her say always take care of you; better than her ever had."

"Why didn't she say anything to me?"

"Her not want to ruin you day," she advises me with empathy in her eyes.

I take a long swig of my beer and look out into the ocean. "I already knew it was something. She looks so bad. I wish there was something I could do." I grasp the pendant around my neck in hopes of it giving me a sign.

"Her want to die. Her say her will anyway since her disease is much worse. Say her has the AIDS now and her not want treatment cause it don't help," Lucia continues.

I take another swig of my beer. Lucia and I remain quiet for a moment as we both enjoy our beers and the view. We hear the elevator beep and turn to see Bella running towards us, "Serenity, come quick! Your mother has passed out on the dance floor and won't wake up!" Bella yells in perfect English, unlike her mother. Lucia and I look at each other and dart for the elevator. A knot forms in the pit of my stomach as we take the ride down.

When the door opens to the lobby, we see the paramedics pushing a gurney into the ballroom. We rush to the dance floor to see my mother lying breathless. Then, the impossible happens; my mother takes her last breath right in front of me, as if she was waiting for me to get there. The paramedics try CPR but soon pronounce her dead. Lucia holds me as I stand in disbelief. Not caring who sees me in this robe, my knees hit the floor and I pray silently as the tears flow. It's the only thing I could think to do at the moment.

When my eyes open, Victor is on his knees holding me. Savannah, Lucia, and Bella are all close by. I'm in a state of shock. Not because my mother just died, since this day was intended to come, but because she died on the dance floor at my wedding reception. It only confirms what Lucia just told me to be true.

Mother knew she was dying, so she came to see me before it happened. Why didn't she just take care of herself; she could've lived a long life if she had gotten the treatment she needed. Why she didn't believe it would have helped her, I don't know, and I'll never know. But what I know is she no longer will suffer, and this is what she wanted.

I sit Indian style on the floor, deep in my thoughts, and watching as the paramedics place my mother on the gurney and cover her entire body with the white death sheet. A piece of me leaves as they roll her out. My body is so limp that when Victor tries to stand me up, I fall back to the floor. My soul has gone numb and my mind blank. Lucia comes to my side and sits with me.

More tears fall as the remembrance of my mother at her best develops in my head. As evil as she might have been, she was still my mother, and it didn't take away from the love I had for her. She may not have done a magnificent job showing me love, but that didn't stop me from trying to love her. An image of her before she left for treatment appears in my psyche. I see her jamming on the dance floor with Sam at the New Year's Eve Ball. And in the blink of an eye, the image disappears, and she's gone. She's gone… gone forever.

Lucia's eyes fill with tears and I repeat my thought, "She's gone."

"Me know, baby. Let's go lay down," she says as she tries to help me to my feet.

My body doesn't move. Victor stares at me and I repeat, "She's gone." Then demand, "Take me to the hospital." He attempts again to stand me up, but my body slumps back to the floor. He picks me up as if he's carrying me over the threshold, takes me to his SUV, and lays me in the back seat. Lucia climbs in the front and I curl up like a baby as we ride to the hospital.

Chapter 31

I sit at the middle aisle of the front pew with Lucia, Bella, and Victor all to my left. My mother lies peacefully in her purple casket with white roses surrounding it. It's sad to say, but she looks better in there than she did at my wedding. The doctor stated that the cause of death stemmed from her weakened immune system and combination of legal and illegal drugs. He told us that her immune system was as weak as an unformed fetus. Her heart stopped, and there was nothing they could do when she arrived at the hospital. I reach up and clench the diamond pendant around my neck as the doctor's words replay in my head. Victor grabs my other hand and squeezes it. He kisses me on the cheek. His kiss produces a smirk. We didn't take our honeymoon, but he promised to make it up to me whenever I'm ready. Lord only knows when that'll be. What I know is that we deeply love my mother. They pack the church with her co-workers, Dr. Ivanovsky, Raven and her parents, my boss Felicia, some of my co-workers, customers, and hundreds of people from all over.

The service is over quick, and now it's time to view the body. I'm not sure if I can do this. My body feels paralyzed from the waist down when I attempt to stand. The bags under my eyes hide behind my shades. I make another attempt to stand. No response. Victor grabs one arm and motions for Lucia to grab the other. My body moves, but not for long before the pew catches me. I just want this all to be over so I can crawl in my bed. Victor and Lucia sit with me—one on each side—as if they understand I don't want to do this. Lucia puts her arm around me and lays her head on my shoulder. I place my head on her head and we sit until everyone has viewed my mother's sleeping body.

The preacher says a closing prayer as they all stand to exit. Lucia and Victor, still one on each side, both take an arm to guide me out. We walk slowing down the aisle and I see my father in an orange prison jumpsuit with shackles on his hands and feet, standing between two officers and Malik on the other side of one officer. When I make it to his pew, I suddenly stop, causing a traffic jam behind me. He attempts to approach me, but the officers don't allow.

We come face to face. "I'm so sorry, baby girl."

I attack him with every ounce of energy that I have and spit at him. "You did this to her!" I raise my hand to hit him again, but Victor sweeps me off my feet and carries me out of the church. That doesn't stop me from kicking, yelling, and screaming at my father. His voice follows me, apologizing over and over.

Agony overcomes me as I'm placed in the back seat. Lucia gets in and holds me. "Let all out, Serenity, let all out."

"Why did they let him in there," I cry harder.

"Me don't know, baby. Him was still she husband."

"I hate him! I hate him! It's his fault she had that stupid disease, anyway."

"Me know, baby, me know. Let all out."

"Mom, is Aunt Serenity going to be okay?" I hear Bella ask.

With a straight face, I look at her and say, "I will be all right, sweetie. Come sit next to Auntie." I wipe my tears. Bella comes to sit next to me as Lucia scoots over and gives her room. I put my arm around her and begin talking, "Allow no one to cause you to forget who you are on the inside. I know Sam tried to hurt you a while back, but don't allow that to hinder you from living your life. He was… I mean *is* a dead beat that has no one and nothing. He's a miserable, hurt person who tried to take his pain out on you. As long as you're here with me, you'll never have to worry about that again. You're a beautiful person and you always remember that."

"I know, Aunt Serenity. I don't allow what that bastard did to me hinder me." I look at her. "I forgave him that night because I know he'll get his karma one day. Mama told me to use all the strength I have to move forward from that, and I did. Teaching other kids English language while in Cuba is what keeps me, what's the word... occupied? Yes, occupied is what is has kept me." She throws her arms around me, and then says, "I love you, Auntie. You'll make it through this. I'm a teenager now and I can love you the same way you loved me when we lived in the house. I learned so much from you, I bet you didn't even know it." She lets go of her long embrace and lays her head in my lap, just as I used to do with her mother.

"You're so smart," I tell her as I stroke her hair.

"Don't that look familiar?" Lucia asks with a grin.

"I learned from the best."

The door opens and Victor climbs in. Lucia and Bella move to the other side of the limo as Victor scoots close to me and begins holding me. "You okay, Baby? I didn't know he would be here."

"It's okay, Love. I'm a little better now. Maybe I just needed to let all of that out." I wink at Bella and she smiles and tries to wink back.

It's always obvious when Lucia is around, because the smell of food awakes me if I'm sleeping. I ease out of bed, put my robe on and go to the kitchen. She's made my favorite and Bella is sitting at the table with her phone in hand, earbuds in, and an untouched plate of food in front of her.

"Afternoon, Serenity." Lucia hugs me.

"What time is it?"

"Almost one."

"How long have I been asleep?"

"Since after burial yesterday. You was tired, me knew."

"Obviously. Either that or… never mind."

"Hungry?"

"Not really, but I know I should eat something."

"Victor says going to office. Call when you wake."

"I will in just a second. How long has he been gone?"

"This morning." Lucia giggles.

"What's funny, Lucia?"

"Him love he some Serenity. Him hold you all night long. You not move."

"How do you know?" I smirk.

"Me check on you overnight."

I grin as she places a plate of fresh fruit, bacon, eggs, smothered potatoes, and a bagel in front of me. She thinks I'm smiling at the food when I'm really smiling at the thought of her checking on me throughout the night.

"You know we have to go to the lawyer's office tomorrow morning?"

"Me know. Insurance company too."

Truth sets in at that very moment. My mother is gone. As bad as I need to eat, my appetite hasn't been right, but I force myself to eat something for the first time since my mother's death.

"It's okay, Aunt Serenity. You can cry some more if you need to." Bella has finally taken her headphones off.

"You were so into your phone and had those headphones on, that I didn't think you even noticed I was in the room." I chew slowly and then force myself to swallow.

Bella reaches over and takes a strawberry from my plate and mocks my actions. "I always notice your presence, Aunt Serenity."

"Your English is so good. You should try teaching your mother some." I laugh and so does she. Lucia peers at the both of us with a raised brow.

"Mom will never understand the English rules. As long as we

understand her Spanglish, she'll be fine. Right, Mom?" Bella looks
at Lucia for confirmation.

I eat a little more of my food and excuse myself from the table.
In bed is where I end up with my robe and slippers still on. I remove
my journal from the nightstand drawer, and I blow the dust from the
lack of writing off. I pick up the nearby pen and begin expressing all
the emotions and feelings that consume my body.

Sunday, April 18, 2010

1:39pm

*Three years is a long time to go without writing my thoughts and feelings
down. That's probably because Victor has been sexing them out of me. I
have had little time to even think about me and my fucked up emotions
because work and my recent husband has taken up the majority. Yes,
MY husband. He told me three years ago that I would be Mrs. White,
and I took it as a joke. Let's just say he didn't win me over easily. After
my mother and Lucia left, I felt alone. That's what drew us closer. He
seemed to be a great friend, or sex partner, and the more we had sex,
the more I loved him. He's an only child raised by a single mother and
was born with a silver spoon in his mouth. Victor explained to me it's
the reason he works so hard for everything he has; his mother taught him
to. She was a trust-fund baby and didn't have to do much working, but
she did. Said she wanted to teach him the value of a dollar and not give
him everything he wanted hand and foot, but wanted him to know how
to earn it. It all makes sense to me now.*

*I enjoy having my time while he's at work, but I'll be the one to
admit, being alone is old. This is when I miss Lucia the most. It's too
bad I can't say or feel the same way about my mother, and now that she's
gone, I miss her more now than ever before. Unable to take back all the
negative things I said or felt about my mother, no matter how much I
wish I could, hurts me deep. If only I'd appreciated her a little more*

and understood her a little more, my grieving wouldn't be so bad. She had her fucked up issues and situations, but it's clear that she desired unconditional love. She sought and found them in all the wrong places. Kind of like I do. I sometimes wonder if I had known about her drug use and the severity of her illness, if I would've done things differently. Like, treated her differently or reached out to her when Malik told me where she was. Could it have been me who saved her? Our relationship was financial and materialistic, and as much as I tried to love her, she wouldn't allow me in. That didn't stop me from trying, though. Could I have tried harder? It all makes me wonder about the foundation of love. How can I love someone, especially her, when I know nothing about love BECAUSE of HER? Losing her is bittersweet. Bitter because she's my mother and I miss her, as crazy as she was. Sweet because she'll no longer be able to harm her body the way she did...

"Baby?" Victor creeps in the door.

"Yes, dear." I close my journal and place it back in the drawer.

"I have something for you." He comes and sits on my side of the bed.

"I'm not in the mood for sex, sweetheart."

"As bad as I want to make love to you, that's not what it is." He pulls a box from his inside blazer pocket. "My original plan was to give you this on our honeymoon." He gives me the square Tiffany & Co. box. I untie the ribbon and open it slowly. The diamond bangle bracelet is beautiful. "Look inside," he points. It's engraved "*4-9-07 Three Years Later... Mrs. White.*" My mind flashes back to the day he told me he would remind me of that day, and I smile at his thoughtfulness, and his ego.

The bracelet looks good on my wrist as he slides it on and kisses my lips. A gift like this *makes* me want to give him a little cookie; maybe that'll numb the emotions I'm going through right now. "Is this your way of telling me you told me so?"

"And you know it." He smiles.

"This may earn you a little." I straddle his lap and kiss his lips again.

"Who are you trying to convince? Me or you?" He laughs at his own sarcasm.

"You."

"You don't have to convince me, baby."

"Well then myself." One thing leads to another. When he enters me, all of my emotions become insensate for the moment.

Chapter 32

It wasn't easy bouncing back into the swing of things. It's been over two years, and I still mourn the death of my mother as though it were yesterday. Sitting in the kitchen at the island, Lucia brings me this month's issue of InSyle Magazine. She points to the lower right corner. The title reads, "Power Couple Steals the Show Again" above a picture of Victor and I on the red carpet at the 2012 Grammy's some weeks ago. We both look stunning. I wore a red Valentino, long fitting, off the shoulder gown, with my hair in a chic, side-parted, ponytail. Victor complimented my attire with an all-white Armani tuxedo that fit him perfectly.

Lucia looks at me and says, "You always make he look more good."

I chuckle. "I do. Don't I."

"Humph. Him just not know what him get." She picks up the magazine and points at me in the picture. "Sweet Serenity more just this."

Her statement makes me question who I'm laughing at. Me or Victor. "Maybe one day I'll be more than just his "trophy wife"." I use my first two fingers on each hand to represent the quotation marks. "I know Victor loves me beyond my beauty. He's just too busy to show it. My love for him is un—." The phone interrupts our conversation.

Lucia picks up the receiver, "White residence." The look that overcomes her face sends a blow to my stomach. She tells them they have the wrong number in Spanish, hangs up, hurries to me, and pulls me through the kitchen onto the patio. "Him say speak to Melody Moore."

My feet go numb, then my knees. I try to move, but I'm unable to. Lucia helps me to the sofa and closes the sliding window that separates the outside from the inside to ensure our conversation remains discrete. She comes back and sits beside me, places a pillow on her lap, lies my head on the pillow, and begins rubbing my hair. I'm stuck. My eyes dry out as I cannot blink. I feel like my body has a mind of its own. No matter how much it tells my eyelids to blink or my body to move, the communication is not connecting one to the other.

I try to speak, "Di—,". My throat dries out completely. Lucia lifts my head and sits me up and gets me water. I drink and try to speak again, but I forget what I want to say.

"It be alright, maybe it be old friend?"

How did they get this phone number? How did they know my name? Questions flood my brain. Then suddenly, the numbness disappears, my eyes water, so I blink, and swallow. "Did you say *he?*"

"Si." She cups my hands in hers. "Me call Malik see if he trace call?" After my mother's death and they distributed the inheritance, I let my father keep the house that he and my mother made a home. If that's what you want to call it. Malik lives there and takes care of everything on behalf of my father. We keep in touch with him often, just in case we need his services.

"That's a brilliant idea, Lucia." I mumble with my head down. Maybe it was my father? But he knows my new identity, I answer my thought and then look up and repeat it to Lucia for clarification. "Could it have been Papa?"

"Papa know she Serenity." She confirms my answer.

My head falls as I try to come up with another solution. Who would be bold enough to call my home looking for Melody Moore?

Thank God Victor is never home. How would I explain to him who Melody Moore is? Would he leave me? If he truly loves me the way he says he does, then he would understand. Does that make me selfish? I'm feeling overwhelmed. "I will lie down for a little while." I leave Lucia seated as I remove my shoes and lie down.

~

"I wish I could get you to make those same noises when I'm making love to you," I hear my husband say. I open my eyes and he's in bed, lying next to me on his side, with his head propped up on his hand. He still has his work clothes and shoes on. He gently uses his forefinger to move the flying hair strands out of my face.

I stretch and moan before rubbing my eyes. "What do you mean?" I ask in a soft, confused tone.

"You were moaning in your sleep again." Victor stands and begins removing his clothes, starting with his shirt and tie. I undress him with my eyes before he does. "You still can't remember them? Not even when you first wake up?" He sits next to me and I slowly sit up. I've been having some weird dreams for the past two or three months. They sometimes wake me up out of my sleep and have me up for the rest of the night. There have even been several times I've awaken to wet panties and a rising cookie dough… wet vagina. In the dreams, it's me having sex with a faceless woman.

I wonder what that means. It's been years since I've been with a woman. Not just any woman, though. She was the love of my life. The woman of my dreams is shaped just like her. I wonder if it is Carmen that I dream about. What does it all mean? Does this mean she's coming to find me? What does it mean? I will someday have to tell Victor of my past life. Today isn't the day.

"Now, you wouldn't keep anything from me, would you?" He asks as he pecks on my lips, chin, then neck so delicate, that it causes my neck hairs to stand on end. He knows how to turn me on. One thing starts another, and lovemaking becomes my escape from reality for the next hour.

Afterwards, I lie in his arms, playing with the few hairs on his chest. He speaks and I listen. "You know how much I love you right?" I nod my head. "Good. Because I don't want you to feel you're not the love of my life when you are. I have loved no one how I love you. I may have a hard time showing it, but please be patient with me. And please never leave me." He kisses my forehead and gets up to shower. I unlock the drawer to my nightstand and get my journal and pen.

Saturday, August 11, 2012

8:23pm

Victor sure knows how to ease my mind. Even if it is only for the moment. Lucia was Team Victor until she moved back home and saw the interior of our relationship. Mother always told me that "You never truly know a person until you live with them." She wasn't lying about that, let Lucia tell it. She thinks I deserve more. She feels as though he spends more time at the office, studio, or social events than he does at home with me. I agree, but I also understand he has to work. This is his dream. I would never ask him, nor will I ever distract him from fulfilling his dream. I've learned that in life, make sacrifices. Lucia says I'm sacrificing true bliss by staying with Victor. Could it be that I've become so complacent in the relationship, that I've settled? I think I'm happy… but what is happiness? I married Victor for Victor. I sometimes question if he married me for me. Does he even know who I am… or what I like, besides wonderful sex? Why do I do this to myself? Am I just his "trophy wife"?

My husband knows me. My husband loves me. Of course, he married me for me. What other reason would he have to marry me? Sex is my escape from reality. My husband is my connection to the sex. My body has become dependent upon him. Like he has a magnet to my cookie, and it's pulling my heart in the direction my mind is telling it not to go. Is that love? He asks me to be patient with him, but how much longer does he expect me to wait for him to show me his undying love.

These dreams I've been having confuse me because it's like I'm there, and the dream is real, but then when I wake up, aside for me being horny as fuck, I remember very little.

MM

Chapter 33

Twelve plates fill the distance between Victor and I, but only the two of us sit. This is the usual dinner for Victor and me—distance. From one end of the table to the other, I gaze at my husband as he tells me about the new artist his record label has just signed. Since we've been married, I've never seen him so intrigued by another woman's beauty or talent. He's going on and on about how she's shaped like an hourglass with legs as long as a giraffe. How her overlong hair flows when she walks in a room and commands attention without uttering a single word. Not to mention, her skin is bronze and as flawless as a piece of fine silk.

I sit staring at him. Not jealous, but curious… interested. Sure enough, we've had our bumps in the road, and my question of love or lust remains, but I've convinced myself that he is trying, and his attempts do not go unnoticed. We still have our differences, such as the distance, but jealousy is one thing that I have no reason to be.

"Do you love me as your woman or as your wife?" I ask to break his rant and entertain my own thoughts.

"Is that a question?" He stops ranting in mid-sentence and re-directs his focus.

"Yes. Do you have an answer?"

"Well, I can show you better than I can tell you." He pushes back from his plate, removes the napkin from his lap, stands, and walks toward me without blinking. As he gets closer, his Light Blue cologne by Dolce & Gabbana stimulates my senses. Every one of them. Midway, the gravidity from his magnet pulls every being of my body. My legs wrap around his waist once he reaches me, picks me up, and carries me to our bedroom. He lays me on the bed and loves me until the early morning.

The rising sun wakens me before the alarms go off. I look at Victor. His eyes are barely open. I plant soft kisses on his lips and go to the shower. Today is a busy day for both of us. My clientele at the bank has tripled, and Victor's company promoted him. Out of all the years he's been with the company, he has succeeded, but the company's success didn't rocket until his promotion to CEO.

While in the shower, my husband comes into the bathroom and steps in the opposite shower. From the other end and through streams of flowing water, Victor yells to me, "You will love her." Based on the description he provided last night, an image of her develops in my head as I turn and allow the water to pour down my spine. He rambles while we both freshen up front of the double mirrors.

Dressed, Victor comes over and embraces me around the waist and kisses me softly on the neck. "I've made reservations at Mr. Chow's for seven o'clock. Wear something short and sexy in case we need to make a quick getaway." Victor grabs his blazer and briefcase and turns to walk out the door.

His statement replays in my head as I examine myself in the mirror. The words linger as I select the backless, purple, thigh-length Valentino dress and silver Jimmy Choo stilettos for today's attire. I pull an additional pair of flats out since today is a walk-to-work day.

My thoughts drift to mine and Victor's relationship as I finish putting on my attire for the day. I quiver at images of our all-night lovemaking. Not because of how good the sex is, but more so at the thought of not having every aspect of a relationship. He reminds me that patience is what he needs, but I believe it is my patience that have run out. I wish we talked more about us and less about business. A lot of women on the outside looking in desire for a love connection like ours, or what they think is a love connection. To them, our relationship is the perfect. For me, it's merely wonderful sex. I'm finally able to admit that after all these years.

The day is lovely, and the walk to the office is enjoyable as the breeze prevents the glaring sun from scorching me. I take the fifteen-minute stroll often. Mostly, when I need to clear my mind from all my cluttered thoughts. Lately, they've been on love and the meaning of *genuine love*. Victor is a great husband to me, but I often question his love for me, or if the great sex is what he loves. Is the sex what holds us together? We do little communicating outside of making love or him telling me about a new artist, and we only go out to business functions together. Since I've known Victor, business is always his number one priority. I occasionally wish I could talk to him about my thoughts, but since he always turns the conversation to himself, my wish immediately goes faint.

I love my husband, but am I truly in love with him? Does he make me happy mentally, physically, emotionally, and sexually? There are so many questions I should've asked prior to marrying him. Have I settled because I was lonely? Was I desperate? I know it's not love that made me say yes to marrying him because I don't know what love was. Is it too late to take it all back? If only I could turn the hands of time. Do I know what love is now? Is sex love? These thoughts stay consumed in my brain since I've been too busy to express them in my journal.

"Good morning, Serenity. You have a message from your husband," Savannah informs me.

I'm at the office before I realize it. Lately, I become so confined in my thoughts that I either lose track of time or I'm at my destination sooner than expected. At my desk, I listen to Victor's message, "What's up Baby! I've changed our dinner reservations to lunch reservations. I got an important dinner meeting I must attend after work. I'm not sure how long the meeting will be, but I don't want to cancel any plans. I'm sure you understand. See you soon."

I hang the receiver up and stick my head out my office door. "Savannah, can you make sure you clear my lunch schedule and arrange for a car to pick me up at 11:30, please?" Mr. Chow's is too far to walk, so I'll have my driver, Mark, take me.

"I've already cleared your schedule, and I will have a car ready."

I run through my appointments and send my clients on their way, and as usual, time does not wait for me. It's already 11:10, which means there's only twenty minutes left to fix my make-up, change my shoes, and get downstairs. I wore the dress I picked out this morning as a shirt because I dare walk down the street in it. In my walk-in work closet, I remove my pants and the dress transforms from a nice shirt to a sexy dress. I'm wrinkled. I skim through the garments and choose a similar Valentino dress; same color, length, and style, but reveals more cleavage. Dressed and ready to go, Savannah speaks through the intercom, "Mark is downstairs waiting."

"Let him know I'm on my way down." I pick my purse up and leave my office.

"Well, don't you look stunning," Savannah says as I pass her desk on the way to the elevator. I wink at her and laugh on the inside as I take in the gasps from the other assistants.

"Nice dress Serenity," Felicia says as she joins me on the elevator. "What's the occasion?"

"Victor and I are having lunch at Mr. Chow's. I'm meeting his new artist, and, well, you never know what may happen afterwards."

Felicia laughs. "Oh, I understand that, trust me. Have a wonderful lunch, which I'm sure you will," she tells me as we exit the elevator into the lobby and go separate ways.

Riding in the back seat, my mind wonders to my husband's new artist and a ball of anxiety suddenly hits me in the abdomen. My interest grows, but I try to disregard the fact that I'm so intrigued.

I've never met her, but stress takes over not just my stomach, but my entire body.

We reach Mr. Chow's and Mark comes around, opens my door, and extends his hand to help me out. "Have a great lunch, ma'am," he says, then asks, "Shall I wait, or will you text me when you're ready?"

"No, Mark, you don't have to wait. I'll text you if I don't catch a ride with Victor." His eyes remind me of someone, but I can't put my finger on it. I've never paid attention to that until today.

I glide through the restaurant with the supermodel walk that would slay anybody's runway. My curls bounce on my breast as I sway from side to side in the perfectly fitted, size six dress. All eyes are on me. At the table, Victor sits with the most beautiful woman I've ever laid eyes on. The same emotion of anxiety occurs again. She looks familiar, and it feels like we've met before, but I can't recall when or where.

"Hazel, this is my wife, Serenity White. Serenity, this is Hazel Brown," my husband introduces us. As Hazel shakes my hand, chills run through my body, causing every hair on the back of my neck to stand on end. I know her. Did we go to school together? She reminds me of Carmen. Could this be her? Could she have found me? Is she the woman of my dreams? Am I dreaming?

I sit nervously as we order lunch. Victor does his usual babbling of how great an artist she is and how he's excited to work with her, but my mind is not on the conversation. Instead, it's on the weird feeling that I know her. I try to figure out where from, but I'm at a loss.

As my husband speaks, I catch her glaring at me several times. There's something behind those eyes that makes me tingle. This woman is doing something to me. She's doing something to my body, something to my mind. It's a feeling I've never felt, or have just not with my husband. I'm confused. I glance at my watch. I've only been here for ten minutes. Time is drifting for the first time

since I can recall. My armpits sweat. I take a gulp from the glass of
the water in front of me, but that doesn't help, so I excuse myself.

"Is everything okay, Baby?" Victor gets up to pull my chair back.

"Yes. I just need to go powder my nose," I say in a quiet voice
and not showing my anxiety.

Staring in the mirror and trying to calm myself down, I close my
eyes and take slow, deep breaths as an attempt to ease the pain in my
stomach. It doesn't go away. Instead, it speeds up as I feel someone's
breath on the back of my neck. Only Victor knows this is my weak
spot, so my eyes remain closed as I assume it's him taking this as an
opportunity for another one of our perfect getaway sexcapades. His
hands run along my sides, caressing me softly. He's being gentle with
me, considering we're pressed for time. I enjoy the feeling. It's a fresh
feeling that's calming me down, so I embrace it.

"I've been waiting many years for this day," she says in the sweetest, most sensual voice I've ever heard. I open my eyes to see Carmen
standing behind me. *My* Carmen. It's the same Carmen it took me
months to get over, years. How did she find me? My intuition was
right. I'm puzzled. Unable to speak, I refrain from asking questions.

"You left without a word. I looked for you. No one would tell
me where you'd disappeared to." She whispers in my ear. Still unable
to move, I continue to listen. "I refused to give up and then finally,
I saw a picture of you and your husband on a magazine cover while
in the grocery store. You changed your name. That's why I couldn't
find you. But that face, those beautiful eyes, and that smile... I'll
never forget. I've missed you so much. We were young back then, but
there's not a day that goes by when I don't think of you." I'm trying
to process everything she's saying.

"Se-re-ni-ty," she slowly whispers in my ear, allowing each syllable
to roll off her tongue in the sexiest way. I don't move. Holding back
the tears, I blink as they fill up in the wells of my eyes. "Mel-o-dy,"
she whispers just as slowly. She says my name. A name I haven't
heard in so long. A name I thought no longer existed. Melody.

That's me. My knees weaken beneath me. She holds me up. A tear falls. Our bodies face each other. My arms wrap around her as I cry quietly into her neck. We speak no words. Time is still. The room is still. Our hazel and light brown eyes finally meet.

The woman I fell in love with stands before me. The woman I ran from because of my confusion stands before me. My evil mother made me feel like a confused sinner. My feelings made me question myself and my sexuality. I did everything in my power to forget about her and erase her from my mind. Victor was my scapegoat. He helped me forget about her. Thunderstruck, my hands touch her soft hair. It has grown to be long and beautiful. Oh, how she has changed in the physical aspect, but the amazing feeling she gives me remains the same. It's like I'm in my senior year of college again, back when we first met. It's a feeling that's becomes more powerful with this interaction; a feeling too powerful to describe.

My thoughts speed up. Time moves swiftly. My husband pops in my head. Muddle sets in and it shows. She sees the panic, grabs my face, and says, "Don't worry. I have it all figured out." Her demeanor is calm and refreshing. "We have little time. Your driver, Mark, is a great friend of mines. He's waiting out back for us. I've been watching you for the past two years, waiting for the right moment. I don't want to sign with your husband's company. It was all a front. Everything that I'm doing, I'm doing to have you back in my life. Will you come with me?"

Flabbergasted, I think about the love I had for her and how I was ashamed to admit it. My thoughts take over my being again. I think about the malicious things my mother told me about the women she referred to as 'dykes'. I think about how my success is because of my mother. The talks Carmen and I used to have, and the way she made me feel all circle in my brain. I think about my husband and how he would feel. While I'm doing all this thinking, I think about my happiness, its importance, the opportunity to be free, and the opportunity to embrace love; true love. I think about my dreams and desires.

Looking in her eyes, I nod my head up and down, not caring about my husband, my career, or what I'll do. Nothing matters at this point. My body and mind both eases. My heart eases. A safe feeling overcomes me. For the first time in my life, I feel wanted. Not sexually or physically, but more mentally and emotionally.

She takes my hand as we sneak our way through the restaurant, and to the back door where Mark is waiting. We get in the back seat, and as the car pulls forward, I don't look behind me. I fixate my eyes on hers. I realize I'm doing it again. I'm running, just as I have before, but this time, I don't look at it as running. I look at it as trading a life where sex is my only means of staying for a life of freedom.

Chapter 34

Trying to come to terms with what I've just done, I stare out the window, speechless. My phone rings in my purse. It's Victor. Carmen takes the phone and throws it out the window. She squeezes my hand. "I have everything under control. Trust me." She pulls me closer to her and holds me as I bury my head in her shoulders. My tears flow freely.

It then dawns on me. I hold my head up and say, "What about Lucia and Bella? What about Savannah? What about my clothes? What will I do? What have I done?" Panic arises all over again.

"What would you like to do? Do you trust me?"

"I don't know what I would like to do. I don't know if I trust you. I haven't seen you in seven years. You've changed."

"Do you believe that? Or are you just saying that because you're afraid? The only thing that's changed about me is my physical appearance. I'm still the same Carmen that loved you with all my heart and soul back then. I'm still *me*. Trust me when I tell you I have everything under control. Have I ever steered you in the wrong direction?" I shake my head no. "Ok then. I *never* will. Your well-being means more to me than anything in the world. I've yet to move on from you or date anyone else. I've waited for you. So just relax and trust me?"

I lay my head in her lap and cry my eyes out. My Lucia, my Bella, what will they think. I don't want them to feel like I left them. With drenched eyes, I look up at Carmen. She rubs my hair as I drift. Unable to keep my eyes open, I allow myself to fall into a deep sleep.

~

I wake up, I'm lying in a bed with my clothes off and cover pulled up to my shoulders. Where am I? The purple and white room is beautiful. There's a balcony that overlooks an ocean. Long, purple, sheer curtains cover the windows and the balcony door. It reminds me of my mother's condo in Chicago, but with a splash of purple here and there. I remove the covers and breathe in the ocean. I notice a picture on the wall. It's an old picture of me sitting in between Carmen's legs at a football game. The more I inspect the room, the more pictures I see. On another wall there's a picture of me from two years ago, on the red carpet of the 2010 Grammy's. As I swing my feet around, I hear someone coming.

"I see you're finally awake." Carmen enters and sits next to me.

"Where am I?"

She stands and extends her hand. "Come."

I stand and put on the robe that's lying on the bed. She takes my hand and leads me down a beautiful, all white, swivel staircase. When we get to the bottom, she leads me through another room that's filled with all white furniture and gray sheer curtains. The aroma of food is familiar. We go to the kitchen and I immediately fall to my knees, surprised at what I see. Lucia is standing over the stove cooking while Bella and Savannah are both sitting at the table. Skylar is sitting on the patio, and… wait, is that Casey? Carmen helps me up and leads me to the table. Lucia comes to hug me and Bella throws her arms around the both of us.

"If her love you, her will be there… her here." Lucia whispers in my ear, reminding me of her exact words from several years prior.

I look at Savannah, and she smiles and embraces me with a hug. "I hopped on the jet as soon as you left for lunch."

I turn to Carmen, who is joined by Skylar and Casey. "Yo! What up, Mel!" That damn Skylar has not changed a bit. "You rememba Casey, don't you?"

Casey comes to hug me. "Melody." She can't fully embrace me like everyone else, because there's an enormous belly stopping her in her tracks. I look down; she rubs her belly and stands next to Skylar. "This was our third attempt. We lost the first two within the first trimester, but this time, we are fine. Three more months and Baby Sky Blue will be here."

Speechless, I point to Skylar. "That's right, Mel. Neva thought I'd be the one to settle down, huh? Well, believe it. Casey and I been together for five years and married for three. As soon as they started legalizing the shit, we jumped right on it. Ain't that right, Babe." She throws her arm around Casey, and all Casey does is smile like a kid in a candy store. I guess it wasn't so impossible after all for Skylar to rid her whoreish ways.

"Come." Carmen takes my hand and leads me to the balcony. Everyone else stays in the house except for Lucia. She brings me a plate of food that I know I won't be able to eat. She knows it too, but brings it anyway.

"What's going on?" Finally, the words come out. I'm in tears as usual, and she wipes them away with her thumb.

"Now do you trust me?"

"How?"

"This is love. This is my way of showing you just how much I loved you then and I love you now. I didn't want to take you away from the people you love most, like your mother took you away from me. I knew all about your grades, and I wanted to do whatever to make it all better for you. Your mother contacted me and ordered that I never speak to you again. Malik... eventually I found out about him too." She wipes my tears again.

"After I saw your picture, I hired a Private Investigator to locate you. Remember that phone call to your house asking for Melody Moore? That was a PI. He knew Malik and gave me his contact number. Only thing is, I didn't know it was *that* Malik until we started talking. He told me all about you, your mother, your father, your husband, where I could find you, Lucia, everything, and everybody. After I got all the information, I immediately wanted to come take you away, but decided that wouldn't have been an excellent move, so I came up with a plan. The first thing Malik suggested is that I reached out to Lucia, so I did. Barely able to understand her English, it was Bella that did all the talking, and she informed me that Lucia had been looking for me too. She said she *knew* your heart was with me and she needed to figure out a way to *show* you what true love really is. Lucia expressed how she loved you unconditionally—regardless of your sexual preference—and how she wanted you to be happy. She told me she didn't think you were happy with Victor and that you were just tolerating him. She and I then began plotting on how to take you away from unhappiness." She pauses. "Are you following me?" I nod yes. "Are you upset with us?" I shake my head no. "Good, because I don't want you disturbed. I want you to understand." She then leads me down the steps of the balcony, onto the white sandy beach. We walk close to the water and she sits and pulls me down with her.

"Breathe." I take a deep breath in and close my eyes, wishing not to wake up from what I think is a dream. When I open them, I'm still sitting on the beach with my first love. "Are you ready for me to finish?"

"Please."

"I was still in Chicago and Lucia insisted that I move to Miami, so I did. I was connected with Victor through one of my friends that's in the music industry. That same friend recommended Mark to Victor. As time went on, Lucia and I put our money together to purchase and remodel this home just for you. We knew we couldn't make any moves until we had a haven to bring you to. We filled the closet with all of your things from your penthouse. You don't have to worry about him going there to look for you because we have cleaned all of your belongings out and it's empty. It's up to you if you want to sell it or not. Do you know where you are?"

"No. Where?"

"Cuba." I buck my eyes. "Skylar and Casey moved here to make sure the remodeling and decorating was being done how Lucia and I wanted. There's a lot about me you never got to know, but singing was a hobby of mine in college. I never did it around you because I was too shy and it's not something I want to do long term. It's just something I *did* to get what I want and need in my life, which is you. You know Brown is *not* my last name, so all the information I gave Victor was not accurate. The rest is history." She lowers her head.

"There were days when I would watch you come and go and become more eager to hold you. There were days I would cry myself to sleep because I couldn't breathe the same air as you. Now that I have you, I never want to let you go. Will you stay with me? Will you allow me to introduce you to love? True love, unconditional love. If you say no, I'll walk away, only because I love you." Carmen takes my left hand, removes my ring, and throws it in the ocean. "This is not love. Love *should* not and *cannot* be bought." I do or say nothing to stop her. She looks right through me with those beautiful hazel brown eyes of hers. She doesn't blink and neither do I. Tears spill from her eyes and then mine. Neither of us move. We sit facing each other and allow the waves to wash up our tears. She then looks into the water and takes a deep breath. I fixate my eyes on this beautiful woman who has shown me more love in one day than anyone has ever shown me in my twenty-eight years of living. Well, except for Lucia. I wipe her tears and then my own.

"Do you have anything to say?" Moments pass as she places her hand on mine.

"I want to lie down." I stand and reach for her. She looks

surprised and takes my hand as she stands with me. She leads me to the house and into the bedroom. She removes my robe and I crawl back into bed.

"I'll come back to check on you in a little."

"Lay with me."

Carmen stands at the foot of the king-sized bed for several minutes. She then removes her pants and shirt—revealing her laced underwear clinging to her perfect body—and rests her caramel silk body behind me. Her hands are soft as she runs her fingers down my arm and intertwines her fingers in mine. I turn to hold her, and she mirrors my actions. We lie holding each other as all my worriers sail away.

Chapter 35

10:02am

Cuba. Who would have known I would live a wonderful life in Cuba with the people I love the most. I'm finally learning what love is with the help of Lucia, Bella, Savannah, and my beautiful Carmen. Skylar and Casey have the relationship I one day wish to have, which comprises a beautiful home, a baby on the way, and unconditional love. The way they admire each other softens my heart and puts a smile on my face. Carmen looks at me the same way, but I know that it's something that's not reciprocated by me. I'm working on that. With all the things I've experienced in my life, I never really understood what true, unconditional love was. Now that I'm surrounded by it, adjustments are being made. It takes time, though. Going back to Victor or Miami is not an option for me as of right now. Looking back and evaluating my past relationships, I question the love. Even the relationship with my mother and father. There are times I wish I had stayed in Chicago with Carmen, but if I'd done that, I wouldn't have learned the things I've learned over the years, nor would I have met Savannah. She's more than just my assistant. We've grown to be sisters.

I once heard my grandmother tell someone that God makes no mistakes. Never regret the things you do in life because God brought you to it for a reason. Never question your trials and tribulations because God allows them to happen so they can strengthen you for something else. Look at them as preparation, or a setup for a comeback. I fell so hard for Carmen before I left, that it caused me to flunk out of school. Had I not met her and fell for her so hard, I would still be in Chicago forcing myself not only to go to school, but to make good grades and major in something I couldn't care less about. I've found out that when you force yourself to do something, it makes you unhappy and you'll always get a negative outcome from it. Is this happiness? It feels like happiness, and it feels good.

MM

I hug my journal close to my chest and smile at the decision I've made.

～

It's been almost four weeks and I haven't been able to shake this nasty virus, so Carmen made me a doctor's appointment to see what's going on. I pick up the written directions that she left on the dresser on my way out the door. Lucia has made breakfast, but I'm unable to eat. Instead, I get a bottle of water from the refrigerator and tell her I'll return shortly.

"Savannah not drive you?"

"No. Not today. She's handling some other business for me. I'll be all right." I kiss her cheek and go out the door. When I approach the car and reach for the handle, I notice my reflection in the window. I look horrible.

Dizziness and sickness come over me the more I drive. My mouth waters, so I let the window down and spit. My vision is getting blurred, so I take the next exit. I feel faint.

～

"Mrs. White is very blessed to be alive. She has a fractured ankle, and the inflation of the airbag left her with two black eyes. She should be out of here in no time. We just need to run a few tests and make sure the baby is okay." The voice stops.

"How far along is she, doctor?" It's Carmen.

"She's six weeks."

I open my eyes to lie in a hospital bed with a cast from my toes to my knee. Carmen rushes to my side. I look at her in confusion. "What's going on?" It hurts to talk.

"You were in a car accident and you're in the hospital." She kisses my forehead.

The doctor stands on the other side. "Mrs. White, I'm Dr. Shaw. You fell asleep behind the wheel and were in a car accident. Someone must really watch over you. You have a few minor cuts and bruises and a fractured ankle. And so far, the baby is fine. We just want to run a few more tests. You won't have to stay here long," the doctor relays the same message to me as he did with Carmen.

"Baby? What baby?"

"Well, according to your test results, you're with child. Were you not aware?"

I cry as pain takes over my body. The doctor continues speaking, but I hear nothing he's saying. Carmen is holding my hand as tiredness falls upon me. "Why do I feel so drowsy?" I close my eyes to go back to sleep, hoping to wake up on the other side of what I want so badly to be a dream.

"That's just a side effect of the medicine we gave you to ease the pain. Now, as I was saying…" My eyes close while he continues and before I know it, I'm in dream land.

When I wake up, Carmen and the doctor are both gone. Still in this hospital bed with both of my legs hanging on slings, it then dawns on me I was not dreaming. I *am* pregnant and I *have* been in an accident. I look around the room and push the button beside me for the nurse. A second later, someone comes through the door. That was fast.

I can't believe my eyes, so I blink twice. It's not the nurse, it's not the doctor, and it's not Carmen. It's my husband, Victor White.

"You're pregnant. Is that why you left without a trace?" He comes closer to the foot of the bed. I don't know if I should lie or tell the truth right now.

"Yes Sir. I'll make sure she gets plenty of rest for the next few months." The doctor and Carmen walk in side-by-side. She is astounded when she sees Victor, and he is just when he sees her. "Mr. White." Carmen comes to my bedside.

"Hazel?" He clarifies shockingly.

"It's Carmen." She corrects and extends her hand.

"What are you doing here?"

Carmen and I both look at each other and I become sick at the thought of telling him the truth, the whole truth, and nothing but. "There are some things I need to tell you, Victor."

"Why did you leave me? What did I do so wrong that you had to leave the way you did? I thought something happened to you. That hurt me. Was I that bad of a husband?" I see the pain in his eyes.

What have I done? Why did I run from him? What am I supposed to say? What do I answer first? Was I forcing myself to be with him? "Please forgive me, Victor. We need to talk. I didn't know what else to do." I look at Carmen, knowing she understands what I'm going through right now. "Would you mind leaving us alone for a few minutes?" I whisper to her.

"You sure now is the time to do this? Considering what you've just gone through. You need not cause any more stress on your body." she whispers back.

"It's now or never. He's here. I can't run now." Carmen leaves quietly as I watch her exit, then turn my attention towards Victor. "How did you find me?" He's now standing by the window, looking into the sky as the sun sets.

"When you love someone with all your soul, you go through any measures to find them. It's like losing the key to your heart." He turns and pulls the only chair in the room up next to me and grabs my hand. "Look, I know I wasn't the best husband, and that I neglected you in so many ways. I apologize for that. I didn't realize how selfish I had been all along until I lost you. When I lost you, I lost me. I lost my desire to live, but I knew in my gut that you were still alive. I hoped you were still alive. And sometimes, that's all you need." Victory kisses the back of my hand. "I can do better. I can be better. I promise. Tell me what it is I need to do. Whatever it is, I'm willing." I never thought I would see the day Victor White begs. "I don't care about your past. All I care about is you. And our baby. What about the baby? How will you raise a baby alone? I can't let you do that. That would make me feel less of a man."

"I'm not who you think I am." I close my eyes to catch the tears, but it's too late. "There are a lot of things you think you know that are not true." I reopen my eyes to see him looking sad and lost. He's still holding my hand. Here it goes, Melody. *You can do it.* I convince myself before I speak. "My name is not Serenity. I am in love with a woman. That woman is Carmen, but you know her as Hazel." He releases my hand. "She was my love in college, but when I came home for Thanksgiving break, my mother found out about her and changed my identity. She threatened me to never see her again, or else she would disown me."

Victor stands and walks back to the window. He sits on the window seal and lowers his head. "So what was it we had. Was I just something to do for all these years? Do you love me? Did you ever love me?" He looks at me, alerting me to respond.

"What we *have* is a marriage. Love. I'm not sure if there was love in the beginning, or if it was lust. But what I know is that I love you *now*. I can't say if it's *true* love, or if I'm *in* love with you, because I don't even know if I *truly* love myself."

"But you love *her* enough to leave me cold sitting in *our* favorite restaurant. You love her enough to leave with no intentions on contacting me ever again." Victor paces from the foot of the bed, back to the window. Carmen enters the room. He looks at her in disgust. "So all of this was a plan? All of this was a setup just to get back to her?" He points at me. "You never wanted to sign with my company, did you?" He waits for an answer, but Carmen doesn't respond. He redirects his attention to me. "How could you? Why did you? And for these years. Why did you marry me?"

"I married you because I thought I loved you. I love you." Carmen shoots me a look of disapproval. "I love you too. I love you both, but in distinct ways. What I view to be love, anyway." My tears are streaming effortlessly. Carmen comes to my side and grabs my hand. I look at Victor. He looks away. Are those tears in his eyes? I shake my thought and look at Carmen. Tears fill her eyes.

She speaks, "Do what makes *you* happy. What makes you happy? Who makes you happy?"

Her questions linger as I ponder on them. I don't even know what happiness is. What is happiness? What makes me happy? "I'm not sure what makes me happy." I finally admit in confusion.

"Is this what pain feels like? I'm hurt." Victor speaks up. Now I feel guilty. I look at Carmen. I feel even more guilty.

"What will we do?" Carmen says. Did she say we?

"I need time." I say to her, not knowing how true it is.

"I will support you in every and anything you do Melody. I've always loved you and always will. Even though you were physically absent in my life for all those years, your spirit has always remained right here." She pats her heart.

Who do I love? Who makes me happy? Is it sex that makes me happy? Who loves me more? Is it love that I will choose, or will it be lust? Who represents what? "I need time."

"I need answers." Victor says.

Saved by the doctor. "Mrs. White, we will keep you under observation for two days before we discharge you," he informs me.

Chapter 36

I haven't been in the house for five minutes when Lucia and Savannah attack me with hugs and almost makes me fall out of the wheelchair.

"Me worry sick bout you." Lucia tells me while still holding on tight. "Gone few days only, but seem like forever."

"Victor found me. He's here in Cuba," I inform them both.

"Me know already."

"Yes, we are aware," Savannah says.

"But how?" I ask.

"Me know everyting," Lucia reminds me.

"What will you do?" It's Savannah.

"I will decide soon. I told them both that I need time. I need time to figure this out."

"Shouldn't you be going to lie down? Is it not what the doctor ordered?" Carmen comes in with my things.

"Follow doctor's orders. Me come take you tea shortly."

Carmen places my things on the floor and pushes me to the bedroom. I ask her to push me to the balcony. She does and then says, "I'll come back to check on you later."

"Thank you." She bends down and gently kiss me on the lips.

"No, thank you," she softly responds.

She leaves and I turn to face the ocean. The beautiful breeze blows my hair in my face as my mind escapes reality. I have to make a choice. Victor said he wouldn't leave until he got answers from me.

Is this his way of finally showing his love? Why did it take me leaving for him to realize how much he loves me? Carmen came looking for me. She never gave up on me, while Victor had me and neglected me mostly in every way except for sexually. Is it possible to have them both? I can love one, and lust the other. But how, when after all these years, I still don't know what love is. Is love staring me in the face, but I'm too blind to see it?

"Melly Baby always tinking." Lucia interrupts my thoughts.

She sits on the bench next to me. "I've really gotten myself in some mess now, Lucia."

"Where the Mister now?"

"He got a hotel not too far from here."

"Oh. Me see. Me see." She pauses and takes my hands. "Melly, tis not no mess. Tis life, baby. You have choice. You chose wise. Do what make Melly Baby happy. Not else nobody. You be happy in here." She places her hand over my heart. "Him must really love you. Him came find you. Both they love you. I always say take time for Melly Baby when not know. Now, you not know. Me be here for you always. You said always that you not know what love is. Now be time to figure out it. Has start from within." Lucia embraces me with a hug. "Me go made dinner now."

Wednesday, April 4, 2012

3:32 am

These past couple of days have been the most challenging of my life. I have always questioned love and its meaning. Carmen and Victor both have confessed their dying love for me, but I find it harder than I initially let on to walk away from my marriage. I think I love Victor. I think I love Carmen. I know I lust after them both, though. I really wish I knew what love really is. Maybe I need to visit my father and address some underlying issues that have played a role in the development of my well-being. Lucia said I need to take time for myself. Maybe she's right. Maybe I need to find myself. Maybe that'll give me some direction then. How will they take that? Will they be willing to wait?

"Are you ready to lie down yet." Carmen asks as she stands in the patio doorway with her arms folded and as if she's been standing there watching me for a while.

I close my journal. "Yes. I am."

Carmen comes to me, unlocks the breaks on the wheelchair and says, "We will have to get you on those crutches here soon. So you can get the hang of it." When she gets me to the bed, she picks me up, sits me on the edge of the bed, and undresses me from head to toe, being careful with my leg that has the cast on it. "Lie down," she requests, and I do so. Her attentive gentleness is turning me on. Turning me on in ways and places I didn't know a person could get turned on in. My toes are tingling. My fingers are numb. My nipples are solid as a rock, and my heart is skipping beats like I'm having a heart attack.

"Lay with me." I beg.

"Lay with you? I can't do that. You have a decision to make, and me laying with you will lead to other things. Those other things will only fulfill your emotions for the time being, and I don't want you to base your ultimate answer off temporary emotions." She kisses my forehead. "You're vulnerable right now. Take some time to figure out what is happening around you. Allow it to process. Take more time. Love is a powerful thing, and I don't want you to miss out on something so precious because you don't know what it is. You have a beautiful baby inside of you. Understand love because you don't want this to be a repeated cycle with your child. You don't want your child to be like your mother, or your father. You don't want to be like either of them yourself. Take the time you need. I plan to be right here until you figure it out. I love you enough to let you go because I know that if you come back to me, then it is meant to be. In order for you to grow, I have to give you the time you need." She kisses my forehead again, and her soft, full lips send chills right to my cookie. My hormones take over.

"Please make love to me. I choose you. *You* make me happy. *You* give me a sense of freedom. I'll tell Victor tomorrow that he can leave because I choose you, and that we can raise the baby together." I pull her closer to me causing her upper body to fall on mines.

Instead of her saying anything, she kisses me passionately, and it's on. She sits me up, raises my shirt over my head, lays me back down, climbs on top, and plants soft kisses on my neck. She moves down to my collarbone and then to my right nipple. She licks in soft circular motions. This feeling brings back so many memories. She then moves to my left nipple and does the same thing while caressing my clit. My body hasn't reacted to sex like this since the last time she and I had sex. She weakens my body by the second. She is capturing me with her spell. That same spell I fell under and caused me to flunk out of college.

She brings me back to reality when her finger enters my mouth; the same finger she had on my button. I'm frozen. She lets out a slight giggle. She places her finger back on my button and massages it as if she's a professional masseuse. My eyes are closed, and I'm lost in the feeling of being high. I don't smoke, but it feels like I've smoked a pound of weed; however that feels. I'm so lost; I don't realize she's moved her finger and stopped licking and sucking my nipples. Now she's making soft circular motions on my clit with her tongue and my hips move to her motion.

"Yes, baby. Please don't stop," I softly moan. "Oh Victor. I love you so much. Please don't stop." My body is two seconds away from erupting like a volcano when she stops.

Carmen looks at me with so much pain in her eyes, I immediately break down. "I will give you time to decide. You calling out his name, only confirms that your mind, body, and heart are all still with him. I got this place for you, so I will find me somewhere else to go. I'm always here if you need me, but I cannot allow myself to get hurt, when I have the option to choose what route to take." Carmen kisses my forehead and leaves.

I don't go after her. Instead, I make my last decision while laying alone. I reach for my cell phone and send both Carmen and Victor the same text message: *I choose ME. If either of you love me how you say you do, you would not only understand my decision, but accept it. In order for me to love either of you wholeheartedly and unconditionally, I have to love myself wholeheartedly and unconditionally. I do not want to bring a child in this world and not know how to love it. I have to take time for myself before the child enters this earth and learn to love me. Mel.*

Chapter 37

4:29am

Thanksgiving Day and thirty-four weeks since the day I chose myself.
Over the years, I've had a hard time defining who I am because I was
too busy being someone I wasn't. At one point, my actions portrayed me
to be a replica of my mother. I want to be the one to break that cycle.
I don't want to view love as pain, or as neglect. I want to view love as
what it is... love. Victor and Carmen had different definitions of love.
And Carmen has been the only one to show that she truly loves me. After
I told Victor I choose me, he left and had all of my things shipped to me.
He wrote a letter saying how he don't think he is ready for a child, and
he doesn't have the time to wait for me to "find myself". He mentioned
something about not wanting to be heartbroken if he waited and I didn't
choose him. Or I choose no one. Malik told me he has someone new. I
just pray they make him happy and loves him unconditionally. When I
tried to reach out to him, he ignored my attempts. I forgive him for that,
but it only confirms that he did not love me at all. He talked a delightful
game, but when it came time to show up, he chickened out. If I wasn't
so in love with me, and free, it would piss me at him off that he refuse
to stand on his word or respect and accept my decision like Carmen did.
Victor wants me to have patience with him, when I've found out that he
has none for me. I love Victor with all my heart. I love him enough to

know that our relationship would never work unless he changes his work habits. Work always have been his number one priority, and I thought that would change once they married us.

Carmen, she is who helped make my decision easier. She wants me to love unconditionally, and she wants a healthy companionship, and not just a relationship. She understands that my journey is something necessary in order for her to have me the way she wants to have me. She wants me to love my child and myself the same way she loves me. Her love is unconditional, and she's shown it. She has been here with me every step of the way, even during my complications. Something else, among a list of other things, that I have learned over these past few months, is that not everyone is accepting or understanding of my current journey, and I must be okay with that. I cannot force other people to embrace self-love if they're not ready to.

Lucia is here more now than all my years of knowing her. Her and Savannah both. They've been an enormous help to Skylar, Casey, and their little bun too. I never want to be a terrible parent, so I've been attempting to contact Victor. I send him updates every month, but he doesn't reply. I can't believe he's that upset with me. I'm not sure if he realizes it, but it appears he's bitter. I cannot and will not allow that to stop me. It's an obstacle that I must overcome with my head held high. I got a blessing out of this lesson. I got my child, for whom I am thankful for. I now understand what love is.

Love is life. Love is happiness. Love is faith. Love is forgiveness. Love is the ability to have a free mind, body, and soul. Love is something I never knew existed until now. I look down at my growing belling. *For so long, I'd always thought love was pain and neglect and abandonment. Then I became pregnant. Love is life. It brings life to me. Over the past nine months, I witnessed growth within me, mentally, physically, emotionally, and literally. This growth has given me strength that I never knew existed. Is this what freedom is? Something needed to change. I needed to change. I questioned everyone else's love for me, but never did I take a moment to question my love for myself. This time has allowed me to learn a lot about myself and answer most of the questions I asked in the beginning as it pertains to love, and its meaning. Carmen was right about the importance of me understanding love before I give birth. For the first time, I can honestly say that I am in love. In love with me. In love with my child. In love with my life. I am thankful for my life. I am thankful for the ability to understand love.*

To love me, I had to grow with me. I had to let go of a lot of things. I had to understand who was actually for me, and who had my best interest at heart. It hurts me that Victor didn't, because now that I know what love is, I loved him. He was just unaware of it. I couldn't hold on to that hurt though, I had to take it as a lesson, and be thankful for the blessing. I will continue to send him messages every month, updating him on our child.

I don't want the baby to grow up the way I did. I want her to feel love, so by the time she gets older, she'll know what it is. I want her to understand her self-worth. I want her to understand her values. I see a lot of young ladies that wish so desperately to be like the "reality stars" they see on television. I see how they degrade themselves for a check and diminish their characters. I don't want her to be like that. I want her to understand that she can be whatever she wants in life, and she can have whatever she wants in life, as long as she remains loyal to herself first. I want her to understand the importance of knowing and understanding self, to know and understand someone else. I want her to see more than what's on the television. I want her to know that women are the essence of the world. A woman's worth is based on and determined by the woman herself.

Never allow another person to degrade or diminish your self-worth. If you believe in love, you will have love. Carmen loves me, and so does Victor, but both in unique ways. All it takes is for me to have faith, and to believe that it will happen. Then it happened. I had to believe that I could change. I had to admit my issues. I had to take accountability for my actions, both old and new. I had to understand the power in the tongue. What you say, and what you believe, determines how your life will go.

So many people get into relationships looking for just that… a relationship. I was one of those persons. Nobody understands or have the desire to wait for companionship. I now seek companionship. I desire freedom. I need to live free for the safety of my child. I can't consume in any relationship and lose focus of my child. I don't want her to grow up the way my sister and I did. I want her to feel my love for her without me saying it all the time. Carmen has agreed to be the Godmother, and I don't know what I would do without her. Will I eventually make a choice? If life forced me to choose, who would I choose? Carmen has always given me a fresh feeling. Like we connect differently. I still find it hard to believe that she's here and Victor isn't.

The games individuals play to fulfill their own desires are selfish. We've all played the game, and now it's over. I played with Victor to fill my sexual desires, and to fill that void. I played with Carmen to fulfill my sexual desires also, but her being her free-spirited self gave me encouragement and motivation throughout this entire process. No one really won, because in the game's process came heartache, and other emotional pain. I've learned that my value and self-worth have no price tag. If everyone understood this, the world would be a better place. I want my daughter to grow up understanding this. I don't want her to grow up unaware of herself, her choices, or her environment.

There's a knock at the door. It's Lucia and Malik, accompanied by two police officers. What is going on? Did they find out about Sam? Oh shit! What will happen to my baby girl? Lucia reaches for Victoria, "Me take she." She's lying on my lap, so I pick her seven-pound, twenty-one-inch body up and pass her to Lucia, who then sits in the rocker she has turned to face the window.

Malik greets me with a hug. "Long time no see Melody.

Congratulations on your bundle of joy. I know you probably don't care, but your father sends his well wishes. He prays that one day you will find it in your heart to love him again." I must go visit my father, so he understands and feels my forgiveness and love. I'm a different person, therefore, I can visit him and have a relationship with him without all the resentment. I look around Malik and eye the police officers. He notices and continues, "There has been a tragedy, Melody. They found Victor dead in his office early this morning. It appears he committed suicide by taking a mixture of prescription drugs and alcohol and then hanging himself. He left this letter for you." Malik tries to give me the envelop, but I cannot move my hand to receive it. As I sit up in the hospital bed, everything moves in slow motion. I recompose myself as Bella, Savannah, and Carmen returns from the gift shop with pink balloons and several beautiful flower bouquets. Bella and Savannah join Lucia and baby Victoria at the window. Carmen notices my blank expression, looks at Malik, then comes to my side. Malik gives her the letter from Victor. "They found Victor dead in his office this morning. I got here as fast as I could. He left this letter for her, and according to the letter, a lot of other things. I will go now." Malik looks at me and grabs my hand, "Everything will be all right Melody. Just hang in there. You have been through a lot these past few years, but things will get better." He pats the back of my hand with his free hand before he exits with the two officers.

Carmen comes and joins me on the bed as I lie back. Bella comes over and embraces me with a hug. "I'm so sorry this happened to you, Aunt Serenity. Look at it this way, God allows everything to happen for a reason. He took something from you and replaced it with a greater gift, baby Victoria." She releases her embrace. "I'm so glad I had time to see her before I left for school. I will come home every month just to love on her and give her kisses. She is the baby version of you." Bella squeezes me again. I squeeze her back.

"I am proud of the young lady you have become. Always remain true to yourself, and allow no one to change you, your dreams, or your ambition." I whisper in her ear.

"Do you want me to read this letter?" Carmen interrupts the moment.

Reality sets in and I must face it. "Yes, please." Bella sits on the bed and holds my hand.

"My Love Serenity. I could no longer live without all of your love. You can have everything I own. Please take care of the greatest gift a person could ask for. Victor White." She folds the letter back up.

"Is that all he said?" I ask.

"Unfortunately, yes."

Lucia and Savannah join us, and both find a spot on the bed as they place baby Victoria in my arms. I look down at her and my tears overflow uncontrollably. I look around the bed at the people who have loved me and supported me most of my life. Tears of gratitude and humility pour out. God doesn't make mistakes, does He. Maybe he removed Victor out of my life so I could have the companionship I desire with the person who is best for me. Maybe Carmen has loved me all this time and has shown nothing but love for me. Maybe she is the one for me. Now that I know what love is, maybe I can love her the way she has always loved me.

A tear falls from my eyes onto baby Victoria's cheek. She smiles. "Love meet Melody. Melody, meet love." Carmen says as she comforts both me and my baby in her loving arms.

New Year's Eve 2013

12:00am

FREEDOM

Straight... Gay... Lesbian... Black... White... Fat... Skinny...
Attractive... Ugly... Mean... Real... Fake... What are these? These
are terms used to categorize an individual. To judge an individual and
place them in a box where they don't deserve to be. It happens so often
that we begin to believe that it's who they/we are.

We often gossip about what someone else may have referred to us as
and are most times offended or defensive. Why? Because we feel there
might be some truth in what's been said. If not, then why waste our
energy gossiping about it? We allow ourselves to become so rational to
the things we hear about self, that we become immune to it. And that is
the BOX you've placed yourself in and others.

Try calling someone beautiful regardless of the color of their skin,
or their weight and size, or their sexual preference. Try looking in the
mirror every day you wake up & remind yourself how beautiful &
wonderful you are. Free yourselves from this judgmental society. Free
you from what or who someone else wants you to be. LOVE has no color,
size, or sexual preference to it. Free yourselves to LOVE. Free yourselves
to LIVE!

Lesbian is a word. Do not define me by that word. I am a woman
first. A woman who's learning my desires and passions. A woman who
is more than what you will ever know if you place me in a box.

You may not agree with who I am or what I stand for, but that
doesn't stop me from learning. It doesn't stop me from being who I am.
When you tell me I'm "going to hell" for being who I am, reality check,
you're judging me! Which is a sin, and no sin is greater than the other!
Please, please stop telling people that "they don't look gay"! Question?
How does a gay person look? I'm not gay, I AM ME!!! If I was to never

share my sexuality, you wouldn't know. No, I'm not boastful about it, and neither am I ashamed. I am happy in the skin I'm in. I laugh, I smile, I share, I care, I love, I respect just as much as a heterosexual person does. No, I'm not your average individual, but I am an individual.

So now that I've stepped out of the box and into a world where I am free… free to live… free to love… free to grow… free to be me, I can learn how to let others love me freely. I challenge you to try it.

MM

I tear the pages from my journal, walk to the ocean with an empty bottle in hand. Standing alone, I roll the pages and place them in the bottle. I release the filled bottle into the ocean, and yell to the top of my lungs, "I AM FREE!" Captured by the breeze, a chilling emotion comes over me as I close my eyes and embrace… freedom.

Printed in the United States
By Bookmasters